ROMANCING THE WEST

by Beth Ciotta

Jewel Imprint: Sapphire
Medallion Press, Inc.
Printed in USA

DEDICATION:

For the mavericks at Medallion Press. Thank you
for bringing the stories of my heart to life.

Published 2007 by Medallion Press, Inc.

The MEDALLION PRESS LOGO
is a registered tradmark of Medallion Press, Inc.

Typeset in Times New Roman
Printed in the United States of America

10 9 8 7 6 5 4 3 2 1
First Edition

ACKNOWLEDGMENTS:

They say a writer's life is a solitary one, but there are many who encourage and support me daily, reminding me that I am never alone. My husband, Steve, my family and friends (you know who you are!), my buds, critique partners, and fellow writers, Mary Stella, Julia Templeton, and Cynthia Valero, and my agent, Amy Moore-Benson. From the bottom of my heart — thank you.

CHAPTER 1

Territory of Arizona 1878

You understand that this is top secret."

Seth Wright reflected on the official document signed by U.S. President Hayes. The one he'd tucked into the pocket of his black frock coat alongside his new reading spectacles.

Sequestered in a private room of George T. Becker's bath and hair dressing emporium, he lit a Cuban, sank deeper into the steaming water and glanced at the man soaking in the adjacent washtub. The smooth-talking politician who'd summoned him to Phoenix to celebrate a mutual friend's birthday. At least that had been the pretense. "The appointment or my association with you?"

"Both." Athens Garrett flashed a practiced smile then shifted his green gaze to the rough-hewn table wedged between the brass tubs. He ignored the wooden box stocked with premium cigars, reached for the crystal decanter of brandy. Pouring liquor into two snifters, he laid out specifics. "The Peacemakers Alliance is a pet project of President Hayes's. PMA's mandate is to investigate sensitive or hard-to-solve cases pertaining to taming the west."

Seth absorbed the idealistic dictate with a wry grin. He'd been tangling with outlaws for years. He'd ridden with the Texas and Arizona Rangers. Served consecutive terms as County Sheriff. He'd kicked a canyon-full of miscreant ass. Regardless, ruthless cutthroats prevailed. No wonder, what with all the crooked lawyers and judges mucking up frontier justice.

The mere thought of those shifty pricks made him mad as a peeled rattler. Outraged by the recent outcome of a murder investigation, he'd opted not to run for reelection as Sheriff of Pinal County. It wasn't the first time a guilty man had been declared innocent. But it was the last time he aimed on witnessing such blatant injustice.

Yesterday, he'd walked away from the jailhouse pondering his future. He needed a break. Or a change. Something to reawaken his passion for the law. For living. Frustration was only the tip of the iceberg. Boredom had wormed its way into his being and he'd be damned if he'd roll over, accepting complacency or cynicism as part and parcel of growing older.

Today, he'd been offered the position of elite government agent.

Maybe it was the cure for what ailed him.

Optimism buzzed through his veins for the first time in months.

Then his daddy's voice rang in his ears, compromising the rush. *Take it slow, son. Get the facts.*

"I thought Hayes was concentrating on reforming the South."

"The President is concerned with this nation as a whole," Athens said. "Last year he focused on encouraging economic development in the arid regions. I assume you're familiar with the Desert Land Act."

Seth puffed on the cigar. "Nice plan in theory. Six-hundred-forty acres of land to anyone willing to pay and promising to irrigate the land within three years. Heard tell there were a goodly number of fraudulent proofs."

"Possibly as high as ninety-five percent."

"So Hayes's nose is out of joint."

"He's disappointed." Athens dragged a forearm across his moist brow. "But it's the outlaw mentality, the senseless loss of life that's driven the President to initiate PMA."

Seth detected a flash of anguish in the other man's eyes before he looked away. He didn't know Garrett well enough to ponder the reason. During the awkward silence he soaped up his hair and reflected on the man with the plan, a man of vision—President Rutherford Hayes. Known for being honest, levelheaded, and a man of action, he'd earned Seth's respect by striving to secure rights for people of color in addition to warding off a border war with Mexico through negotiations with that buzzard-ass dictator Diaz. The more he thought about it, the more he could imagine Hayes cooking up the Peacemaker Alliance. Still, something didn't sit right. Mainly, the man to his left.

Seth exhaled a plume of smoke and studied Garrett through wary eyes. "How do you figure into this?"

"I've been appointed acting Director of PMA. I'll be your primary contact. Codename: Fox."

He raised a brow at that. Fox implied shiftiness, trickiness. Someone prone to scheme and outmaneuver. Unlike his brothers, Rome and Boston Garrett, two Wells Fargo detectives who maintained order with flying fists and lead, Athens was a diplomat. A man who settled arguments with brains, not brawn. For sure and certain, not with a gun. Smart as a steel trap, his reputation was that of a silver-tongued do-gooder. A former citizen of California with a background in law, he'd climbed the political ladder to State Senator. A widower and the father of two young children, most folks had pegged the unshakable mediator as the state's next governor. Now he was supervising an agency whose mandate was to tame the west?

It wasn't the Peacemakers Alliance that gave Seth pause, but the man Hayes had put in charge. Athens Garrett lacked experience in the field. Grit. The man sipped brandy and had the vocabulary of a Bible thumper. Taking orders from a man who substituted dad-blame-it for goddammit made Seth's ass twitch.

He snuffed the cigar. "Thought you moved to Phoenix to be near your sister."

"I did."

"To escape the political dust-devil so you could spend more time with your kids."

"That's right. When the President heard I was relocating to Arizona Territory, he offered me a supervisory position with PMA."

Seth drained his drink in one swallow. The President wouldn't entrust this job to a man he didn't deem capable. Maybe he knew something about Athens's character beyond the reported. "Just so I'm clear, PMA doesn't exist." He set aside the glass and indicated the two of them with a flick of his hand. "*We* don't exist."

"Not officially, no."

He reached for a shaving mug and brush and whipped the contents into a lather. "I'm listening."

Athens nodded. "President Hayes is fed up with the lawlessness west of the Mississippi. He wants the citizens safe, the outlaws handled. Cattle rustlers, road agents, train robbers, guns-for-hire, and such."

"What about the Rangers and local and federal law enforcement?" Seth asked as he scraped a straight-edged razor along his jaw.

"Special cases call for special skills. Peacemakers are authorized to act creatively to ensure success."

His motions slowed. "*Creative* a codename for illegal?"

"Let's just say special rules apply."

A license to bend the law. He imagined his daddy, a by-the-books town marshal, rolling over in his grave. Then again Hershel Wright had never tangled with the likes of the cutthroat gangs and crooked politicians currently plaguing the west.

"Might entail undercover work," Athens continued. "Aliases, disguises. Figure you could assume another man's identity convincingly?"

He thought about it, shrugged. "Reckon I can do whatever I set my mind to."

"You an arrogant man, Wright?"

"Confident."

Athens smiled.

Seth glanced at the man alternately sipping brandy and scratching soap through his hair, blond, and in need of a trim . . . much like his own. "Why me?"

"The President wants the best of the best. Your history with the Rangers and local law enforcement speaks for itself. So happens you and I are acquainted."

"Because of Josh." Athens's brother-in-law and Seth's best friend. A former Ranger and the current Sheriff of a boomtown called Chance. His enthusiasm swelled at the thought of working alongside Joshua Grant, a man he trusted with his life. "You bringing him on?"

"I'll be utilizing his expertise in an advisory capacity. Right now Josh is focused on wife and family."

"Seein' his wife is your sister, I'm guessing you're pleased with his priorities."

"Let's just say he's inspired me to adjust my own."

Seth didn't ask how. Wasn't his business.

"So are you in?"

"Tame the west, huh?"

"That's right."

"Sure."

"Good."

Seth poured a celebratory round. "When do I start?"

"Tomorrow. Your first assignment involves relaying a message and relocating a VIP."

Not exactly what he had in mind. He tamped down his disappointment and scrubbed his arms and pits with the bar of aromatic soap. After this he'd go out on a spree, starting with Fletcher's pleasure palace. He hadn't been with a woman in over two weeks, what with personal and professional obligations. No wonder he was wound tight. "What about those hard-to-solve cases you mentioned?"

"Who said this assignment is simple?" Athens traced his finger around the rim of his glass. "Ever heard Paris mention her friend Emily McBride?"

The swift change of subject surprised him. "Sure." He swung his thoughts around to previous conversations with his best friend's wife. The longer Paris lived in Arizona Territory, the more she reminisced about her childhood friend. "I know she misses Miss McBride." The woman lived a world away in northern California.

"Those two grew up tight as ticks. Now they keep in touch via the U.S. postal service. A few days ago Paris received a letter from Emily, canceling an upcoming visit. She was supposed to be here for the birth of the baby. I expected my sister to be upset, but she's been unnaturally agitated and close-mouthed on the matter. Josh prodded. I prodded. All we got was that Emily's in a financial bind."

"Sorry to hear that."

"She's had a rough time of it lately. Lost her ma a few months back. Her pa not long after. Now this." He angled his head as if pondering the matter. "Emily's a smart girl. Fanciful, like Paris, but she wouldn't squander the family savings. I'm thinking she trusted someone she shouldn't have, made a bad investment.

She believes the best in the worst of people."

"So send her some money."

"Tried. But she's a proud one." Leaving his brandy unfinished, Athens climbed out of the tub and commenced to drying and dressing. "Emily's misfortune got me to contemplating my own life. I've been selfish," he said, without looking at Seth. "Not wanting to remarry because I'm still in love with my wife. Or rather, the memory of my wife." He fastened his trousers, donned a tailored shirt and vest. "Thing is, Zach and Zoe need a mother. Emily needs a protector. I've always been fond of her. Shy, but good-hearted and intelligent. We'll make a good match."

Seth hauled his body out of the tub and nabbed a towel. He felt for the man—a widower with two kids—but *damn*. "So my first assignment is to fetch your intended bride?"

"President Hayes is counting on me to organize and supervise PMA. I'm counting on you to deliver Emily safely to me so I can concentrate on doing that. When you think about it, this matchmaking venture is of national importance."

Seth suppressed a grunt. Wouldn't want *Fox* thinkin' he was unpatriotic.

"I've penned a proposal of marriage. I'm hoping, after due consideration, that she'll agree."

He jerked on his shirt, poleaxed by what he was

hearing. "You mean you haven't discussed this with Miss McBride? Don't you think she'd like to hear the proposal from *you*?"

"I can't leave Phoenix or my children. Not now. If she balks, you'll have to plead my case. Explain the advantages of a practical, amiable marriage." He shrugged on his frock coat, his actions and tone matter-of-fact. "Rumor has it you can talk any woman into anything. I'm counting on you to persuade her."

"Am I to take it she's not as *fond* of you as you are of her?"

"She's fond of Zach and Zoe and she likes me just fine. Problem is she fancies herself in love with Rome."

"Your *brother*?"

"Been moony-eyed over him since she was a kid. Rome has no interest in her, trust me."

Seth jammed his feet into his boots, cursed a dull throb at the base of his skull. "This has disaster written all over it."

"I have faith in your abilities." Athens slicked back his hair, pocketed the comb. "Another thing. Paris is to know nothing about this."

"PMA or Emily?"

"Both. At least for now. I don't want her to get her hopes up in case you come back empty handed."

Seth smirked. "I thought you had faith in my

abilities."

"I also have faith in fate intervening and sabotaging my life."

"You a bitter man, Garrett?"

"Realistic."

Fully dressed, they exited through the rear door of the bath and hair dressing emporium. They agreed to meet up for dinner to celebrate Josh's birthday. Naturally, Paris would be there as well as Zach and Zoe.

"Remember," Athens said, "if Emily comes up in conversation, you're to say nothing of your impending mission."

Seth didn't figure bride-fetching counted as a mission, but held his tongue. He shook hands on the matter, and the two men parted. Avoiding talk of Emily this evening should be simple, so long as the men controlled the conversation. He wouldn't be lying to his best friend's wife, just omitting information of *national importance*. Besides, once he returned to Arizona Territory with Emily, Paris wouldn't mind that she'd been kept in the dark. All she'd care about was that her friend was no longer thousands of miles away. She'd be happy which meant Josh would be happy. Emily and Athens's problems would be solved and Zach and Zoe Garrett would have a ma.

By the time he rounded the corner and hit Washington Street, he'd convinced himself he was on a *mission* of good will, ensuring the happiness of Emily and the Garretts, and the wellbeing of the honest, hard-working folk of the west. This time next month he'd be kicking criminal ass Peacemaker style.

CHAPTER 2

With the meeting behind him and free time ahead, Seth surveyed the wide street bordered with cottonwood trees and adobe buildings. In addition to a couple of respectable hotels, assorted general merchants, a schoolhouse, a library, and the newly erected National Bank, Phoenix boasted sixteen saloons, four dance halls, two monte banks, and one faro game. Just now, the colorful side of this booming oasis appealed to him most.

Specifically, Fletcher's pleasure palace.

He sauntered up the boardwalk, aiming on celebrating his new job by riding a feisty dove. Best to see to his needs now. Calico Queens would be sparse in Heaven, California, a town whose citizens, according to Paris, had been raised on prunes and proverbs.

"Just the man I'm looking for."

Seth stopped short as a freckle-faced half-pint blew across the street and blocked his path. He touched the brim of his hat in greeting. "Be more pleased to hear those words if you weren't my best friend's lovely wife."

Paris Grant waved off his innocent flirtation with a snort. "I'm not lovely. I'm fat."

"You're with child and you're glowing."

"You mean sweating." She fanned her face with her hand. "It's hot as the devil's kitchen."

Seth guided her into the shade. She looked flushed and anxious. Couldn't be good for the babe. "It's the middle of the afternoon, hon. You should be wearing a bonnet or—"

"—carrying a parasol. I know. I forgot. I was in a hurry."

Impetuous as always. "Where's Josh? Ain't like him to let you walk around town alone."

"He took Zach and Zoe for a buggy ride so I could take a nap. Only I couldn't rest because I'm agitated."

"I can see that."

"I knew you'd arrived and I wanted to talk to you. You weren't at the jailhouse so I figured I'd find you in one of the saloons."

"Seeing that you often tread where you don't belong, I'm relieved you ran into me on the boardwalk." Imagine if she'd stormed Fletcher's? Although, if she caught him with his pants down, she'd probably declare them even. Several months back, he'd walked in on her and Josh. *Don't think about your friend's woman in the all-together.*

"I need to talk to you regarding an urgent matter."

Damn. "Why don't we go back to your brother's house and—"

"Why don't we slip in here?"

Before he could protest, Paris nudged him inside a merchant's store. Café Poppy. A fancy bakery of sorts. He smelled something sweet. Cookies? Cake? Almost as delectable as the tasty morsel rounding the counter. She was new in town. New to the region, given her sophisticated appearance. Her bustled blue gown and fancy up-do were more suited to a cotillion than a café. She reeked of elegant grace and cake batter. Intrigued, Seth considered spending the afternoon here rather than Fletchers. Then he noticed the wedding band. Damn.

"Afternoon," he said with a pleasant smile. Hard not to smile at a rare beauty, hitched or otherwise.

"Thank you for frequenting Café Poppy." She bested his smile and escorted them to one of six tables. "I'm the proprietor, Mrs. Kaila Dillingham."

Her accent—British?—caught him off guard, as did her enthusiastic greeting. He'd expected reserved, stuffy. Instead, she was friendly. Friendly *and* beautiful. "Pleasure, ma'am."

He wondered about her husband. Were he the law in this town, he'd inquire outright. Keeping the peace meant knowing a piece about those in your jurisdiction. Given his new appointment, he supposed that included everyone west of the Mississip.

Mulling that over, he eased Paris into a padded chair. Calico cushions to match the calico tablecloths and curtains. Sure was a frilly place. "Name's Seth Wright. This here is—"

"—a woman dying of thirst," Paris finished. "Could I bother you for a cup of tea, Mrs. Dillingham? And maybe some of whatever smells so good? Seth will have coffee," she said before he could order. God forbid he prolong the conversation. "Thank you," she added, dismissing the woman with a polite smile.

Apparently, the urgent matter was for his ears only. The best he could do was hear her out and hope this urgent matter concerned anything but Emily McBride.

"It's about my friend Emily."

Naturally. He settled back and listened as Paris relayed the same story Athens had shared minutes before. "I understand that you're disappointed," he interjected. "But, honey, things don't always go according to plan. You'll see Emily again. The timing's just off."

She shook her head. "It's not that simple. She's in trouble."

The hitch in her voice summoned a pain in his

neck. He massaged the telling ache with a frown. "What kind of trouble?"

"I can't say precisely. It involves a secret and I made a promise. Promises are sacred."

A belief that had gotten her in a passel of trouble in the past. "Why are you confiding in me and not Josh?"

"Josh wouldn't do what has to be done because he won't leave me when I'm in this condition. He'd send you. When I learned about this, you were still Sheriff and I didn't want to impose so I sent Phineas Pinkerton."

"The poet?" Seth had seen the pretty boy recite his flowery prose in various theaters, including the Desert Moon, the opera house owned by Josh and Paris. Didn't care for the man's delivery, though the poems were clever.

"In addition to a professional poet," Paris informed him in a hushed voice, "he's an intuitive detective."

"A what?"

"Someone who solves crimes by reading or hearing a recounting of the case."

"Does he have a background in law? Practical experience in enforcement?"

"He doesn't need it. His deductive skills come naturally." She frowned. "You look skeptical."

"I am skeptical." That was putting it mildly. "Paris, two of your brothers earn livings investigating and apprehending criminals. They've known Emily all their lives and when they're not on the trail, they live in the same town as your friend. Why not alert them?" He thought back on Athens's theory that Emily had made a bad investment. He'd mentioned her trusting nature and now Paris cited criminal types. Was it possible the preacher's daughter fell prey to a flim flam man?

Paris shook her head so hard, her bun came loose. "Rome and Boston can't know about this. *None* of my brothers can know."

Naturally. "What about the local authorities—"

"Loose-lipped ninnies. Not an option."

"Hence Pinkerton."

"Hence my problem. Yesterday, I received a telegram from Mr. Pinkerton. He's been offered a lucrative northeast tour. Regrettably, he said, he cannot continue his journey to Heaven. He's heading back to New York!"

Tears sprang to her big brown eyes as she spewed the rest of her hushed tale. "If I don't send help, Emily will take action herself. She's *that* desperate to keep her secret and what does she know about thwarting blackmailers? She's resourceful, but *still*. I'm beside myself with worry, Seth. Emily's had a powerful run of bad luck. If you don't go, something awful is going to happen. I just know it!"

"Hold up." He pressed a clean bandana into her hands, hoping she'd stem the tears before they flowed. Weepy woman gave him heartburn. "Someone's blackmailing Emily?"

"Don't ask me why. I can't tell you. I promised I wouldn't tell anyone and promises are—"

"—sacred. I know." He should've begged off Josh's birthday celebration and taken an overdue holiday. He should have known better than to get mixed up with the Garretts. A pain in his neck, all of them, including, no, *especially* Paris. "How am I supposed to help Emily if I don't know the problem?" How was he supposed to deliver a proposal to a woman mixed up in some sort of scandal? PMA was a government agency. Low profile. Athens expected to hook up with a preacher's daughter, an angel. A respectable mother for his children.

"You understand women more than any man I've ever met, Seth. Use your imagination."

He leaned forward, incredulous. "Are you suggesting that I seduce your friend into revealing her secret?"

"I'm suggesting you earn her confidence." She blew her nose into his bandana. "Besides, you couldn't woo Emily. She's in love with Rome."

He'd yet to meet a woman he couldn't *woo*, but that was beside the point. "Maybe that's just a girlish infatuation. Maybe she's meant for someone else."

Paris pursed her lips, studied him for a spell then smiled. "Maybe."

He started to give her an earful then Mrs. Dillingham walked over with a loaded tray and stole away his breath. Gorgeous. Mr. Dillingham was one lucky son-of-a-bitch.

"Tea, coffee, and French macaroons," she said, setting dainty cups and a plate of cookies between them. "Freshly baked. Do enjoy." She spun away and greeted Doc Gentry as he lumbered into the café mumbling something about crumpets and jam.

Seth watched her go.

Paris kicked him under the table. "About you and Emily . . ."

He focused back on the half-pint. "Swear to God, Paris, if this is some sort of elaborate matchmaking scheme—"

"Of all the . . . honestly! You're the one who brought it up. I was just thinking that if you chased off the person who's making her life miserable and she just happened to fall in love with you at the same time— and you with her—well, I was just thinking I'd be all right with that. Better you than Mr. Bellamont."

Never mind that she'd just insulted him, again. "Who in the devil is Bellamont?"

"Claude Bellamont. He proposed two weeks after Preacher McBride's funeral. Emily turned him down, thank goodness. But what with her financial difficulties . . . Let's just say she's not herself these days. I'd hate to see her marry someone for the wrong reasons."

Seth's head threatened to explode.

Paris reached across the table and grasped his hand. "It's not like you have anything better to do. You're in between jobs, right?"

"Right," he was obliged to say. He tasted his coffee. Black and strong. Good, but just about now a quart bottle of whiskey would be even better.

"Besides, you owe me."

That coaxed a smile out of him. "How do you figure?"

"You forced me to marry Josh."

No way, no how did he feel bad about initiating a shotgun wedding. Besides, he'd never known two people more in love. "Sweetheart, if I hadn't hurried along the proceedings, your brothers would have. Josh compromised your reputation."

"All he did was—"

"I don't want to hear it."

"Then hear this. If you don't go, I will."

He wouldn't put it past her. "I'll go." He was going anyway. Only now his mission was twofold.

She blinked back more tears. "I don't know how to thank you."

"Stop fretting. And stop doing fool things like disappearing on Josh."

"Mercy! What time is it?" She wrapped the macaroons in a napkin and bolted to her feet, the tea untouched. "I need to get back to the house before he discovers I'm missing and calls out the Rangers."

Seth left money on the table, sorry he hadn't gotten to taste one of those cookies. Glanced over his shoulder at Mrs. Dillingham, sorry he wouldn't be getting a taste of her. Damn. He really needed to visit Fletcher's.

He led Paris out onto the boardwalk, groaning when she tugged him into the alley. "What now?"

"I have an idea."

"God, help me."

"I'm thinking you should pretend you're Phineas Pinkerton," she whispered. "Emily's already expecting him. Instead of staying at the local hotel, I suggested he rent a room in her house. She's taking in boarders to earn extra money because of, well, you know. I'd feel better if you stuck close. That is until you dupe her tormentor, because who knows what he's capable of? People won't talk, because Mr. Pinkerton is, well, that is to say he favors . . ." She cleared her throat. "Let's just say he'd be smitten with the likes of, well, you."

"Forget it." That Paris even knew about such

things amazed him. Then again she was in the theater business. She'd probably seen it all. "Write to your friend and tell her there's been a change of plans."

"But . . ."

"No." Yes, he'd just told Athens he could take on another man's identity, but in this case—thankfully— it wasn't necessary.

She blew out a dramatic breath. "Fine. But you better take care and not compromise her reputation, Seth. She's got enough to worry about. Oh, and remember, if Emily comes up in conversation tonight—"

"—I'm to say nothing of my impending . . . trip." He tugged on his hat, frowned as she fiddled with her hair, twisting, untwisting. He stilled her nervous actions. "Emily's secret, whatever it is, is safe with me."

"Promise?"

He looked into those doe-like eyes thinking she was slicker than a clay hill after a rainstorm. He did, however, respect her motivation and loyalty to her friend. "Sure."

Twenty minutes later, Josh stormed Fletcher's. "I need a favor." He didn't care beans that Seth had one hand on a bottle of whisky and the other on a dove's bodacious ass. The matter, he said, stopping his friend midway up the stairs, was urgent.

Five minutes after that, Seth had issued a third promise. To deliver Emily McBride to Arizona Territory by hook or crook and before his friend's wife worried herself bed sick. He'd done so without revealing his previous conversations on the matter with Athens or Paris. He didn't like withholding information from Josh, but a promise was a promise and the objective was the same.

He told himself that he hadn't given his word to anyone in vain. First order of business: clean up whatever mess Emily had made. A preacher's daughter. A librarian. A woman the Garretts described as a shy woman with a heart of gold. How bad could it be?

Clean up the mess then deliver Athens's proposal and escort Emily to Arizona Territory. If he was going to tame the west, he could sure as hell save one tarnished angel.

CHAPTER 3

Napa Valley, California – Two weeks later

Damnation!" Emily McBride covered her mouth, shocked she'd blurted the curse aloud. In the library of all places. Thankfully, no one was within earshot. Well, except God. He heard everything. He also saw everything, knew everything, and she couldn't help wondering if this was part of her punishment.

She envisioned her father shaking a condemning finger, imagined his slurred voice. *"This is what you get for being deceitful."*

"Drat!" She paced between the non-fiction stacks, told herself to get a grip. Being asked to read an I. M. Wilde dime novel aloud at the Lemonade and Storytelling Social Club wasn't divine punishment, just bad luck. "Snap out of it, you ninny. You're paranoid." She bumped up her spectacles and pinched the bridge of her nose. "You're also talking to yourself. You really need to stop doing that."

Townfolk whispered words like *dotty* and *moody* whenever they spoke of the late Preacher McBride's daughter. They used to call her *shy*. Only she'd never really been shy, just content to dwell in the background, nose in a book, head in the clouds. She'd spent countless hours committing her own stories to paper, although she'd learned early on to keep the tales to herself. Her imagination cooked up scenarios unbecoming of a preacher's daughter. Or so many said, including her father. Her mother, an avid reader herself, had cut her most deeply. *"Listen keenly to my words and remember this always, daughter. Emily McBride must channel her talents in a more respectable direction."*

That night her heart had cracked, and never since healed.

"No one understands me," she'd cried into her pillow. No one except Paris, a fellow artistic soul. The day the townfolk shunned the only female in the Garrett clan, they shunned the only child of the McBrides as well. *"Artists have to stick together,"* Emily had said, comforting her friend with a hug. Used to being around four older brothers, Paris suggested they shake on a lifetime friendship like men. So, they'd spit into their palms and clasped hands.

Paris became a recluse and Emily with her. She'd

been the subject of hurtful gossip ever since. The other day she overheard someone call her crazy. Just because she'd swapped her conventional gowns for men's shirts and split-riding skirts and started practicing sharp shooting. Just because she'd turned her father's rural home into a boardinghouse and taken in Mrs. Dunlap, a forgetful widow with a knitting obsession. She had good reasons for these actions, not that she felt compelled to share them. For the first time in her life, her business was her own.

At least it had been.

An anonymous busybody was currently making her life a living . . . Hades.

I know your secret.

Those four little words, typewritten on ordinary writing paper, delivered a mighty blow to her brave new spirit. The taunt filled her with guilt and dread. Now she wasn't the old Emily, or the new Emily, just a confused Emily stuck in between. These days, she didn't know whether to amend her Grand Design or ditch it. Her nerves were threadbare and things were about to get worse. Thanks to Paris, she was supposed to welcome a poet into her home. A *man*.

Her friend's missive had arrived two weeks ago, give or take a few days. Mrs. Dunlap had misplaced the mail. By the time Emily read the letter, it was too late to relay her objections. The man was on his way.

Though Emily appreciated what Paris was trying to do, she simply couldn't accept the gesture. Or, rather, Mr. Pinkerton. She'd have to send the gentleman packing and that's all there was to it. No matter how badly she needed his money. No matter how tempted she was to pick the intuitive detective's mind as Paris suggested.

Confiding in him meant entrusting him with a secret. It meant putting her life in someone else's hands, giving over control. The mere thought made her chest ache. She wanted to live life on her own terms. She wanted to voice her thoughts without fear of being struck by a lightening bolt or chided by opinionated prudes.

No, sir. She wouldn't be leaning on Mr. Pinkerton or anyone else. Besides, she couldn't take on a male boarder, even one with delicate sensibilities. She couldn't withstand the added speculation as to her good sense, or lack thereof. If she didn't mind her actions, her narrow-minded neighbors would pack her off to Napa State Asylum for the Insane.

Those same neighbors circulated a few feet away in the magazine and newspaper section of the library, gossiping over lemonade and cookies as they awaited the official start of the meeting.

Wound up from her agitated pacing, Emily rounded the corner and rested her forehead against the shelf stocked with the works of Charles Dickens. If only the committee would've voted *Nicholas Nickleby* as today's feature as opposed to *Showdown in Sin-town*. Was it possible that her anonymous tormentor, the cause of her financial and emotional woes, was on the Lemonade and Storytelling committee?

"There you go being paranoid again." On the other hand, she had good reason to be wary. Two good, cryptic reasons signed, *Your Savior*. Dwelling on the gut-twisting mystery just now would only add to her immediate anxiety, so she blocked it from her mind. One crisis at a time. She clutched the dime novel to her chest, a swarm of emotions buzzing in her belly. The illustrated cover featured a heart-pounding sketch of Rome and Boston Garrett—Wells Fargo detectives and hometown heroes—in a showdown with a notorious road thief. It wasn't the gun blazing scene that tripped Emily's pulse, but the sight of Rome. She'd had a fearsome crush on Paris's brother since she was nine. Unfortunately, the attraction was one-sided. Even though she was now twenty, he still regarded her as Preacher McBride's bookish little girl. Emily McBride, the socially backward daydreamer.

Sighing, she sneaked another peak at the dime novel cover. The artist's rendering of Rome was exquisite. So handsome in his brown duster and Stetson, menacing holster slung low on his lean hips. These days he wore his fair hair longer, making him look all the more rakish. She'd spent many a night wondering how it would feel to kiss a rake. Specifically, Rome Garrett.

"Mooning over your fantasy beau?"

Emily whirled. Mary Lee Dobbs, formerly Bernbaum. The woman Paris had once humiliated in song at a Lemonade and Storytelling Club picnic as payback for Mary Lee calling her Goofy Garrett. Self-conscious, she pressed the dime novel into the folds of her buckskin skirt. "I wasn't mooning."

"Yes, you were. Dream on, Emily. Men like Rome Garrett don't fall for women like you. You look like Calamity Jane, for pity's sake."

Like that was a bad thing. Emily liked wearing her wavy blond hair in two braids. She liked dressing similar to the frontierswoman who'd ridden alongside legends such as Wild Bill Hickok and Charlie Utter. An accomplished horsewoman and a crack shot, Calamity Jane was courageous and adventurous and Emily admired her with all of her heart. She didn't care what Mary Lee liked. She didn't like Mary Lee.

"Those Garrett boys prefer pretty, sensual women," the judgmental vixen said. "Women who know how to please a man."

You should know, Emily wanted to say, but didn't. Ten years ago she and Paris had caught Rome and Mary Lee canoodling by the creek. Rumor had it she'd dallied with London, the eldest of the four Garrett brothers, as well. If Athens hadn't intervened, Mr. Bernbaum would've instigated a shotgun wedding. No doubt Mary Lee's fondest wish. Now the woman was a bitter hussy, married off by her pa to a man twenty years her senior. A hussy in search of a new lover. No one talked about Mary Lee's secret rendezvous, but a few suspected. Emily *knew*. She brushed past the woman, without making eye contact. "Excuse me, please. It's storytelling time."

Mary Lee snorted. "I can't wait to hear your delivery of page three."

She kept walking, knowing in her queasy stomach it must have been Mary Lee who swayed the committee to choose *Showdown in Sintown* over a more literary work. She didn't need to peek at page three to know what it said. She'd read the story so many times she had it memorized. Page three offered the scene where Rome saved a west coast socialite, a victim of the stagecoach robbery, a woman with more backbone than sense, with the kiss of life. Upon revival, the damsel thanked Rome with another kind of kiss altogether.

When embarrassed, Emily babbled. Mary Lee knew full well when it came to reading this scene aloud in front of faithful churchgoers, she'd become flustered.

The shrew.

Chin held high, she walked past the reference

shelves, two reading tables, and the upholstered wing chair donated by Doctor Kellogg. So what if she rambled? So what if people found humor in her discomfort? She'd lived through like situations many a time before. "I can do this," she vowed to the scuffed toes of her leather boots.

She reached the meeting area just as Ezekiel Thompson, proprietor of the general store and this year's elected club president, called the late afternoon social to order. Members quieted and jockeyed for seats. Emily stood by, pulse racing. She caught Cole Sawyer staring at her and frowned. He'd been annoyingly attentive since her father's passing. Annoying, because she had no romantic interest in the man. She thought she'd made that clear, so last week's marriage proposal had been a shock. When she recovered her wits, she'd declined.

Unlike Mr. Bellamont, who'd proposed several weeks before, Cole was disinclined to take "no" for an answer. He'd promised to win her heart. But that was impossible since her heart wasn't up for grabs. Besides, whereas Mr. Bellamont had been motivated by good intentions, she suspected Cole wasn't so much interested in her welfare as her womb. The eldest of three, his pa was bent on him marrying and producing a grandson. Unhinged by his blatant attention, she focused on the committee table.

Mary Lee mouthed, "Page three," and smiled.

The shrew.

"Welcome, ladies and gents, to our bi-monthly meeting of the Lemonade and Storytelling Social Club." Mr. Thompson patted his potbelly, stifled a burp then gestured to his left. "Special thanks to Miss Frisbie for providing the baked goods and to Mrs. Dobbs for her delicious lemonade."

The membership applauded in appreciation.

Emily's pulse thrummed with dread. *Don't think about page three. Don't think, just read.* "I can do this."

Bam!

All creation started and turned at the sound of the front door slamming open.

A strong breeze fluttered the pages of the periodicals as a square-shouldered individual crossed the threshold. "Beg your pardon," he said, his soft voice laced with a Texan drawl. He scanned the audience, noted the committee, and their president who stood with arms akimbo, pointy-toed boot tapping in irritation as he closed the door. "Am I interrupting something?"

"Yes, sir, you are, sir," said Mr. Thompson. "The bi-monthly meeting of the Lemonade and Storytelling Social Club."

The membership muttered as they shifted in their seats for a better view of the intruder.

Emily felt obliged to intercede, seeing as she was

the assistant librarian and closer to the door than her boss, the incomparable Fannie Frisbie. Maybe he'd come to borrow a book. She pushed away from the wall and was afforded a better view of the stranger.

The wide brim of his Stetson shadowed his face, masking his expression and age, but his posture and clothing declared him a man of confidence and good taste. Brown frock coat, matching vest, a crisp white shirt, dark trousers—store bought and tailored. He held a folded newspaper in one hand, a leather traveling bag in the other. His gold-wired spectacles, much like her own, gave him a scholarly air. Maybe he was a professor or an encyclopedia salesman or . . . Oh, no. Could it be? "May I help you?"

He secured the newspaper beneath his arm and removed his hat. Shaggy, blond hair framed a breathtaking face. She'd never seen an honest to gosh angel, but she imagined a warrior of God would look much like this. Powerfully beautiful. Stylish and scholarly with a hint of arrogance. Mercy, he was an enigmatic presence. He raised a tawny brow. "Miss Emily McBride?"

She nodded, dumbstruck. Paris must have provided Mr. Pinkerton with a description of her. That made sense, of course. But she hadn't expected the poet so soon. She certainly hadn't expected to make his acquaintance in front of a portion of Heaven's most judgmental folk.

He flashed a dimpled smile. "I'm—"

"A friend of the family. I know." Startled out of her appraisal, she addressed the social club, "Excuse us, please," then rushed forward and shooed the man back outside. Since he was moving too slow, she nabbed his jacket sleeve and hurried him across the library's front lawn. "Please forgive my rudeness," she said when they reached the shade of a tree, "but you caught me at the worst of times."

He planted his expensive boots in the plush grass, angled his head. "Paris did notify you that I was coming?"

"Yes, although she didn't say when, not that it matters." She twisted the dime novel in her hands, glanced at the tree, her boots, the library. As if reading *Showdown in Sintown* wasn't bad enough, now she had to deal with an unwanted visitor. "Have you seen her recently? How is she? She sounds healthy and happy in her letters."

"I saw Paris a couple of weeks ago. She's fit as a fiddle, happy with her domestic situation, but miserable regarding you, Miss McBride."

"Yes, well, I'm sorry for that. I shouldn't have burdened her with my problems. I very much wish she would not have burdened you."

"No burden."

"Kind of you to say, but be that as it may, I cannot

. . . that is, I'm sorry but . . ." *Just say it*. "I'm afraid your trip was in vain, sir."

"Have your troubles disappeared?"

She bit her bottom lip. "I'm not sure."

"Then my trip wasn't in vain."

"Forgive my bluntness, but I don't want your help."

"Why not?"

"Because I want to handle this on my own."

"Why?"

His persistence, though amiable, irritated her. She thought about Calamity Jane and straightened her spine. "Because I'm an independent woman. Because everyone, including my best friend, thinks I need a keeper. I may not have the best judgment in the world, but the last thing I need is someone deciding what's best for me. I've had enough of that for three lifetimes, thank you very much!"

"No need to yell, Miss McBride."

"I'm not yelling!" Then she realized she was and blushed. The trials of the last year had whittled away at her polite sensibilities. "Damnation," she blurted and began to pace. "I'm not angry with you. I'm per-turbed at life."

Just as Paris had written, Phineas Pinkerton was kind and patient. She'd unleashed her frustration and he'd taken it in stride. Embarrassed by her outburst, she took a calming breath and restated her view. "I know you're an expert on criminal matters, but I'd prefer to solve my own problems. Now, please excuse me. I must get back inside. They're expecting me to . . ." She faltered. "You're staring, sir."

"I am." He angled his head, a quizzical expression on his Gabriel-esque face. "You're not what I expected."

Her cheeks flushed with embarrassment then anger. "Sorry to disappoint," she said, not sorry at all. She was weary of trying to live up to other people's expectations.

"On the contrary, Miss McBride. I'm intrigued."

Her cheeks burned hotter. Was he commenting on her unladylike attire? Her abrasive behavior? Instead of asking for clarification, she pointed. "The Moonstruck Hotel sits at the north end of town. You can catch a train back to San Francisco tomorrow. Good day, sir, and safe travels." There. That sounded assertive. Didn't it?

Nerves jangling, she took her leave, congratulating herself on handling at least one of the day's calamities with grace and success.

One crisis at a time.

CHAPTER 4

Emily's victory was short lived. She thought she'd left Mr. Pinkerton in the dust. He merely lagged behind. He caught up to her on the threshold and gently grasped her elbow. "Miss McBride."

Stomach fluttering, she turned to face him. She indicated the gawking audience with the tilt of her head. "Yes?"

He gestured toward the door. "Can we go someplace quiet, sit and talk?"

"For Pete's sake, Emily," Mr. Thompson said, "we're completely off schedule now."

"I've got fifteen minutes 'fore I have to git back to the store," Frank Biggins griped. Then again Mr. Biggins was always whining about something or another.

Emily could feel a dozen pair of eyes boring into her back. She could hear wheels turning—speculation, gossip. Even more, she was acutely aware of Mr. Pinkerton's touch. Although he held her elbow lightly, casually, her entire being tingled. She stood wide-eyed, momentarily crippled by confusion.

The situation worsened.

Suddenly Cole was standing next to her and glaring hard at the stylish stranger. "I'd appreciate it if you'd unhand my intended, mister."

Instead of releasing her, Mr. Pinkerton held firm. Part of her wanted to shake him off. Part welcomed the support. She was shaken by Cole's outrageous claim. She wasn't his, or anyone else's, *intended*.

The poet looked from Cole to Emily. "I'm confused."

"That makes two of us." If she flushed any hotter she'd set her clothes aflame. "I'm sorry, Cole," she whispered with all of the dignity she could muster, "but as I told you before, my heart belongs to someone else."

"Rome is a wanderer and a rake. He doesn't deserve you," Cole said. "He doesn't even know you're alive."

She knew that. But now so did Mr. Pinkerton and those sitting within earshot. Surely, Cole hadn't meant to be cruel, but his words had cut all the same. Her stomach pitched. Could a person expire from embarrassment?

Mr. Pinkerton subtly tugged her closer to him, farther from Cole. "This hardly seems the time or place to discuss Miss McBride's romantic preferences."

Cole jerked a thumb at the poet, his attention on Emily. "Who is this man?"

She sighed. "Phineas Pinkerton."

The poet furrowed his brow and rubbed the back of his neck. "For the love of—"

"Thirteen minutes and counting," Mr. Biggins hollered.

"Leave 'em be," Mary Lee called. "This is better than I. M. Wilde."

"Are you ailing, Mr. Pinkerton?" Emily asked, eager now to escape the social club. "Maybe I should walk you over to Doc's."

"Maybe he should git goin' on his own," Cole said, balling his hands at his sides.

Mr. Thompson pounded his gavel against the table. "Take a seat, Mr. Sawyer."

"Yes, please be seated, Cole," Emily pleaded then regarded the gentle poet with dismay. The rowdy son of a local rancher, Cole was known for settling arguments with his fists. "I'll just walk Mr. Pinkerton over to—"

Mr. Thompson pounded his gavel in protest. "Emily McBride, you are the featured reader. You can't leave!"

"You can't traipse off with a strange man," Cole said. "You may have no regard for your reputation, but I sure as hell do."

"I'll thank you to watch your language, Cole Sawyer," Miss Frisbie called.

He mumbled an apology, but his gaze—riveted on the poet—sparked white-hot fury.

Thanks to Cole, Emily was as uncomfortable as a camel in the Klondike. She had to nip this nonsense in the bud once and for all. Although she couldn't meet the rancher's eyes, at least her voice didn't crack. "Your concern is appreciated, Cole, but unnecessary." There. That sounded firm. Didn't it?

"I beg to differ. As I've said before, Emily, I only want what's best for you. As your husband, I could make your troubles disappear."

She thought about her *Savior* and shivered. Still . . . "I have a lot of living to do, Cole. The last thing I want or need is a husband."

Mr. Pinkerton mumbled something under his breath.

Cole narrowed his eyes. "You're the daughter of a preacher. I'm thinkin' you don't know diddly about real life. Otherwise, you wouldn't allow this stranger to lay hands on you."

It was then that she sensed a change in Mr. Pinkerton. A softening of sorts in his expression, his posture. "I assure you, I represent no threat to Miss McBride's reputation." He smiled, released her, and addressed the membership. "Pardon the interruption." He gestured to the wing chair. "I don't need a physician, but

I would like to sit a spell."

"It's a public facility," Mary Lee piped in, no doubt intrigued by a new man in town. "We can hardly turn him away."

"Fine, fine," Mr. Thompson said, glancing at his pocket watch. "Hurry on in then, Mr. Pinkerton. This meeting's running late. Cole, dad blame it, plant your keester."

The denim-clad rancher worked his jaw then graced Emily with a tight smile before retreating. "Looking forward to your reading, Emily. Knock 'em dead."

She'd prefer to knock some sense into him, specifically, as well as Mr. Pinkerton who seemed oblivious to danger. Instead, she waited until her unwanted suitor was halfway to his seat then turned on the good-natured, sweet-smelling poet. "You don't want to get mixed up in this. It's . . . tawdry."

He raised one brow, smile steady, gaze tender. Kind and trustworthy, Paris had written.

She didn't care. She wouldn't risk it. After the reading, she'd pull him aside and convince him to go away. Just like Cole, the man was annoyingly persistent. "Just don't say anything about my . . . troubles."

"Wouldn't dream of it." He acknowledged her with a nod then strode toward the wing chair.

Goodness. He even walked pretty—confident, controlled. She'd trade her treasured edition of Cooper's *The*

Last of the Mohicans to be that comfortable in her skin.

"Now then," Mr. Thompson said. "This afternoon we are setting aside our more literary pursuits to partake in a reading of I. M. Wilde."

Mumble. Murmur.

Emily pinched the bridge of her nose.

Mr. Thompson tapped his gavel. "Now, now, we all read the dime novels and penny dreadfuls. Ain't nothing wrong with sensationalized adventure. I know for certain we all read stories featuring the exciting tales of our homegrown heroes, Rome and Boston Garrett. Past year or so, most of them stories have been written by I. M. Wilde."

Grumble. Whisper.

At this point, *Showdown in Sintown* weighed mightily in Emily's heart and hands. Soon as she started reading, folks would get hot under the collar as this was a hot topic. She had the sweaty palms to prove it. She glanced at Mr. Pinkerton who sat rigid in the chair, his hat resting on his knees. He looked intrigued and annoyed at the same time. She wondered if he considered dime novels an inferior genre. Her temper flared at the notion. She'd never had patience for literary snobs.

Mr. Thompson paced in front of the committee table, his pudgy hands clasped behind his back. "Now I'm sure most of you read that little item in the Napa

County Reporter regarding Mr. Wilde's next publication. Apparently, it's a full-fledged novel. A historical novel with unsavory content."

Frank Biggins pumped his fist in the air. "You mean s-e-x. Just say it, Ezekiel. We're all adults. Sinful, that's what it is. I'm voting to ban it from this town."

"Firstly, you didn't say the 'S' word, you spelled it out, Frank." This from Miss Frisbie, the head librarian and an energized ball of sunshine even at fifty-one. "Secondly, how can you vote to ban a novel you've yet to read? Not that I believe in banning books, period. And lastly," she said, jabbing a finger at him, "if I recall, the article touted Mr. Wilde's novel as a historical romance."

"Historical romance with erotic elements," said Mr. Biggins.

"Exotic elements," Miss Frisbie countered. "I'm almost certain it said, exotic, not erotic."

"Same difference."

She rolled her river-blue eyes at the silver-haired cobbler. "That's why you're single, Frank. No woman wants to hitch herself to a man who doesn't know the difference between exotic and erotic."

The library exploded into a cacophony of rude noises.

Again, Emily pinched her nose and stole a glance at the poet, whose brows were raised in amusement . . .

or shock. She couldn't get a bead on this man.

Again, Mr. Thompson pounded his gavel.

Honest to gosh, Emily wanted to rip it from his hands. Between the gavel pounding, the poet's presence, Cole's unwanted attention, and Mary Lee's snooty looks, she had a considerable headache.

"Let's get on with this, shall we?" said Mr. Thompson.

Yes, let's, thought Emily. She hurried forward, whipped open the dime novel with a determined nod, and read. She did fine, real fine. Then she reached page three.

"Dread snaked down Rome's spine," she read aloud, "as he bent over Miss Sarah Smith. His gut clenched at the sight of her swollen, discolored temple. What kind of a man buffaloed a woman? A coldhearted pissant, that's what. She'd refused to hand over her reticule when threatened at gunpoint. That called for admiration, not a damned clubbing."

Assorted grunts and titters caused her to falter. Maybe she should have glossed over the vulgarities. Then again, Wilde had used those specific words to emphasize Rome's anger. Anyone who knew Rome knew his predilection for swearing. In the upcoming showdown with Four-fingered Angus, Wilde had peppered dialogue with *son of a bitch* and *bastard*. Truth told she'd overheard Paris's brothers say worse.

Perspiration beaded on her upper lip. She resisted the urge to sleeve it away. Purposely refrained from making eye contact with anyone in the audience, especially Mr. Pinkerton. A professional scribe. A gentle man.

"Go on, Emily," Cole urged. "I, for one, am eager to hear the outcome."

Was this part of his plan to win her favor? A public display of approval and support? She couldn't get a bead on him either. Clearly, she was inept where men were concerned. Her stomach contracted and her voice warbled as she picked up where she'd left off. "Swearing Four-fingered Angus to the devil, Rome brushed tendrils of fine coal-black hair from the woman's slack features. Dead to the world she was, so the Wells Fargo detective bestowed upon her the kiss of life. He pressed his mouth to hers and . . . and . . ."

She swallowed, tugged at the collar of her shirt. Gracious, the room was warm.

Mary Lee sniggered.

"Grow up, Mary Lee," Miss Frisbie whispered. "Keep going, Emily. You're doing fine."

She told herself to rally. She so desperately wanted to be the new Emily. Outspoken and fearless. Mary Lee deserved a pop on her powdered nose or, at the very least, a lecture on compassion. The woman was a bitter menace. Emily knew she could shut her up, by telling everyone she'd seen the woman kissing a ranch hand down by the stream last week. But Emily didn't have it in her to humiliate another human being. Mary Lee's husband and father would suffer as well. She just couldn't do it.

Squashing down her discomfort, she plowed on. She choked out one more line before reverting to the old Emily. She stared down at the print, at the romantic scene, hopelessly tongue-tied. How could she not say the words? She knew them by heart.

Mary Lee sniggered. "Prude."

"Hussy," Miss Frisbie rallied in Emily's defense.

Mr. Thompson cleared his throat. "Ladies, please."

Someone coughed into their hand. Wooden chairs creaked with fidgeting bodies.

Then silence prevailed as the audience waited for her to continue with the story. Mr. Biggins, the stuffy cobbler. Sheriff McDonald's pious wife. Mary Lee, the uncharitable hussy. She imagined them, along with a scattered intolerant few, scooting to the edges of their seats, making mental wagers as to whether she could get through *Showdown at Sintown* without succumbing to the vapors or a babbling episode.

Gaze riveted on the dime novel, Emily's skin burned. The wings of a thousand butterflies ravaged her stomach. It's not that she was embarrassed by the scene. She believed in the passion behind the words. Trouble was folks expected her to behave in a certain manner.

Like a preacher's daughter. A puritan. A *prude*. If they only knew. Well, actually someone did know.

Her *Savior*.

Now why did she have to go and think of that wretched soul? Everything inside of her seized. Her vision blurred and her hearing buzzed. She heard voices but couldn't distinguish words. She stared at page three, paralyzed.

"Pardon me."

The roaring in her ears grew louder.

"Excuse the interruption, but . . ."

Mr. Pinkerton's accented voice rose above the din, breaking Emily's trance. She glanced up just as he started toward her and went down hard, face first, with an undignified yelp.

Though the membership turned, not a soul offered assistance. They probably figured the stranger would get up and dust himself off, only he didn't. Concerned, Emily passed the dime novel to Miss Frisbie and rushed forward. She dropped to her knees and touched his shoulder. "Mr. Pinkerton. Are you all right?" When he didn't answer, she nabbed his arm and tried to flip him over. Mercy. For a soft-spoken, sweet-smelling man, he certainly was solid. She could feel sculptured muscles beneath his jacket sleeve, and couldn't help but wonder how he'd come to be so fit. One didn't develop rock-hard biceps from pushing a pen or pencil across paper or solving crimes from an armchair.

"Out cold," Mr. Biggins declared as he stooped and helped to turn Mr. Pinkerton onto his back.

"Must've hit his noggin hard." Miss Frisbie leaned over Emily's shoulder. "Maybe I should fetch Doc Kellogg."

By now the whole membership had huddled.

"Give him a sec," Mr. Thompson said, shooing everyone back. "Give him some air."

"Sure does smell pretty," the senior librarian noted as Emily readjusted the man's specs. Knocked askew in the fall, it was a wonder the lenses hadn't cracked.

"Looks pretty, too," Mr. Biggins said, hands on hips. He looked over at Cole. "Don't know what you got so riled for. This Nancy boy doesn't look like much of a threat."

"His name is Phineas Pinkerton," Emily grit out. "He's a poet in search of inspiration." A half-truth, but better than the whole truth. She couldn't reveal why he'd really come to Heaven.

Several people repeated the word *poet* and chuckled.

Their intolerance for anyone who marched to a different beat struck her anew and with a vengeance that had her grinding her teeth. She tapped the scribe's clean shaven cheeks in hopes of reviving him. The longer he was out, the more she worried he'd suffered serious harm.

Bones popped and creaked when Mr. Thompson hunkered down for a closer look. "A poet. Guess that would explain his prissy clothes and delicate constitution."

Blood burning, she locked gazes with the proprietor of the general store. An essentially good man, or at least she'd thought until this moment. "Mr. Pinkerton doesn't seem to be coming around, Mr. Thompson. Miss Frisbie's right. We should fetch Doc."

Duly contrite, he nodded and rose with another series of snaps and creaks. "Cole, would you mind? You move a mite quicker than me."

Cole spared Emily a look that caused her stomach to flutter . . . and not in a good way. "I'll be right back."

Emily would've told him to take his time, except she wanted him to hurry along Doc.

Mary Lee, who'd probably never regretted a word or action in her life, kneeled across from Emily. "Mr. Pinkerton looks right peaked." Her lip twitched. "Maybe his heart gave out. Maybe you should give him the kiss of life."

Miss Frisbie waggled an arthritic finger at the shrew. "Maybe you should—"

Emily touched her champion's arm to cut off whatever verbal bullet she was about to shoot. A shouting match in the library wouldn't do. Besides, this was her

fight. Mary Lee had been egging her on all afternoon.
If she leaned forward she could sock that smirk off of
the woman's puss. But that wouldn't be nice, and if
Emily had had anything drilled into her spirit, it was
to be good. Besides, if she took a poke, Mary Lee
might collapse on top of Mr. Pinkerton, making it even
harder for him to breathe.

Kiss of life.

She'd never pressed her mouth to a man's. Didn't
it figure her first kiss would be of a practical nature and
not with the love of her life? She placed her hands on
either side of the poet's face, conscious of his sharply-
cut features, of the warmth of his skin. Or maybe it
was she who was overheated. Lord knew she was
burning up with awkwardness as she dropped her face
close to his. How many times had she dreamt of touching Rome like this?

"Mr. Pinkerton," she whispered. "Phineas. Come
back to us. Come back or I'll have to . . ." She cleared
her throat. "Please don't make me do this."

No response.

Drat.

She leaned closer, lips hovering inches from his
mouth. A nice mouth, she mused. Not that it mattered.
This wasn't about pleasure, but life and death.

She heard a collective intake of breath, could feel
the membership hovering over her and the unconscious

man, could sense Mary Lee's amusement.

Just then Mr. Pinkerton's tawny lashes fluttered. He opened his eyes and, startled by her proximity, jerked upward. Their foreheads knocked and they yelped in unison. "Good heavens, Miss McBride," he rasped. "You scared the dickens out of me."

She palmed her smarting brow, eased back. "Are you all right?"

He sat up, and casually adjusted her crooked spectacles. "Are you?"

Her heart galloped at the brush of his fingers. She nudged away his hand and flipped her braids over her shoulders. "I'm fine." Knowing everyone was staring, she scrambled to her feet and offered Mr. Pinkerton a hand up.

He squinted at her as if he didn't understand the gesture.

Miss Frisbie squeezed her elbow. "I'm thinking he's still dazed, Emily. Probably shouldn't get up until Doc examines him."

"I'm quite well, madam," Mr. Pinkerton said. "Merely chagrined. It's not every day a man trips over his own feet." With that, he rose and swooned.

Mr. Biggins caught him and eased him into a chair. "Whoa there, Percy."

"It's Phineas," Miss Frisbie corrected, moving forward to fan the poet with a copy of *Harper's Bazaar*.

Mr. Biggins studied the groaning man with a disgusted sniff. "Same difference."

Mary Lee joined Miss Frisbie, and suddenly every woman in the room was fussing over Phineas Pinkerton. Emily stood in the background, amazed. First impressions could certainly be deceiving. *Warrior of God, my foot.* She'd never met a more fragile man in all her born days. Apparently, Frank and the other men agreed as they rolled their eyes and drifted back to the cookies and lemonade.

Cole and Doctor Kellogg burst into the library and Emily knew two things for certain.

One: She wouldn't have to finish reading *Showdown in Sintown.*

Two: She'd have to look out for Paris's friend until he left town. Once word got out that he was *delicate,* Phineas Pinkerton would become the subject of petty, hurtful gossip.

It occurred to her that they had a lot in common.

CHAPTER 5

Seth considered himself an expert on two things in life: wrangling criminals and seducing women. The trick was getting into their minds, learning what made them tick, and anticipating their actions and reactions.

Emily McBride was a brain buster. Hard to make sense out of a woman who made no sense at all.

Seated in the passenger seat of a ramshackle buggy, he glanced sideways at the young woman in possession of the reins. She didn't dress, talk, or behave like a preacher's daughter. Instead of wearing her pale blond hair in a conservative style, she'd woven the waist-length tresses into two sassy braids, tying off the ends with leather thongs. Her attire was equally unconventional. A buckskin skirt, flat-heeled boots, a man's white ruffled shirt, and black suspenders. She looked more like a circus sharpshooter than a librarian. The only bookish thing about her was her spectacles. She wasn't homely or beautiful. Quietly pretty, maybe. Tall for a woman, though not as tall as Seth, and thin as a desert grasshopper. She wasn't overtly sensual and yet, since meeting her, he hadn't been able to take his eyes off of her. He'd told her he was intrigued. That, for sure and certain, was the truth.

"A concussion. Of all the rotten luck," she grumbled as she slapped the reins to the backside of the harnessed mare in a bid to hasten their trek out of town.

"Possible concussion," Seth corrected, though he had no such thing. "If you're uncomfortable about me staying with you—"

"I am, but there's no help for it. Someone needs to watch over you for the next twenty-four hours and I can't leave you at the mercy of the innkeeper at the Moonstruck. Boris tends to frown upon men with delicate constitutions, if you know what I mean and I think you do. Forgive my bluntness."

The absurdity of the statement caused Seth to smile. Good thing he was confident in his manhood. "I appreciate your candor, Miss McBride." Mighty worldly for a preacher's daughter. Athens's description of a shy, trusting soul had been a tad misleading. Although she avoided eye contact, Emily spoke her mind fairly well. On the other hand, she *was* painfully polite and overly concerned about what other people thought. To top things off, she was dead set against marriage, except maybe to Rome Garrett. Once again, the Wells Fargo agent was proving a pain in Seth's ass and he wasn't even present.

He'd met Rome, had instantly recognized a fellow skirt chaser. In addition, he'd heard about the man's fickle ways from his sister and had read about them in those exaggerated dime novels. Emily wasn't his type. She wasn't Seth's type either. Apparently Athens, Sawyer, and Bellamont had a weakness for outspoken, flat-chested virgins.

Paris had tipped him off regarding Bellamont's interest. Cole Sawyer had been a surprise. After meeting the arrogant prick and sensing Emily's distress, he'd jumped on her mistaken assumption he was one Phineas Pinkerton. It had been a split-second decision, one he aimed on using to his advantage. Obviously Paris, the interfering minx, hadn't informed Emily of the change in plans as agreed. Josh was operating on the sly. Athens hadn't forewarned her of Seth's arrival, wanting to catch her off balance with the marriage proposal.

Turns out, Seth was the one caught off balance.

"You're going to have to stay with me. Which is what Paris intended. I can't believe this," she lamented to the horse's behind. "She's not even here and she still got her way."

He was thinking the same thing.

"Just promise me you won't interfere in my problems."

"Can't do that."

"Why not?"

He'd already given his word to the contrary to three other people. "I'm not big on promises."

"Well, I'm not big on saviors!"

Seth studied her with curiosity and concern. He heard more than anger in her tone. He heard fear. "No need to raise your voice, Miss McBride." He winked in a conspiratorial manner, as if they shared a special secret. "Delicate does not equal deaf."

The smile he'd hoped for in return did not appear. "I'm sorry," she said, her gaze riveted on the winding trail. "I just . . . I don't want to be saved."

That statement bothered him though he couldn't say why. Not that it mattered. No way, no how was he going to let her tangle with a blackmailer. He wouldn't allow a woman to put herself in harm's way. He sure as shootin' didn't aim on twiddling his thumbs while she played amateur detective. The sooner he fixed this mess, the sooner he could return to solving real crime.

Tawdry.

What had a she gotten herself into?

"Is this your first time in California?" she asked in a blatant attempt to change the subject.

It was. But he figured Pinkerton had probably toured the regional theaters, maybe even The Gilded Garrett, a San Franciscan opera house owned and run by Paris's oldest brother, London Garrett. "First time this far north."

"Paris mentioned you've been creatively blocked. Maybe this trip won't be a total waste. Maybe you'll find inspiration in the hills and valleys of Napa County."

Seth had learned long ago he could often glean information by remaining silent. As such, he settled back and allowed Emily to ramble. She pointed out the vineyards of one of her distant neighbors, a hard-working entrepreneur, suitor number one, Claude Bellamont.

"He's a good neighbor, and a good . . ." She cleared her throat. "*Was* a good friend of my father's. He and his sons run Bellamont Winery and . . ."

Seth took it all in. The names. The history. The scenery.

He was damn near mesmerized by all the serene green. Gentle hills and lush lowlands. Densely wooded areas of oaks, pine firs, and varieties of trees he didn't recognize. Vineyards. Orchards. According to his chatty companion, Napa County was rich with grapes, olives, apples, oranges, and walnuts.

Then there were the flowers. Abundant, colorful petals exploding amongst miles and miles of green.

She identified those, too.

There was an almighty difference between Northern California and the desert wilds of Arizona Territory, where mostly everything, aside from the cactus and mesquite, was one shade or another of brown.

He didn't mind the scenery. Change was good. He'd repeated that mantra on the journey from Phoenix to Yuma, from Yuma to San Francisco, and from that sprawling city to the quaint one-horse town of Heaven. He was just about sold. If not good, then change was at least interesting. These days he appreciated anything out of the ordinary.

The bridge of his nose throbbed from a slight, but annoying, pressure. Damned spectacles. Mostly they were for up-close work. It chafed that he needed them. A sign of aging, the spectacle peddler had said. Completely normal, he'd added, as if that was supposed to make Seth feel better. The traveling salesman had made him feel a half century older than his thirty-one.

Frowning, he gazed over the top of the oval-wired lenses and continued to study the land as he memorized the trek from town to Emily's country home. After his fall and the Nancy boy references, she'd changed her mind about taking him in fast as a Deacon taking up collection in church. Add gullible and softhearted to her vast and varied characteristics.

Deception, though not his original intention, now seemed key to ensuring a successful mission. He wasn't keen on masquerading as an effeminate scribe, but Paris was right. Her friend's reputation wouldn't suffer overly much under this guise. The ass over tea-kettle incident, though an ego bruiser, had strengthened his ruse. Now the citizens not only thought he was a dandy, but a klutz. Only one other person knew he wasn't a total buffoon, and that was the person who tripped him. Cole Sawyer. Instead of saving himself and cold-cocking the bastard, Seth had milked the fall.

Kissing the floorboards had been a sure-fire way of diverting attention from Emily. When it came to cussin', she didn't swallow her tongue none, but describing a steamy embrace struck her speechless. He'd feigned unconsciousness longer than necessary, luring her into that kiss-of-life business. He couldn't get a fix on her and he wanted to explore the extent of her inhibitions. Now he knew. The woman dressed on the wild side, but when it came to physical intimacy, she was wound up tighter than a toad's ass.

He felt a little guilty about the ruse, but not much. A passel of folks' happiness depended on his cleaning up Emily's mess and delivering her to Arizona Territory. He'd fess up as soon as he judged her willing to accept his true identity without ordering him back to Phoenix, *alone*.

She'd declared herself capable of handling her own trouble. Like hell. No way, no how was this woman up to handling a low-down extortionist. As for relying on the local law, Paris's description hadn't been far off. He didn't know about the loose-lip part, but ninny applied. He'd stopped by the jailhouse on the way to the library to scan the wanted posters. A career habit. If there was trouble in the area, he wanted to know who to look out for.

Heaven's sheriff had been sitting out front, feet propped up, hat tugged low. He jerked out of his nap when Seth's boot heels hit the boardwalk. He didn't get up, didn't spur introductions. But he did note Seth's interest in the posters. "Looking for anyone particular?"

"Just looking."

"You're new in town," he'd said, wiping drool from his mouth.

"Yup."

"You a troublemaker?"

"Nope."

"Then welcome to Heaven."

He'd pointed Seth in the direction of the library without inquiring as to his name or business. Hard to tell if the man was completely incompetent, but he was sure as hell lax.

"So, what did Paris tell you about me?" Emily

asked, jolting him back to the present.

He racked his brain. "That you have a fierce love of literature. Your preferences run the gamut, from Shakespeare to Dickens to . . ." he flattened his mouth. "I. M. Wilde."

"I suppose you disapprove of dime novels."

"Why would you suppose that?"

"You frowned at the mention of Wilde."

What he disapproved of was Wilde's penchant for portraying the Garrett brothers as indestructible paragons of justice. No man was indestructible. The Garretts weren't saints by a long shot. He'd butted heads with three out of four when they'd come after their sister last fall. The oldest brother, London, was a bossy son of a bitch, but Rome and Boston in particular were destined to meet their maker due to arrogance and lack of self-restraint. Though he didn't think Emily would appreciate the observation seeing that she was smitten with Rome. "I don't have a problem with Wilde. Precisely."

"Can you elaborate? Is it the writing in particular that troubles you? The style? The pacing?"

He didn't rightly know why she cared what he thought, then he remembered he was Phineas Pinkerton—poet. Also that Emily, according to Paris, dabbled with writing herself. "I'm leery of glorified violence," he answered truthfully.

Her shoulders relaxed and she nodded. "Oh."

Seth fixated on her crooked smile, experienced a pull in his gut. Well, damn.

"I can respect that," she said.

She dressed tough, talked tough, but when it came right down to it, Emily McBride was sweet. He suddenly understood why she was the object of several men's affection. Angel and hellion rolled into one. Men connived to get a woman like that in bed. The appeal did not escape Seth.

"About that Cole fellow," he ventured.

"Cole Sawyer. His pa owns the Rocking S, a cattle ranch up north. Mr. Sawyer's ailing and looking to secure his legacy. Cole's anxious to comply. I don't know what's worse, knowing ahead of time that a loved one's going to die or just waking up one day and . . ."

"Paris told me about your parents," he said as a flush crept up her neck. "I'm sorry for your loss."

"Thank you." She looked everywhere but at him. "What did she tell you exactly?"

"No specifics. Just that you lost them a few months apart and that their deaths were unexpected." He could almost see the tension whooshing out of her body. Interesting.

"The adjustment has been challenging and full of surprises. Some good, some bothersome. About Cole," she said, redirecting the conversation. "I do apologize for his ill manners, Mr. Pinkerton. He's gotten it in his head that . . . well, he wants to marry me."

"I gathered. When do you expect he'll pose the question?"

"He already did. Last week. I declined. I mean, it's ludicrous. I'd rather hitch myself to a donkey. Not that I used those express words. I mean, I wouldn't want to hurt his feelings."

His lip twitched. "Heavens, no."

"It's infuriating, I tell you, Cole's persistence. At least Mr. Bellamont accepted my refusal with grace."

Seth feigned surprise. "The winemaker. Your neighbor. He proposed as well?"

"Several weeks ago." She focused back on the road. "I've never had a beau. Then Pa passes, and two men propose in less than two months. Everyone thinks I need a keeper. I don't."

"So you've said."

"I'm perfectly content being single."

"Forever?"

"For now."

So there was hope. It was all in the timing and choice of words. He'd make her see the wisdom in marrying Athens. In turn his boss's faith in his abilities would be confirmed. If he could pull off this poet persona, he could pull off anything.

Emily sighed. "I apologize for bending your ear, Mr. Pinkerton. I don't usually unburden myself to strangers, to anyone, well, except Paris. I don't know what got into me. Although, she did say you're a good listener. Which you are." She scraped white teeth over her full bottom lip. "Can we not talk about this anymore?"

Suited him fine. She'd given him plenty to think on. He folded his arms over his chest, relaxed against the seat, and studied his hostess from the corner of his eye. He'd wanted a challenge. He'd gotten one. This woman was as hard to pin down as smoke in a bottle.

She glanced sideways, her blue-blue eyes telegraphing her discomfort. "You're staring again."

"Pondering. You're a mite different than what I was led to believe."

"That's the second time you've said something like that." She focused back on the road, squared her shoulders. "I shudder to think what all Paris shared with you."

Actually, he was contemplating Athens's description of a meek woman. Paris had called her resourceful. He remembered then that Emily had been the one to persuade Paris into running away from home to pursue a songwriting career. "She told me that if it weren't for you she wouldn't have met Josh."

She fidgeted in her seat.

"Told me you advised her to dress like a boy and to use an alias in order to elude her brothers."

"It wouldn't have been safe for her to travel all that way alone as a woman."

"She shouldn't have been traveling alone period." He bit back a lecture on the numerous perils awaiting an unescorted woman. He doubted a man like Pinkerton had witnessed the same atrocities as a career lawman.

"She needn't have traveled any farther than San Francisco if it weren't for her pig-headed brothers," she said. "Her family owns an opera house. London runs the place. If he would've allowed her to perform her original compositions at the Gilded Garrett, like she asked in the first place, she wouldn't have been forced to explore alternatives. Personally, I'm proud of Paris for following her heart and defying convention. She's an artist. A composer. Life experience inspires passionate prose."

"Strange talk coming from a preacher's daughter," Seth noted, truly fascinated. "I would have pegged you more conservative."

"Strange talk coming from a poet. I would have pegged you more liberal."

She delighted the hell out of him with her grit. He would've smiled if not for the sudden feeling they were being trailed. He glanced around, saw nothing, but experienced a tickle of apprehension all the same.

Oblivious, Emily nudged him. "We're almost home."

Guinevere—what kind of a name for a horse was

that?—whinnied and quickened her gait of her own accord. They rounded the bend and he got his first glimpse of Emily's sprawling two-story house. Carpenter gothic, he thought they called it. A wooden monstrosity with scrolled gables. It looked like a storybook gingerbread house and it was painted, Christ Almighty, various shades of *green*.

"I know it looks worse for wear," she said. "But it's comfortable on the inside."

As they drew closer, he realized worse for wear meant that the paint was chipped and peeling, the front door window was cracked, and one of the porch posts was plumb broken.

It looked like a palace compared to his one-level, four-room adobe.

In the distance, branches rustled and the hairs on the back of Seth's neck stood. His fascination with Emily took a back seat to Paris's dire plea. *"If you don't go, something awful is going to happen."* He pretended interest in the property while surreptitiously scanning the wooded area to their left.

No doubt about it. They were being watched.

CHAPTER 6

Territory of Arizona

The hair on the back of Athens's neck prickled. Parker. His assistant, though competent and fearless, had a vexing habit of entering the room like a ghost. Unseen. Unheard. An admirable quality in a covert situation. Irksome in everyday life.

"How long have you been standing there?" he asked without turning. Hunched over his desk, he continued to read a file on Bulls-eye Brady, a notorious road agent and cold-blooded killer.

"Not long, sir. Sorry to interrupt, but—"

"Yes?"

"I have a telegram from your brother."

"Which one?"

"London."

Athens held out his hand, his gaze still pinned on the report. Two train heists and three stagecoach robberies in less than two months. Six deaths. He cursed Brady to the bowels of the devil's lair.

"It's good news, sir," Parker said, prompting Athens to close the outlaw's file and open the telegram.

Good news indeed. The eldest of the Garrett clan had agreed to relocate to Arizona Territory. Athens smiled. All of his plans were coming together. Seth was in Heaven, procuring a mother for his children. London would be setting up shop in Phoenix, providing a front and operation base for PMA. If Lady Luck continued to look favorably upon him, he'd have the alliance up and running by the end of the month.

Unlike Alan Pinkerton's National Detective Agency, a veritable private army, the Peacemakers Alliance would rely upon the talents of eight qualified agents— all former law enforcers in one or another regard. He'd enlist Rome and Boston, for they were certainly among the best, but they had two things working against them. Their hotheaded nature and the fact that they were nearly as famous as Wild Bill Hickcok, the first dime novel hero of the west. I. M. Wilde's romanticized tales had catapulted the two youngest Garrett Brothers to celebrity status. Fine for Wells Fargo. A liability for PMA.

He folded the telegram, grateful that London had retained a certain degree of anonymity. Though owner of one of the most successful opera houses in

San Francisco, he led a quiet life. Unlike their father, London didn't crave attention. Nor did he sleep with every starlet who hit the Gilded Garrett stage. His low key existence proved of little interest to gossipy folk and sensationalists like Wilde. What they didn't know was that London possessed the same skill with his fists and gun as Rome and Boston. Athens knew. He also knew his older brother was looking for a prime excuse to shake up the life he'd never wanted.

"I need you to send a reply," Athens told Parker, but before he could dictate a telegram, the office door slammed open.

Sammy Kirk, the blacksmith's nine-year-old and a schoolmate of Zach's, burst in wide-eyed and out of breath. "You best come quick, Mr. Garrett. Zach's really gone and done it this time."

Parker sighed.

Athens wanted to sigh. He was weary of his son's explosive temper, but he rose calmly and reached for his coat and hat. "Another fight?"

"Yes, sir. A whopper, sir."

"Injuries?" Since moving to Phoenix last month, Zach had suffered assorted scrapes and bruises and a chipped front tooth.

Sammy braced his hands on his knees, attempting to catch his breath. "A shiner."

"Well, he's survived a black eye before."

"Wasn't Zach that got clobbered, sir. Was Zach that did the clobberin'."

Athens blinked at the freckle-faced kid. "My son punched someone?"

Sammy nodded. "Mrs. Wilson."

"The schoolmarm." Parker whistled. "Holy—"

"Lock up the files, Parker. I'll be back as soon I handle this situation."

"You might be away a good while, sir," Sammy called, just as Athens breached the threshold. "Zoe's missing."

Kaila Dillingham's mood was bright despite a slow day at Café Poppy. At least she *had* Café Poppy. A business of her own, not that she needed the money. What she needed was independence, purpose. She'd found that when she moved from Kent, England to the land of opportunity. Specifically, the American west, an untamed region that stirred her noble blood. For the first time in her adult life, she was truly happy. She had I. M. Wilde, the American dime novelist, to thank for that.

Since business was slow, and since she could afford to close early, she did. Thereafter she'd indulged in a bit of shopping. Wilde's latest tale, *Showdown in*

Sintown, presently burned a hole in the satchel of supplies she'd purchased at the general store. She looked forward to afternoon tea on her veranda, coupled with an exhilarating read. Later, she'd enjoy a quiet meal and a scenic sunset. She'd been working very hard since her arrival in Phoenix. Had she truly been here a month already?

A cloudless sky and a refreshing breeze prompted a leisurely walk home. Pedestrian and equine traffic diminished the further she strolled from the town's center. An invigorating combination of serenity and excitement pulsed through her body as she viewed vast desert and distant hills.

Somewhere out there lived a man who could make her soul sing. A handsome, rugged lawman, or maybe a rakish frontier man. Each morning she awoke wondering if this was the day he'd ride in and sweep her off of her feet. She wanted an adventure. A romantic adventure. Oh, to be a heroine in one of her beloved dime novels.

Tales of intrigue, specifically Wilde's tales as they always involved a dashing hero and a damsel in distress, played through her mind as she walked the edge of a wide sandy road. An arranged, loveless marriage had left her yearning for what she'd never experienced—heart-tripping passion. A girlish notion and she was a widow of twenty-eight. Still, she harbored hope that a cowboy would take her on a lustful ride, even if only for a moment in time. One passionate moment could make for a lifetime of contentment, or so she'd read.

Two blocks from her humble residence, she heard the rustling leaves crying. Perplexed she lowered her parasol and peered up at a massive cottonwood tree. She caught sight of white petticoats amongst the green foliage and two wee dangling feet. A small girl, surely no more than five or six, was nestled in the branches, sniffling and talking to herself.

Kaila couldn't make out the anguished words, but the stilted sobs and hiccups tore at her heart. Her biggest concern was that the girl would slip and fall. "Young miss," she called softly so as not to startle the tyke. "Are you hurt?"

The girl peered down at Kaila with teary green eyes. She shook her head no, her blond curls bouncing with the effort.

"Are you stuck?"

Another shake of the head and more sniffles.

"Perhaps you could climb down then and we'll discuss whatever is causing you distress."

She set her chin at a stubborn angle, clapped onto the next branch and climbed a little higher.

Heart fluttering, Kaila tossed down her satchel and parasol and edged closer to the trunk of the tree. She wanted her arms free in case the girl fell. When the blond monkey settled safely on yet another limb, Kaila looked over her shoulder for help. No one was around. "Oh, dear." She tilted her head back, smiled up at the girl and kept her voice as calm as possible. "My name is Kaila. What's your name?"

After a long moment she sleeved tears from her cherubic face and croaked, "Zoe."

"Pleased to make your acquaintance, Zoe. I have homemade cookies in my satchel. They're quite delicious, if I do say so myself. Would you care for one?"

She bit her lower lip, nodded.

"Excellent." Kaila's shoulders sagged with relief. "Come down then. Slowly and . . . no?" Blast.

The sniffling tyke summoned Kaila with a crooked finger. "Could you bring a cookie for Sparkles, too?"

As the child was quite alone, she had no clue as to the identity of Sparkles. Regardless, Kaila took a napkin full of cookies from her satchel and stuffed them in the reticule looped over her wrist. She couldn't fathom climbing a tree in her cumbersome ensemble. She didn't want to scale the tree at all, but felt she stood a better chance at reasoning with Zoe face to face, ginger cookies in hand.

Again, she surveyed the area.

Deserted.

Before she could second guess her actions, she

took off her ostrich-plumed hat, shimmied out of her bustled skirt, and, dressed only in bodice and bloomers, worked her way toward the wide-eyed girl. She did so with surprising ease. The branches were strong and plentiful, and she was fit and limber. *Well done*, she thought as she positioned herself on a branch opposite Zoe. To pull such a stunt on her native soil would have been scandalous. Women of title simply did not climb trees. She supposed her actions would raise a few eyebrows even here in Arizona Territory. Not that she'd shimmied a tree, but that she'd done so in her bloomers. Best to talk Miss Zoe down before anyone happened along. Though she'd abandoned her title, she still possessed dignity.

She dipped into her reticule and passed Zoe a cookie.

The girl thanked her and pointed. "Sparkles is sitting right next to you."

"I see," she said, even though she didn't. She imagined, however, as she guessed Zoe was doing. "I'll set your cookie on this branch, Sparkles. Help yourself and do enjoy."

Zoe pursed her lips and nodded to the empty space next to Kaila. "Sparkles says you talk funny."

"I'm from England. Do you know where that is?"

"Far away."

"Indeed."

"Sparkles comes from far away, too. She's a forest fairy."

Kaila smiled at the space that was Sparkles. "A very pretty one, too. As are you, Miss Zoe. Lovely creatures, the both of you."

She smiled at that and nibbled on her cookie. Her cheeks were tear streaked, but her eyes were now dry. Progress.

"What were you and Sparkles talking about before I interrupted?"

"My brother."

"Is he all right?"

"He's in trouble."

"For what?"

"Hitting our teacher."

"Oh, dear."

"Wasn't his fault," Zoe said with her mouthful. "Them mean boys called him liar."

"Hmm."

"And our uncles figmans."

Kaila furrowed her brow. "Figmen?" Was that anything like a forest fairy?

"Said someone made them up."

She pondered that then nodded. "Ah. Figments. Those boys said your uncles are *figments* of someone's imagination."

Zoe swiped crumbs from her plaid dress. "That's

what I said."

"Indeed it is." Kaila angled her head. "So why are you up here?"

"If Papa's busy lookin' for me, he can't whup Zach."

"Zach's your brother?"

She nodded. "Papa told him if he got in one more tussle, he'd get a whuppin'."

Kaila frowned. "Is that so?" The bully.

A dog barked at the base of the tree and she made the mistake of looking down. Her vision blurred. Oh, dear. She hadn't realized how far up she'd ventured. She blew out a breath, focused back on Zoe. "Yes, well, it's most noble of you to protect Zach, but your mother must be terribly worried."

Zoe wrinkled her nose. "Do angels worry in heaven?"

"Pardon?"

"Papa says mama lives in heaven. Says she's an angel."

Kaila blinked. "Oh. I, well, I . . ." The branch she was sitting on creaked and her heart leapt to her throat. She wiggled closer to the trunk and grasped the limb above.

"It's cuz you're heavy," Zoe said, though not un-kindly. "You should get down."

"Yes, well, you go first. Don't worry about your brother. I'll walk you home and make certain your father understands the situation and does not . . . whup."

"Maybe we should bring him a cookie."

Kaila blew stray hairs out of her eyes, tried to steady her nerves. "Excellent idea. I have plenty in my satchel. Can you make it down on your own, Zoe?"

"Yep. See ya later, Sparkles!" She scrambled to the ground in a heartbeat, leaving Kaila in the care of an invisible forest fairy.

"You wouldn't allow me to fall would you, Sparkles?" Kaila asked through clenched teeth. Fighting a bout of vertigo, she swung her body to a lower branch and . . . "Oh, no."

"What's wrong?" Zoe called from below.

"I'm caught. My bloomers, they snagged and . . . Bloody hell."

"You said a bad word."

"I know. I'm sorry, but I'm a bit flustered at this moment."

"Want me to climb back up?"

"I do not!" Just what she needed. A little girl risking her neck to free *her* bloomers. "Maybe if I wiggle . . ." She slipped, heard a rip, and yelped as she clung to a branch.

"You loose now?"

"No, Zoe." Kaila said, tamping down her panic. "I'm still stuck."

"I'll get help. Look. There's Papa!"

"No, wait! Wait!" But she was gone.

The dog, however, was rooting in her satchel, no doubt in search of ginger cookies.

"Shoo, you meddlesome hound! Go away!"

The long-nosed mutt stared up at her and licked crumbs from his snout. Then to her utter horror, he snapped up her skirt and took off running.

"Bloody hell."

Morbid thoughts assaulted Athens as he searched high and low for his five-year old daughter. It wasn't the first time she'd run off, but it was the first time he hadn't found her within ten minutes of looking. After checking in to make sure Mrs. Wilson was all right and learning what had precipitated Zoe's disappearance, he'd delivered his son to Parker for safekeeping.

"We'll talk later," he'd told the ill-repentant boy, struggling to contain his exasperation. Zach had accidentally clipped the schoolmarm when she'd tried to break up a fight between him and another boy. Soon after Zoe had gone missing. His children were driving him to an early grave with their constant shenanigans. The sooner Seth delivered Emily, the better.

He'd schooled his frustrations and set to fetch his daughter, a girl who talked a blue streak to animals and imaginary friends, but clammed up around strangers (which constituted the whole of Phoenix). He'd expected to find her at the livery hiding out in a stall and playacting with the blacksmith's new litter of pups. Or sitting in a tree swapping tales with Sparkles, a conjured fairy. Half an hour into the hunt and his nerves were shot. The same helplessness, the hopelessness that had pulverized him upon hearing of Jocelyn's murder snaked up and strangled his spirit.

He was getting ready to enlist the sheriff's aid when he spotted Zoe in the distance, standing at the base of a tree and shouting something up to the branches. He didn't know if she was talking to a bird or Sparkles. He didn't care. Relief fueled his steps as he sprinted toward his daughter.

She spotted him at the same time, raced forward waving her tiny arms.

He'd almost reached her when the little polecat swiveled round and ran back for the tree. Winded, fuming, he caught up to her and swooped her into arms. "God*dammit*, Zoe. Are you trying to give me a heart attack? Don't ever . . . how could you . . . ?" Emotion clogged his throat.

Eyes wide, she flicked a nervous tongue across her lips. "You said a bad word."

"I know, baby. I'm sorry."

"Are you flustered?"

"What?"

"Kaila's flustered. She's stuck in the tree."

Please, God, not another imaginary friend.

He heard a creak and a curse. He glanced up and saw a woman, a stunningly beautiful redhead, straddling a gnarled limb and clinging for dear life. "What the . . .?" he lowered his daughter to the ground and surveyed the situation.

"I'll thank you to avert your eyes, sir," she said in an accented voice.

With Zoe safe, curiosity doused his anxiety, leaving him oddly relaxed. "Why?"

"I'm in my . . . my . . ."

"I can see that and again I ask, why?"

"Because it's difficult to climb trees in tiers of stiff frills and yards of silk," she ground out.

Athens braced his hands on his hips and studied the red-faced woman with a smile. "Climb a lot of trees, do you?" Staring was ungentlemanly, but, by God, she was lovely, even with that distressed expression. Teasing her was ungentlemanly as well, but he couldn't seem to help himself.

She narrowed her enormous, sultry eyes. "You're incorrigible."

Zoe poked him in the thigh. "What's that mean?"

"Means I'm rude," he said with a grin. He'd never been rude to a woman, not once in his thirty-one years.

This was a first. It was also the first time he'd flirted with a woman in years. He swept off his hat. "Beg your pardon, ma'am. I'm Athens Garrett, Zoe's pa."

She blew out a breath. "Kaila Dillingham."

"Proprietor of the Café Poppy. I've heard about you." He angled his head. "Huh."

"What does that mean? What did you hear?"

That men and women alike were intimidated by her beauty and fancy airs. All except the local doctor who'd developed a hankering for some pastry called crumpets. That everyone wondered about her absent husband. He was suddenly curious on the matter himself. "Never mind about that." He moved directly beneath her. "Let's get you down."

She set her gorgeous jaw and gripped the limb tighter. "I'm not leaving the shield of this greenery without my skirt. Bad enough you've seen me in this state of undress."

"I've seen a woman in bloomers before, Mrs. Dillingham."

"Well, bully for you."

He laughed. "Where's your skirt?"

"A mangy mutt ran off with it, after he had the bad manners to eat my cookies."

"She makes good cookies, Papa," Zoe said. She pointed past the tree. "I see him! I see the dog. I'll get your skirt, Miss Kaila!"

His heart pounded as he watched his daughter giggle and skip off. He glanced back up at the redhead. "I assume Zoe was hiding in the tree. She does that a lot. I assume you climbed up in order to get her down." He turned his hat over and over in his hands. "I don't know what you said to her, but thank you. I haven't heard her talk that much, haven't seen a spring in her step for quite some time."

"Perhaps if you'd refrain from *whupping* your children."

His back went up. "I've never laid a hand on Zach or Zoe."

"But you threatened to. Zoe said—"

He held up a hand. "Zoe either misunderstood or misspoke. I don't threaten my children."

"Oh." She winced. "Oh!" The branch snapped and she plummeted.

Athens caught her in his arms. One-hundred-and-some, voluptuous, luscious pounds of the most beautiful woman he'd ever laid eyes on. Stunned, breathless, she blinked up at him and his heart raced like a schoolboy's. His body pulsed with awareness. Good God.

She licked her lips, fought for an even breath. "Thank you, Mr. Garrett."

"You're welcome, Mrs. Dillingham." He tried not to stare at her heaving breasts, and failed. "About your husband . . ."

"I'm a widow."

He met her mesmerizing gaze and his mouth went dry. "I'm sorry."

"I'm not."

Good God.

CHAPTER 7

Napa Valley, California

"*What have you done, Father? Why? Why?*"
Grief and smoke choked Emily as she tried to beat out the flames with a horse blanket.

Walt McBride slumped against the outside of the barn, his eyes glazed as he stared at the pile of burning books. "Those stories filled her head with notions. Those notions lured her away. They're evil, Emily, and I've committed them to hell."

"You're the one who needs to be committed," she sobbed as the blanket caught fire and her mother's cherished adventure novels turned to ash. "I'll never forgive you for this. Never!"

"I should have taken her to Europe," he said in sing-song voice.

"Let it go," she implored. "Let her go."

"Let her go. Let her . . ." Emily woke with a start.

"Go." She stared at the ceiling a full minute trying to calm her runaway heart. "Let her go," she said softly and more to herself than her conjured father. She closed her mind to the bad dream, the unwanted memory, and took a calming breath.

She squinted at the ceiling, not her bedroom ceiling, she realized. Achy and disoriented she surveyed her surroundings. Sunlight filtered in through a crack in the closed drapes. Worn drapes that had faded with the years like her good vision. She kicked off a threadbare quilt and pushed herself up on the sofa. She'd fallen asleep in the sitting room.

She rolled a kink out of her neck while tightening the sash of her mother's green silk robe in a bid for modesty, even though she appeared to be alone. Blurry-eyed, she nabbed her spectacles from the end table and shoved them on. Her vision cleared but her mind was still fuzzy. Last she recalled she'd been playing chess with Mr. Pinkerton.

No, wait. That had been directly after dinner. Mrs. Dunlap had been sitting in the rocker, knitting yet another afghan, and Emily had goaded the poet into a sixth board game. Anything to keep him alert as advised by Doctor Kellogg.

An hour later, Mrs. Dunlap had taken herself off to bed and Mr. Pinkerton, proclaiming himself weary of chess, had perused the bookshelves. He'd noted a lack of poetry in her private collection and she confessed a preference for medieval romances and adventure novels. To which he'd commented, "I can see that."

"I know what you're thinking."

"Do you?"

"*Sir Gawain and the Green Knight. The Three Musketeers.* Sword play and chivalry. Romanticized violence. You disapprove."

"You don't have to defend your reading preferences to me, Miss McBride."

You're right. I don't, the new Emily proclaimed, albeit to herself. "Old habits die hard. I'm sorry if I sounded churlish."

"I assume your father frowned upon this collection."

"He didn't know about this collection." She didn't elaborate, and thankfully, he let the subject drop. If only he'd stop fingering her shelves and books. His scrutiny made her nervous.

After a few moments, he settled in an armchair with Jules Verne's *Around the World in Eighty Days.* Breathing easier, she curled up on the sofa with a pencil and her journal. Only she didn't write about her day, but a fictional heroine's encounter with a swashbuckling pirate, not that she confessed as such to Mr. Pinkerton. Even though Paris had described him as open minded, his statement regarding Wilde and glorified violence stuck in her craw.

They fell into companionable silence. Next thing she knew it was past midnight. Her lids were drooping and Mr. Pinkerton was yawning, so she'd locked her journal in her desk and asked him to read aloud. Better sleep deprivation than succumbing to a concussion. He'd smiled at her request, a small smile, but one that had made her stomach flutter. Most distressing to have a man in her house, especially one as handsome as Phineas Pinkerton. Not that she was attracted to him in the romantic sense. She was, however, keenly aware of his charismatic aura.

He read very well, though she shouldn't have been surprised what with him being a professional who recited poetry on stage. But it was the sound of his voice, deep and rich with character, that mesmerized her. He brought new life to a story she'd read a dozen times. Regardless, she must've drifted off somewhere in the middle and now it was morning.

Morning.

Emily bolted to her stockinged feet. Where was Mr. Pinkerton? On instinct, she whirled to her rolltop desk, jiggled the lid. Still locked. She checked for the key hidden in the locket hanging around her neck. Still there.

Mr. Pinkerton, however, was not where she'd left him. Had he gone to bed? Fallen asleep never to wake up again? Had he experienced another dizzy spell, tripped on the stairway, and knocked himself out? Her vivid imagination spun wild and disastrous scenarios as she scrambled out of the room and up the steps. There were three bedrooms on the second floor. They were all empty. Even Mrs. Dunlap was out and about. What time was it anyway?

She hurried back down the hall, slipping and sliding over the polished wood floor. Mrs. Dunlap was not only a knitting fanatic, but fussy neat. Since her memory was spotty, she often scrubbed and straightened a room twice in one day. Although this house and its furnishings were worse for wear, everything was in its place and dust-free.

The hems of the long robe clutched in her fists, Emily rushed down the stairs, toward the smell of coffee. She burst through the kitchen door and found Mrs. Dunlap standing at the sink scrubbing a griddle. "Have you seen Mr. Pinkerton?"

"Yes, of course, dear. You introduced us yesterday, remember? Handsome young man, don't you think?"

Emily's heart thudded. Not because she was envisioning the poet's dashing profile, but because she was imagining him dead! "Mrs. Dunlap, I'm wondering if you've seen Mr. Pinkerton *today*."

"Certainly. He made me breakfast." The grey haired woman looked over her shoulder at Emily and smiled. "Handsome *and* handy in the kitchen.

Unmarried, too. I asked."

"Of course, he's not married, he's . . ."

"What?"

She couldn't say it. She could barely think it. She could imagine a lot of things, but homosexuality was a little, no, a lot out of her scope. Her father would've declared Mr. Pinkerton a sinner. Emily viewed him as an enigma. She could not condemn what she did not understand. "Love is never wrong."

"What, dear?"

Emily started and refocused on Mrs. Dunlap who'd resumed her vigorous scrubbing. "Nothing. I was just . . ." She crossed the room and placed a hand on the elderly woman's sturdy shoulder. The only thing feeble about Iris Dunlap was her mind. "I need to speak with Mr. Pinkerton." There. That sounded direct. Didn't it?

"Why didn't you say so, dear? He's in the barn."

"The *barn*?"

"Yes, he said he'd be in the barn. Or was that yesterday? No, wait. When did he arrive? I . . ."

Emily raced out the back door and across the vast yard toward the listing barn. The grass was slick with morning dew. In her haste, she slipped and fell twice to her knees. By the time she reached the dilapidated building she was winded and hopelessly frazzled. What if he'd found her treasure chest?

"Mr. Pinkerton!" She burst inside full speed, full panic, screaming when she plowed into a half-naked man brandishing a gun.

He pulled her into his arms and into a stall, shoved her down in a corner then peered over the chest-high wall.

She gasped for air, focused, and massaged her pounding heart as she realized the half-naked man was Phineas Pinkerton. Shirtless, sweating, and holding a Colt .45 like he knew how to use it. What in the world?

"Did he hurt you?" he asked in a low, even voice, eyes keen on the entrance to the barn.

"Who?" she squeaked.

"Whoever you're running from."

"I'm not running from anyone."

He glanced over his shoulder, his broad, *bare* shoulder, and pinned her with a stern expression. "You're not in danger?"

"Why would you think I was in danger?" Her pulse galloped all the same.

He silently slid the gun into a worn holster hanging from the gate post, yanked off his spectacles and squeezed the bridge of his nose. Specs in hand, he crouched in front of her, his normally tender green eyes hard as a gemstone. When he narrowed them, she had the urge to back away, only her back was up against the wall.

Emily scraped her teeth over her bottom lip. This moment he didn't look scholarly or delicate. He looked rugged and, *gulp*, dangerous. Her insides twisted and her mouth went dry. She'd never been this close to a half-naked man and though she knew she should look away, she could not. His muscled torso was most impressive. She'd seen paintings and sketches of nude men, but the real thing . . . Mercy.

He dipped his chin, took a calming breath. "You screamed my name. You blew into this barn like the devil was on your tail. You looked frightened and," he gestured to her clothing, "quite frankly as though you'd been accosted."

She looked down. The sash was gone and the robe gaped open. Her white chemise was sullied with soil and grass stains. She snatched closed the silk wrapper, blew meddlesome curls out of her eyes, and realized her hair was loose and most probably disheveled from the frenzied sprint. She closed her eyes and groaned.

"I thought maybe Sawyer or your blackmailer—"

"I don't want to talk about him."

"Which one?"

"Either one." Her pulse slowed to a lumbering run. It helped that she wasn't looking at his bare chest. Still, the outright mention of her blackmailer was distressing. Pinkerton had refrained from bringing up her troubles last night. She'd been grateful, thinking he meant to honor her wishes, and not to interfere. Now, between the .45 and his being in the barn, she feared otherwise. "Why, pray tell, do you have a gun? Do you even know how to use it? I thought you were against violence."

"Protection. Yes. And it depends."

She blinked.

"The west is overrun with scalawags, Miss McBride."

"I'm aware of that."

"Which brings us back to your blackmailer."

She swallowed a frustrated groan. The man was tenacious. She almost wished he'd have another dizzy spell. "How much did Paris tell you?"

"Not much. I know he or she is demanding payment in return for silence. Other than that . . ." He shrugged, slid his spectacles back in place. They did not diminish his appeal. "Just that whatever he's got on you, it's tawdry. Your words, not Paris's."

She gave herself a mental kick for sharing that information. She'd meant to warn him off, but realized now she'd only fanned the intuitive detective's interest. "Mr. Pinkerton."

"About my name—"

"You have to leave. I don't . . ." Her gaze flew to his. "What about your name?"

"Why?"

"Why, what?"

"Why do I have to leave?"

Her skin burned and she looked away.

He stood, removing his upper body from her line of vision and she released a pent up breath. "Because you saw me without a shirt?" he asked.

There was that. But mostly she didn't want him snooping around her barn, her business. Bad enough her *Savior* had violated her privacy.

"Or because I saw your—"

"What?" Was her chemise that sheer? Had the neckline dipped, exposing a, *gulp*, breast? Or maybe he was referring to her other chest. "Saw my what?"

"Your nightshirt." His green eyes softened as did his expression. "You have nothing to fear, Miss McBride. I'm not interested. No disrespect intended."

"None taken." Of course he wasn't interested. She had the wrong, well, parts. Still, she tensed when he grasped her elbow and pulled her to her feet. Clutching the lapels of the robe with one hand, she used her other cuff to wipe her lenses which had fogged up. Goodness, it was warm in here. She flinched when he stepped in and touched her hair.

He frowned and drew back, producing a sprig of straw from the tangled mass.

"Oh," she whispered, embarrassed by her over-reaction.

"Miss McBride."

"Yes, Mr. Pinkerton?"

"Have I given you reason to fear me?"

"I'm not afraid of you."

He raised a brow.

"I'm just a little uncomfortable. I'm not used to being . . . touched."

"You mean by a man."

"By anyone." She'd always been envious of the way Paris's brothers showered their sister with affection. Hugs and hair ruffling had been commonplace in the Garrett household. When they'd been alive, her friend's parents had been equally demonstrative. Perhaps because they were theater people.

Emily's people, her parents, had been less . . . warm.

Realizing Pinkerton was looking at her with curiosity, and knowing she'd revealed too much about herself, again, she went on the offensive. "Why *aren't* you wearing a shirt, Mr. Pinkerton?"

"I worked up a sweat."

She could see that. His entire torso glistened with the evidence of physical labor. She attributed her dry mouth and erratic pulse to rising panic. What if his exertion was due to him nosing about and finding her treasure chest? Although, these days her treasured collection felt more like a curse. "Doing what? I'm sorry, but, this *is* my property. What business do you have—"

"Repairing the stalls?"

She swallowed the word *snooping* and her tongue with it. She stared at the man and flushed from head to toe.

He snagged his shirt, and eased it over his head. "Yesterday, I noticed your porch steps were loose. I'd hate to see you or Mrs. Dunlap take a spill. Easy enough to fix but I needed tools." He spread his hands wide. "Figured I'd find them in here. Thing is, once I looked around, I noticed the disrepair of the stalls. Your horse is fine in the pasture for now, but come a storm, come winter—"

"I had every intention of hiring someone to handle repairs," Emily butt in, lest he think she was neglecting her human and animal boarders.

"But you lack the funds."

Her skin flushed hotter. She needed to escape this inquisition and the rising mid-morning heat, but she refused to leave him behind. In the barn. With her chest. "Presently, yes."

He gathered and placed several rusty tools into a splintered box. "I'm surprised a member of your father's congregation didn't offer his services."

"Someone probably would have if they knew the property was in need. I don't get many visitors."

"A neighbor then."

"Mr. Bellamont sent over his sons. I sent them away. I was polite about it, of course."

"Naturally."

"Cole offered and I declined. I don't want to be beholden."

"To your neighbors?"

"To anyone."

"I'm not just anyone, Miss McBride. I'm a friend of the family."

"All the more reason I can't impose."

"You're not imposing." He regarded her with a sidelong glance. "Truth told," he said after a long moment, "the manual labor spurs my creative thoughts."

She blinked. "It does?"

"I composed a poem while reinforcing the loose boards of the stall," he said, while setting the tool box on a warped workbench.

"You did?"

"Fiddled with an idea for a short story while tightening the hinges of the gate."

Thoroughly sidetracked, she edged closer to the man she wanted to escape just seconds before. "Would you mind sharing?"

"The poem or the short story?"

"Either one." Talking craft with a fellow writer. She'd never been in this position.

He tilted his head as if giving her request serious consideration then balked. "I'd rather not. They need work and I'm not fond of sharing anything less than my best."

I know what you mean! she wanted to cry. She felt the same way about her own writing. She obsessed over every word, every aspect. Sharing one's creation meant opening oneself up to criticism. Oh, yes. She understood his trepidation very well. She wanted to offer her help. Lord knows she could stand a fresh perspective on *her* current story. But what if he laughed or took exception? Wary of rejection, the old Emily held her tongue. Still, even the thought of exchanging ideas with another writer greatly lifted her spirits.

He buckled the holster around his waist and started for the main door, toward fresh air and sunshine. She followed, wondering how else to engage him in artistic conversation. She was thinking about the pacing of a short story versus a novel when he stopped and turned. "About your frantic entrance."

Drat.

"You do understand my initial reaction? You burst in here in your nightclothes, shoeless, no less."

"Yes, well . . ."

"Why?"

She stared down at her damp stockinged feet, trying to conjure a rational explanation without revealing the truth. She licked dry lips, cleared her throat, and spun a tale. "Imagine my distress, Mr. Pinkerton, when I woke to find you gone. I thought maybe . . . I was worried you'd succumbed to that concussion. I thought maybe, that is, when Mrs. Dunlap said you were in the barn . . . I thought about the . . . *disrepair* of the building and worried you'd slip, trip, hit your head or something."

"You were rushing to my rescue?"

"That's right." She met his glittering gaze. "You think that's funny?"

"A little."

"Because you're a man and I'm a woman?"

"Something like that."

"I can take care of myself and Mrs. Dunlap. And you, too, if need be," she added for good measure.

"And the blackmailer?"

"Him, too."

"Paris was afraid you'd feel that way." He braced his hands on his hips. "I apologize for catching you unaware."

"Pardon?"

"Shirtless."

"Oh."

"I'll do my best not to make you uncomfortable if . . ."

"Yes?"

"Allow me to stay on for awhile. As a paying

boarder. Paris will be appeased, knowing I'm contrib-
uting to your flagging funds. Maybe your blackmailer
will perceive me as a threat and fade away. Lastly, you
were right. Something about this region inspires me."

Something about the way he looked at her made
her jumpy. "It does?" Her voice sounded hoarse. She
fingered her throat, cleared it.

"Creatively speaking."

The clarification didn't help. Every time he said the
word *creative* or anything of a literary nature, her skin
prickled with excitement. She didn't want to confide
in Pinkerton regarding her blackmailer, but she was
dying to connect with another writer. "Creatively?"

"That's right. I'd be obliged. I know you're not
interested in my deductive skills, but if I can assist you
in any other way . . ."

She glanced at his holster. "How good are you
with that gun?"

He smiled.

"That good, huh?" Suddenly, she wasn't so miffed
with Paris for sending along Phineas Pinkerton. Suddenly, she saw an advantage or two to his being here.

"You should do that more often," he said.

"What?"

"Smile."

Her joy was genuine and she didn't try to curb it.
She so seldom laughed these days. Scenes from last

night flashed in her head. Pinkerton engaging Mrs. Dunlap in lively conversation at the dinner table. Pinkerton listening intently as the forgetful woman told the same story three times in two hours and reacting as though he were hearing it the first time every time. How engrossed he'd been in *Around the World in Eighty Days* and how he'd delivered Verne's prose with passion.

She realized now that she'd felt safe enough with her guest to fall asleep in the same room. Her physical reaction to his naked torso and handsome features were unsettling, but she'd gladly weather the discomfort if it meant exchanging creative ideas. She hadn't felt this inspired, this connected to a person since, well, Paris.

Artists have to stick together.

Maybe, just maybe, her luck was changing for the better. "I suppose it wouldn't hurt if you stayed on a week or so." She had the ridiculous urge to whoop and kick up her heels. Instead, she walked calmly outdoors, toward the house, Pinkerton at her side. "About your name," she ventured.

"What about it?"

"You brought it up earlier. As if there was a problem."

"Ah." He rubbed the back of his neck. "I was going to suggest that we dispense with formalities."

She pondered that. "I feel funny calling you Phineas. Somehow it doesn't suit you. No disrespect intended."

"None taken. Trust me. Not a name of my choosing."

"What should I call you then?"

He grasped her forearm, saving her from another fall when she slipped on the wet grass. "How about *friend*?"

CHAPTER 8

*H*e'd expected her to ask him to put the fear of God into Cole Sawyer. To threaten her blackmailer. To plug a pheasant for dinner. Shooting lessons never entered Seth's mind.

"I have the entire afternoon free," she informed him as she loped down the stairs sporting two tight braids and loose men's clothing.

He fixated on those suspenders. Normally he wouldn't be so all-fired fascinated, but they accentuated her small, firm breasts. Not that he had any business considering the breasts of his boss's future wife, but he'd gotten a peek at them compliments of her thin chemise and they'd been on his mind since. *Stop staring, start detecting.* "Library closed today?"

"Operating hours are Monday through Friday, ten to five."

"Been working there long?"

"A year. It doesn't pay much, but the benefits are priceless."

"Benefits?"

"Being surrounded by books." She breezed past him, wrenched open a door and reached for something in the back of the closet. The trousers stretched and emphasized her backside. Another tantalizing vision he could have done without. Damn Josh for waylaying his tumble at Fletcher's. Surely his over-appreciation of the quirky librarian's physical attributes was due to his lack of physical intimacy with a Calico Queen.

What were they talking about? Ah, yes. Books.

She backed out of the closet, armed. "I've spent the past three months honing my sharp shooting skills."

"With that?" An older-than-dirt 14-gauge double-barrel shotgun. He couldn't imagine her muscling the long gun. He could imagine the kick knocking her on her pretty backside. *Don't think about your boss's lady's backside.*

"It's the only thing I have. Father kept it for protection, although I'm not sure he knew how to use it."

"Do you?"

She smiled.

Okay. He was charmed. Charmed and intrigued. Emily McBride was an enigma. A mystery he wanted to solve. He'd never been able to ignore a woman in distress. Normally, they welcomed his aid. Not this one. She wanted to solve her own problems and that it involved *honing her sharp shooting* concerned and impressed him at the same time.

What had caused her to storm the barn in a panic? Although her explanation had amused him, he knew a lie when he heard it. What was she scared of? What was she hiding? He'd wager she had more than one secret. He itched to learn each one. Paris had suggested that he earn Emily's confidence. Assimilating their conversations thus far, he concluded her weakness was her love of literature. She'd confide in a poet. The lawman she'd send packing.

Pinkerton it was.

She stroked the walnut stock, sighed. "Sorry to say the locking mechanism busted a couple of days ago. I wanted to take it into town to see if it could be fixed but thought better of it. Thought, if someone, you know like a criminal-sort—"

"You mean blackmailer."

"—trespassed, I should have a weapon to threaten them with."

"Only it's busted."

"They wouldn't know that."

He frowned at her reasoning.

"I can argue a gopher into climbing a tree," she said with confidence. "By the time I finished spinning my tale, they'd believe the gun was loaded and that I had no qualms about giving them a belly full."

"Have you had to test that theory?"

"No."

"No criminal-sorts, no trespassers, no one lurking about?"

"Not that I've seen." She turned her back, wedged the weapon into the corner of the closet, and dragged out a box filled with empty bottles and cans. "For target practice," she explained.

Seth nudged her aside and pulled the box into the hall. He eyed the shotgun. "Looks like a Parker Brothers."

"One of their first."

"Locking mechanism's operated by a lever under the breech mechanism. Crude and inconvenient. You'd be better off with a newer model. Better yet, purchase a Remington."

"I wouldn't have expected a poet to know so much about guns."

"I could say the same for a librarian."

She quirked a shy smile. "At any rate, I've decided a shotgun doesn't suit my purpose. I'm interested in purchasing a revolver. Easier to travel with."

"Going somewhere?"

"Eventually."

Mrs. Dunlap waddled out of the kitchen with a picnic

basket. "I made you young'uns something to eat."

"We just had breakfast a couple of hours ago."

"Mr. Pinkerton had breakfast. *You* had a biscuit. Besides, this is for later." She looped the basket over Emily's arm and disappeared back into the kitchen.

"She worries about you," Seth said.

Emily shut the closet door with her hip. "I worry about her."

"What's her story?"

"I'll fill you in later," she whispered. "Her memory's iffy, but her hearing's just fine."

Seth nodded and hefted the box of targets. He doubted she'd hit a third of what she aimed at. A shotgun and revolver were two different animals.

"Speaking of stories," Emily said as they neared the front door. "I do a bit of writing myself."

"Paris mentioned."

"I was wondering if, later, well, if you might be willing to help me with a pesky plot point?"

"Sure." In his youth he'd been an avid reader. Hopefully that, logic, and a bit of imagination would be enough.

"Good. Great. Thank you."

She didn't look at him, but he could feel her pleasure. Yup. For sure and certain he'd know her secrets within two days, if not sooner. Then it was a matter of dealing with the blackmailer. He was used to wrangling murderers and thieves. A spineless bully would pose little challenge. Less of a challenge than delivering Athens's proposal and obtaining a favorable reply. What had she said to Sawyer? *The last thing I want or need is a husband.*

My kind of woman, Seth thought with a wry grin and quickly shunned the notion. That kind of trouble he didn't want or need.

Territory of Arizona

This was a bad idea. He knew it. Yet it didn't stop him. In fact, he'd had to caution himself not to run. Twice between his house and hers, Athens had had the overwhelming urge to sprint. Now that he was standing on her veranda his heart thumped as hard and fast as if he'd done just that.

"You're an idiot, Garrett." Even now, Seth could be reading his proposal of marriage to Emily. Regardless, Athens knocked on Kaila Dillingham's front door.

He knew where she lived because he and Zoe had walked her home yesterday. She'd invited them inside, but he'd declined. He needed to get his daughter home, needed to address that fight with Zach. He also needed to burn the midnight oil, reviewing several criminal cases, only he'd ended up burning for the Englishwoman instead. He'd tossed and turned reflecting on her in those bloomers, in his arms. Imagining her out of those bloomers and in his bed. The images had been erotic and unrelenting. Restful sleep, even after self-satisfaction, had proved impossible.

Since moving to Phoenix, he'd been obsessed with establishing the Peacemaker Alliance, going so far as to work seven days a week. He couldn't focus on those files any more today than he could last night. Maybe if he saw her again, talked to her, maybe the intense infatuation would cease. Maybe he'd learn she was pretentious or ignorant. Or that he'd been blinded by the sun and she was, in fact, butt ugly.

The door swung open.

Or not.

"Mr. Garrett."

"Mrs. Dillingham."

He took off his hat and fingered the brim as he grappled for a sane thought. She was even more beautiful than he remembered. It was more than her striking face and figure. She exuded a raw sensuality that summoned his most primal urges. The devil of it was she personified sophistication. Her green bustled gown was European chic. Her fiery red hair tamed and twisted into, what did they call it, a chignon. He visualized pulling loose the hairpins, one by one, and setting free thick, long ringlets. Erotic images filled his head. The same as last night only more intense because here she was. In the flesh.

She peered around him. "You're alone?"

"Parker, my assistant, took Zach and Zoe over to watch the J.P. Fishburn outfit pitch a big top tent. Although I think they're more interested in catching a peek at an elephant, Parker included. A traveling circus rolled into town this morning," he explained, wondering if he sounded as foolish as he felt.

"I read the posted advertisements regarding their performances. I'm most keen on attending." She fingered a locket around her neck, calling attention to her left hand. Yesterday she'd worn a wedding band. This morning it was conspicuously absent. "You look surprised."

He started to comment on the ring then realized they'd been speaking of the circus. "I would have figured you a fan of more highbrow entertainment."

"Such as the opera?" She smiled, and his heart rate tripled. "I've been to dozens of operas, Mr. Garrett. I've never been to a circus."

That was his cue to invite her, but the words stuck in his throat. He hadn't courted a woman in years. He wasn't free to start now, what with his impending engagement.

"I was hoping you would call," she said, filling the

awkward silence. "I wanted to apologize for my brisk manner yesterday. It would seem I'm not entirely fond of heights."

"Yet you climbed up after Zoe."

"Yes, well, I didn't realize I'd developed a fear until it was too late. Nevertheless, I was, as Zoe pointed out, flustered. Thank you again for saving me from a potentially disastrous fall and the embarrassment of having to walk home in my bloomers. If your daughter hadn't recovered my skirt . . ." She shook her head, laughed. "Although, perhaps the risqué scene would've increased business at Café Poppy. People wandering in for a firsthand look at the scandalous Englishwoman. If I could just get them through the door . . . But I digress.

"To show my appreciation, I baked a sugar cake for you and the children. Zoe seemed fond of my Ginger cookies and I'm rather fond of baking. I was going to bring it over, but here you are and . . ." She waved off her words. "I'm babbling. How did your talk with Zach go?"

Generous, good humored, and sensitive. Just his luck. "I managed not to whup him. Barely." He smiled as her cheeks burned brighter. "Where'd you hear that term anyway?"

"Zoe."

"Ah." Sultry eyes. Sultry voice. *That accent.*

Besotted. He was utterly, hopelessly besotted. He fingered sweat from his brow.

"Where are my manners? We should be having this discussion inside where it's cooler." She opened the door wider, a silent invitation.

"Bad idea."

"Why?"

"Best not to put it into words." He saw mutual desire sparking in those brown eyes, felt himself harden. He subtly lowered his hat to crotch level. Good God.

She smiled. "I had intended an afternoon stroll. Would you like to join me, Mr. Garrett?"

"I would." In truth, he had other ideas, but he'd take what he could get.

"I just . . . I need my parasol." She waved him indoors. "Do step in out of the heat. Please. I'll only be a moment."

He stepped inside, but as she turned away, he nabbed her wrist and pulled her against him, closing the door and shutting out the world in one fluid move. If she'd resisted in any way, signaled or verbalized outrage or disgust, he would have released her.

She kissed him.

He didn't have time to respond. He'd been too stunned and she wrenched back, much too soon, wide-eyed. "Oh, dear. I'm so sorry, Mr. Garrett, I—"

He silenced her apology with his mouth. Lips,

teeth, tongue. Hard, hungry.

She reciprocated, her response fevered, as if she couldn't get enough of him. As if she'd fantasized about him as well.

She set him on fire.

He backed her against the wall, knocking over a footstool and a stack of books along the way. If she noticed, she didn't say, then again her tongue was tangled with his. He pressed into her and explored her curves. Her hips. Her breasts. The more bold his actions, the more eager her response. It had never been like this with Jocelyn.

That thought stopped him cold. He planted his hands on the wall, on either side of her head and pushed away.

"What's wrong?" she rasped.

"This."

"I was too aggressive. You're appalled."

"On the contrary. Your enthusiasm is indescribably . . . attractive. You, Mrs. Dillingham—"

"Kaila."

"—are . . . I'm not sure there are words to describe your beauty."

"Those will do fine."

"Me being here. Like this. I don't want to tarnish your reputation."

She swallowed hard, looked earnestly into his

eyes. "I am twenty-eight years old. I have acted in a responsible and proper manner for each and every one of those years. I am here to tell you that a sparkling reputation is overrated."

He smiled at that.

"I don't want a commitment, if that's what's bothering you. I've experienced marriage and found it lacking. I cherish my freedom. It is why I am in the Americas and not at home. It is why I am here in the west. I'm keen on an adventure, Mr. Garrett."

He dropped his forehead to hers. "Ah, Mrs. Dillingham—"

"Kaila."

"Kaila. You're making this too easy."

"Good."

"There are things about me you don't know."

"A man of mystery. How exciting."

"There's no future in this. In us."

"One passionate moment could make for a lifetime of contentment."

His heart hammered. "Meaning?"

She nabbed his lapels and peeled off his jacket. "You better make this bloody good."

CHAPTER 9

Napa Valley, California

You're making this very difficult, Mr. Pinkerton."

"I thought we decided on Phin."

"We did. But I guess that doesn't work for me any more than Phineas. What was your mother thinking? No disrespect intended."

"None taken. What would you like to call me, Emily?"

Her breath caught just like the first time he called her by her Christian name. Silly. He wasn't being familiar; after all, he preferred men. That didn't work for her either. She couldn't imagine. How could she be so aware of someone so totally unaware of her? Then again, she had the same relationship with Rome. For all her adoring, he couldn't be less interested. Clearly, she was clueless where men were concerned.

"I don't know," she said on a huff. "Poet. When I

think of you I think *Poet* as you surely have a way with words. Anyway, that's beside the point."

"The point being?"

"It's hard for me to concentrate when you're hovering."

"Hovering?"

"Yes. Hovering. Crowding me. As if you're afraid I'm going to cause someone serious harm except there's no one around for me to injure." They were in Weaver's Meadow, a lush open area stretching between her property and Bellamont Winery. Rolling hills surrounded them on three sides. Due north, a dense patch of woods. They were very much alone with the exception of the targets she'd set on stumps and fallen logs. "I'm pretty sure empty wine bottles don't have feelings."

"Right."

"Or empty tin cans."

"Doubly so."

"Can I fire now?"

"Be my guest."

She took aim, jerked the trigger and . . . *yes*! The can flew off of the tree stump even though she only nicked the rim. "I winged it!"

"You can do better."

"Of course I can. With time and practice—"

"You can do better now. Improve your technique

and you'll improve your marksmanship."

Why was he walking on egg shells?

"I can help, but . . ."

"What?"

"I'd have to hover."

"Oh."

"It gets worse. I'd have to touch you."

She looked over her shoulder, astounded and impressed that he had taken words uttered this morning to heart. His sensitivity melted her reserve. "Then by all means, touch me, Poet. I'm eager to learn."

He mumbled something, stepped in behind her, his front flush against her back. "Your stance is all wrong. Look at your feet. Squared off parallel like that? Compromises proper balance. You want a power stance, a fighter's stance. Think of your lower body as a triangle. Left leg forward, right leg back."

She complied, though it was hard to concentrate on the precise directions. His warm breath tickled her ear and his husky tone sent shivers to her toes. His closeness was unsettling and at the same time exhilarating. If she was this distracted by Pinkerton, she couldn't imagine what she'd feel like if Rome were giving her hands-on instruction.

He grasped her hips, adjusted her position. "Pelvis at a 45-degree angle."

Mercy.

"Shoulders forward. Not that much." His hands shifted upward. "Like so."

"Sorry. I'm nervous."

"Do you want me to stop?"

"No! I mean, I'm fine." *Liar.* "Please go on."

His palms glided down her arms. "For now, use both hands. You want a high grasp on the grip for premium control. Thumb curled down for strength, index finger on the trigger like, yes, good."

No, bad. She couldn't breathe. With his hand wrapped around hers, his body pressed against the length of her, his mouth close to her ear. She felt faint.

"Your grip is excellent. A hard grip ensures less kick. Also makes it tougher for someone to snatch or knock away your gun. Emily. Em."

She licked dry lips. "What?"

"Relax."

"I'm fine."

"You're trembling."

"Anticipation. You can step back now," she croaked. "I've got it."

"Not yet. Aim for the first bottle. Focus on the front sight. Got your target?"

"Yes."

"Focused on the sight?"

"Uh-huh."

"I'm going to ease off now. When you're ready,

fire. Slow and smooth on the trigger. Understand?"

"Slow and smooth." She breathed easier when he broke contact, her concentration no longer divided. Strong stance. Tight grip. Focus. Fire—slow and smooth.

Glass popped and shattered.

Emily whistled low.

"Nice," Pinkerton said with a smile in his voice. "Do it again."

There were three more wine bottles lined up on a decaying log. She hated those bottles. Shattering them to Kingdom Come would be a pleasure. But even more, she wanted to impress the man behind her. The approval in his tone soothed an ancient void.

She took a calming breath. Strong stance. Tight grip. Focus. Fire—slow and smooth.

She fired. Once. Twice. Three times. *Pop. Pop. Pop.* Three direct hits.

"Shit."

His vulgar curse only half registered. The shots rang in her ears as did her own inner shouts of glee. She whirled, ready to whoop her joy. Instead, she shrieked. "You're bleeding!"

Pinkerton's shirt sleeve was torn, the white fabric stained red.

"What happened? How . . . ?"

Grim-faced, he stalked toward her, grabbed his

gun and shoved her down in the grass. "Stay here. Stay low."

He disappeared into the woods.

Heart racing, Emily shoved to her feet and followed. She burst into the copse of trees full speed. Her toe clipped an exposed root and she flew forward, plowing into Pinkerton and knocking him into a mighty oak.

"Dammit!"

That curse she heard loud and clear as they'd shouted it in unison. "Merciful heavens," she said when he turned. "You're bleeding!"

"I know."

"No, I mean your forehead." He'd smacked the tree hard, and although it only looked like a scratch, blood liberally trickled down his face. She rushed forward and tried to stem the flow with the cuff of her sleeve. "I'm so sorry. I tripped and—"

"I told you to stay put."

"I was worried. Your arm." She transferred her ministering to his first injury, hurriedly rolling up his left sleeve. "What in the world?"

"Grazed by a bullet."

"What bullet? *My* bullet? How . . . did one of them ricochet? But you were behind me. Weren't you?" Hands trembling, she yanked her shirt tail out of her britches and ripped off a long section of the hem.

Back up against the tree, he sighed and holstered

his piece. "What are you doing?" he asked even as she wound the fabric around his bicep and tied a tight knot.

"Stemming the bleeding."

"It's nothing, Emily. A flesh wound."

Tears welled. "I feel awful. I don't know how—"

He grasped her chin, looked calmly into her eyes. "It wasn't you."

"Then who?"

"That's what I was trying to find out before you waylaid my search. Whoever it was is long gone."

Her brain scrambled to make sense of his words. It was hard to think straight with him holding and gazing at her the way he was, all tender like. As if reading her thoughts, he broke contact and sleeved away fresh blood threatening to drip in his eye. Jolted out of her daze, she ripped more fabric from her tail.

"Keep that up and you'll be as shirtless as I was this morning," he said with a teasing grin.

"How can you joke? You're bleeding something awful."

"I've suffered worse." He pushed off of the tree, grasped her elbow and guided her back into the meadow, looking over both shoulders and across the way.

"Why would anyone want to hurt a poet?"

"Remember how Paris's father died?"

"How can I forget? She was devastated. Mr. Garrett

was shot by a stray bullet. A bullet meant to silence the comedian on stage." She nudged away his hand when he tried to pick up the picnic basket, and looped it over her own arm. "You're hurt."

"I'll live."

"I can't believe people shoot at you in your line of work."

"Believe it." He started the long walk back to her house at a brisk clip.

She hurried to keep pace. "But you're not on stage now."

"No, I'm with you."

She pondered that. "You don't think . . ." She shook her head, pushed her glasses firmly up her nose. "Cole's bullheaded and fights like Kilkenny cats, but he wouldn't shoot you."

"Maybe, maybe not."

"I'm thinking someone was hunting in the woods and a bullet went amiss."

"Or maybe they hit their mark. Maybe they figured on scaring off the likes of me."

"A poet?"

He raised an eyebrow.

"Oh."

"You mentioned Boris over at the Moonstruck frowns upon men who are, how did you put it? Delicate. I'm not saying it was him. I'm saying there are plenty of motives."

She had a hard time thinking of Pinkerton as delicate now. She'd seen him ably handle what he perceived
as dangerous situations twice today. Was it just yesterday he'd tripped over his own feet? "Boris would rib
you. He wouldn't shoot you. Heaven is riddled with
conservatives and hypocrites, but not murderers."

"What about blackmailers?"

She averted her face, not wanting him to see her
distressed expression. The thought of her *Savior* made
her anxious.

He reached over and relieved her of the weighty
picnic basket without breaking stride. "We need to
talk, Emily."

She made the mistake of looking at him. Shirt
torn and stained red, forehead and arm bleeding. The
Pinkerton of yesterday would have fainted dead away.
Then she thought back on her first impression of him—
Warrior of God. Someone who fought against evil. Or
evildoers. Although he hadn't recited a lick of poetry
since his arrival, he most definitely had a silver tongue.
His obsession with her blackmailer spoke volumes.
She wanted him to be an artist, but his true passion
was in detective work. She could see that now. Why
was he only an intuitive detective and not a working
detective? Nothing worse than being unable to pursue
your real passion. She knew that all too well.

Emily felt a sudden and fierce connection with the man as surely as if they were spiritually mated. She didn't know what to do with the feeling, overwhelming as it was. She swallowed a lump of emotion and looked away. "I need to get you to a doctor."

"I don't need a doctor."

"If you let Doc Kellogg examine you, I'll talk."

"Deal."

Territory of Arizona

"This was more than I bargained for."

"Was I too rough?"

"You were everything I've dreamed of and more. Thank you, Athens."

"For ravishing you like a common trollop?"

"Honestly? Yes."

They lay side by side on her tapestry carpet, one of the few things she'd had shipped over from Kent, staring up at the ceiling, and trying to catch their breath. They never made it to the bedroom. They'd torn off each other's clothes and made torrid love in her small, but comfortable parlor. He'd pinned her against the wall and done unspeakably intimate things to her naked body. She'd felt no shock or embarrassment, just wonderment and intense pleasure. Her knees gave way upon reaching orgasm and they ended up writhing around on the carpet like two animals in heat. When he entered her, she'd climaxed again, which only heightened his excitement. The man pleasured her in countless ways before finding his own release.

Her muscles ached and her skin glistened from exertion. Somewhat self-conscious now that the fog of passion had dispersed, she reached for the calico quilt on the sofa and covered herself.

Still splendidly nude, Athens rolled onto his side and gently brushed her hair off of her damp face. "Are you all right?"

"Oh, yes. Just thoughtful. I never knew it could be like this. Sex," she clarified, cheeks flushing. "Although I had hoped." She turned her head and smiled at him. "You are an imaginative and energetic lover."

"You inspire me."

"You're too kind."

"I'm not being kind. I'm being truthful."

"May I speak frankly?"

"Haven't you been doing that since the moment we met? It's very attractive, by the way."

"Few men would agree."

"Why do I get the feeling your husband was a controlling man?"

She dragged her fingers through his fine, fair hair.

"Handsome and perceptive."

"Beautiful and interesting." Propped on one elbow, he traced his fingers over her arm. "What's on your mind?"

"I've never made love in the afternoon. I've never done most of what we just did. Charles was conservative. Cold and conservative, and vaguely disinterested. I feared I was . . ."

"Frigid?"

"Mmm."

"Far from it, honey."

The endearment made her heart flutter. Her husband had been a practical man, sparing with his compliments and affection. Athens Garrett was giving and warm. Far from the dangerous gunslinger she fantasized about, but equally exciting.

"So tell me," he said with a cocky grin. "Was I bloody good?"

She laughed. "Bloody hell, yes."

His green eyes sparkled. "You're an intriguing puzzle, Kaila Dillingham. You're obviously well-born, cultured. Yet here you are."

"In Phoenix running a bakery?"

"With me. Making love on a carpet."

He looked so befuddled. So deliciously handsome. A gentleman with a wild streak. She longed to ask him if he was indeed brother to the famous Garretts featured in I. M. Wilde's adventurous tales. Zoe had mentioned two uncles in a dime novel. She'd put two and two together last night while reading *Showdown in Sintown*. She was terribly intrigued, but feared if she asked he'd think she was merely fascinated by his association with pulp heroes, Rome and Boston Garrett. She knew the wretched feeling of people wanting to get close to you for ulterior motives only too well.

"What's going on in that pretty head of yours, English? What are you about?"

Another endearment. Another flutter. "Would you like me to clear up the mystery?" *Maybe if she opened up first . . .*

"I would."

On second thought . . . "Do you think it's wise? Perhaps the less we know about one another, the better. It would make this, us, less personal."

"Is that what you want?"

"From what you said before, it is how it has to be."

His expression changed from playful to somber. "Unfortunately. I'm afraid—"

She pressed her fingertips to his lips. "I don't want to know. Not now. I don't want anything to spoil this moment. This memory."

He furrowed his brow. "When I walk out that door, are you going to be able to act like this never happened?"

"Absolutely. I've had years of training in the art of denial."

He frowned. "I'm not sure how I feel about that."

She knew next to nothing about this man, but sensed he wrestled with his morals and actions daily. She pushed herself up and kissed him softly. "You are a tormented man."

"We all have our demons."

"Indeed."

"Thank you for taming mine. At least for awhile."

He kissed her slow, deep, leaving her breathless and dizzy with yearning as he rolled away and gathered his clothes.

"What did you mean when you said this was more than you'd bargained for?" he asked while fastening his trousers and shirt.

She leaned back against the sofa, the quilt clutched to her aching chest. "I thought one divinely passionate encounter would satisfy me for a lifetime. Indeed, it only makes me hunger for more."

He bent over, framed her face in his hands. "Your frankness is going to be my undoing, English." He brushed his lips across hers, groaned. With a reluctant farewell, he nabbed his jacket and made use of her back door.

"You are fortunate, Mr. Garrett," she whispered in his wake, "as I fear I am already undone."

CHAPTER 10

Napa Valley, California

Seth wrestled with whether or not to report the shooting incident to the sheriff. It was the right thing to do, but it might focus unwanted attention on Emily. On their way to the livery, he spotted the badge-wearing lard-ass snoring away on the jailhouse porch. That cinched it. No report. The last thing he needed was an inept lawman mucking up his investigation.

After stabling Guinevere, they visited Doc Kellogg. The good doctor wasn't inept, but he did rush the examination. He never looked Seth in the eye as he abruptly applied a smelly poultice and bandages and issued a clean bill of health. He had to know it was a gunshot wound, yet he didn't comment or question. Maybe he was being discreet. Maybe he suspected foul play and chose not to get involved. Maybe he didn't want to help a Nancy boy.

Eager to leave, Seth settled the bill, mindful that Emily lingered after Kellogg showed him the door. Seth *hovered* just outside the office within earshot.

"Are you sure he's okay?" she asked in a soft voice.

"For now. You best keep your eye on Percy there," the doctor said with a snort. "I swan, that man's accident prone."

"His name is Phineas, and it wasn't his fault."

"You would say that."

"What's that supposed to mean?"

"Just that you're always making excuses for other folks' ... eccentricities. Relax, Emily. I didn't mean nothin' by it. Speaking of odd sticks, how's Mrs. Dunlap?"

"Fit as a fiddle. Thank you for asking."

She didn't seem all that pleased to Seth. She sounded pissed. He bit back a smile and eased away from the door when he heard her snap, "Thank you for your time, doctor, and good day."

He was shrugging into his frock coat and wearing his best poker face when she stepped out onto the boardwalk. While Mrs. Dunlap had cleaned his wounds with peroxide, Emily had changed into a fresh shirt and traded her suspenders and britches for a brown skirt and a wide black belt. Her effort to conform, he supposed, since they were coming into town, only she still looked the left side of conventional. Maybe it was the way she tied off her braids with leather thongs instead of satin ribbons. He couldn't put his finger on it, but her style was unique. She was unique.

"Honest to gosh," she huffed, her hands balled into tight fists.

"Anything wrong?"

She marched up to him, red-faced and harried. Damn, she was pretty when her back was up. Her blue eyes flashed behind her oval lenses. "You've been around."

His lip twitched. "Excuse me?"

"Paris said you travel the theater circuit."

"Ah."

"So you've been around. Various cities, regions."

"Sure." That was true enough. He'd ridden with the Texas and Arizona Rangers before signing on as Sheriff of Pinal County. His travels, up until now, had been limited to the Southwest and Mexico, but that covered an almighty chunk of territory.

"Are people like this everywhere?"

"Like what?"

"Intolerant. Judgmental. Mean-spirited. Small-minded!"

With every word her voice boomed louder. She looked madder than a rained-on rooster and he didn't want her crowing in public. The sharp-clawed she-cat who'd ridiculed her at yesterday's social club meeting had poked her head out of the mercantile. Not that

Emily noticed. She was in the midst of a red-hazed rant. Others had stopped in their tracks to view the show, not that it would be long-running. Seth pressed his hand to the small of Emily's back, guiding her quickly down the boards and across the street as she continued to spout mankind's most negative qualities.

"Got a key to the library, Em?"

"What? Of course. Why?"

"Let's take this inside."

"Do you know how many churches are in this town?" she snapped as she jammed the key into the front door and let them in. "Methodist, Methodist Episcopal, Catholic, Presbyterian. Every Sabbath folks put on their go-to-meeting clothes and squeeze into pews to listen to sermons on how to live a Godly life. Meanwhile, the other six days of the week they drink, covet, lie, mock, and cheat on their spouses!"

He closed the door behind them, leaned against it with his arms folded and watched as she paced and lamented under her breath. "Surely, you're not referring to every citizen in Heaven." The name of the town, given their discussion, struck him as ironic.

"Of course not. Just a goodly portion. They shunned Paris. Did you know that? Just because she has this peculiar talent for being able to make up songs on a whim. Songs about people and situations. Like the time we caught Mary Lee and Rome canoodling by the creek!"

That would explain, at least in part, the she-cat's hostility. He'd heard Paris's ditties, as she called them, firsthand. Frank, clever, and catchy, they'd endeared her to the miners and citizens of her new hometown, Chance. If one lacked a sense of humor or possessed a juicy secret, he could see where they'd want to steer clear of the freckle-faced half-pint.

"Mrs. Dunlap is a goodhearted woman who contributed generously to this community for years. But along the way she lost her husband and two sons and slowly but surely her mind. She's not crazy, she's forgetful. Cole's pa took advantage and manipulated her out of her land. Granted, he paid for it. But not a fair price. No one wanted to take her in because they considered her a nut and a burden."

"You took her in."

"It was the decent thing to do. I can't fathom how someone could turn their back on someone in need!"

Seth pressed the heel of his hand to his chest, attributing the twinge in his ticker to spicy stew and heartburn. Mrs. Dunlap had forgotten she'd stocked a picnic basket, although he and Emily hadn't sampled the fare what with his mishaps waylaying lunch. The stew had been waiting on their return and Seth had been unable to deter the old woman. *"It'll make you feel better."* Like hell.

"Then Doc Kellogg," Emily vented, flailing her arms wide. "Could he have been any less concerned with your injuries?"

"I'm fine, Em. Let's talk about you."

"Who cares about me?"

He knew the question was rhetorical, but it bothered him all the same. "I do."

She stopped in her tracks, met his gaze. "That's a mistake."

"Why?"

"Because I'm a lightning rod for ill luck."

"I'm not a superstitious sort."

"I'm not who you think I am."

"And that would be?"

"A good girl."

"I'm intrigued."

"Don't be."

"Too late." He came toe-to-toe with her, hitched his thumbs in his vest pockets so as not to pull her into her arms. He didn't figure she'd cotton to that kind of comfort. "What happened?"

"What do you mean?"

"Something set you off and it wasn't Kellogg."

She shook her head, her blond braids bouncing along with his twitching heart.

Christ.

"Em. If you believe nothing else, believe that I'm

your friend. Can you do that?"

"He won't listen to reason," she said, by way of an answer.

"Kellogg? Sawyer?"

"My Savior."

For once she sounded like the bible thumper's kid that she was. "I'm a little rusty in the religion department, but—"

"I'm not referring to a forgiving spirit, Poet," she said, whirling away. "I'm talking about a judgmental person who's seen fit to condemn my behavior. Someone who's making me pay for my sins. Literally." She slumped into a chair next to a table splayed with various periodicals.

Seth took the seat across from her, angling the chair so that their knees practically touched. "Your blackmailer."

"I sent a letter along with my last payment."

"How many payments have you made?"

"Two, and they depleted my savings. I said as such in the letter, vowed to adjust my ways, and asked that he please leave me alone. I thought if I asked nicely, you know, appealed to his sense of decency. . ." She trailed off with a dejected shrug.

He wished she'd stayed fired up. He cursed his knotted chest. *She believes the best in the worst of people.* Athens had gotten that much right. The thought of his boss and the man's intentions prompted Seth to ease back in his chair. "Decent folk don't terrorize," he told her. *Nor do they console another's intended by gathering her in his arms and kissing the worry from her brow*, he told himself. *Ditch those inclinations, Wright.*

"He wants me to suffer and I'm not sure why."

"You know for certain it's a man?"

"No. I thought maybe, well, Mary Lee crossed my mind." She wrung her hands in her lap, chanced his gaze. "She doesn't like me much. Then again, she doesn't like any woman she views as competition. Ever since Cole showed an interest, she's been downright prickly."

"I noticed."

"Thing is, the letters were mailed from San Francisco."

"Ever been to San Francisco?"

She looked away. "Never been outside of Napa Valley."

He digested every bit of information, every expression, and telling gesture. "When's the last time you heard from this person?"

"Today."

"What?" Distance be damned. He leaned forward and took her hand. It was bold, but he didn't care and besides he was goddamned Phineas Pinkerton. There had to be some benefit to posing as a fancy pants poet. "You've come this far," he said, sensing her withdrawal. "Don't shut down on me now."

She eased her hand from his grasp, withdrew a note from her skirt pocket, and passed it to him.

It nettled that she was still skittish of his touch, but at least it had jarred her into action. He noted the broken wax seal, unfolded the missive, and read.

AS LONG AS YOU REAP BENEFITS, YOU WILL PAY THE PRICE.

He read the words again before examining the note, front and back. According to the stamped wax, the letter had indeed originated in San Francisco. The only tangible clue as far as Seth could tell. The cream-colored writing paper was ordinary, no stationer's mark, patriotic cartoons or any other symbol to make it easier to track. Nor could he analyze or attempt to match the handwriting as the blackmailer had used one of those new fangled typewriters.

The message itself was a bald threat. But it was the signature line—YOUR SAVIOR—that wedged under Seth's skin.

He noted Emily's trembling hands, took it slow and easy. "When did you get this? Where?"

"At first, Doc Kellogg asked me to wait outside while he examined you, remember?"

Seth nodded.

"I slipped into the mercantile, just next door. Mrs. Dunlap asked me to pick up several skeins of yarn. I wasn't expecting, that is, I collected the mail for the library yesterday. But Mr. Thompson said that he had a missive for me. Said it must have slipped his hold when he emptied Mrs. Frisbie's cubbyhole. He found it on the floor when he swept up last night."

Seth spoke directly. "What's this person got on you, Emily?"

"I can't say."

"Can't or won't?"

She snatched back the letter, pushed out of the chair. Without a word, she strode past him and reorganized a shelf of books.

He stepped in behind her, replaying everything she'd said to him over the past two days, factoring in her personality and quirks. *Tawdry.* "Whatever it is, I'm not easily shocked."

She gripped the shelf, lowered her head. "You're asking me to reveal extremely personal information, Poet. I'm not comfortable doing so. Why should I?"

"Because Paris is worried about you."

"A good reason. But not good enough. I told you I'd talk about the blackmail situation and I did. If you're truly my friend, you won't press."

Well, hell. He jammed his hand through his hair. Rolled a cramp out of his neck. Damn. "All right."

"You mean that?"

Her voice, a scratchy whisper, raked over his heart like barbed-wire. "Sure."

She surprised the hell out of him. She turned and hugged him. "Thank you."

In that moment Seth fell in love with Emily McBride.

The breathtaking plunge set his pulse back a spell, a couple of skips and then it settled on a lumbering pace. He'd loved plenty, many, but he'd never been in love and he never imagined it would happen like this. He thought it would be at first sight, if ever. Thought it would be an earth-rocking sensation, like someone buffaloing him with the butt of a six-shooter. But this was quiet and gentle. Achingly sweet and refreshing.

Like Emily.

Her grateful embrace was so brief that, when she walked away, he was left to wonder if it had truly happened. His only evidence—rubber knees and a hard-on.

"I forgot the yarn," she said.

His mind raced and grappled.

The front door opened and closed. "Emily. Mr. Pinkerton."

"Mrs. Frisbie." Seth smiled kindly at the woman who'd championed her employee during the social club fiasco. She'd also defended erotic, or rather exotic, fiction. Backbone, intellect, and heart. He admired her vibrant spirit and smile.

"It's Saturday, dear," she said to Emily. "What are you doing here?"

"I . . . I . . ."

"My fault," Seth said in a sugar-sweet drawl. He pulled a book from the shelf and strode past the senior librarian. "I had a fierce hankering for Lord Byron."

"The man or his works?" She covered her mouth, smothered a smile. "Sorry. Couldn't help myself."

"That's what Byron said when he was caught seducing one of those Mediterranean boys." He winked at the snickering woman while escorting a blushing Emily out the door.

"She didn't mean any harm," she said in defense of her employer.

"No, I don't expect she did." The majority of the town might be conservative, but the librarians, women usually noted for being straight-laced, were outspoken liberals. "I like her."

She looked up at him, graced him with a small smile. "You're a good man, Poet."

He felt like a bastard. He was earning her trust. He could see it in her eyes. He wanted to come clean, admit his identity. He'd had the same urge this morning. But for sure and for certain, she'd resent him and shut him out. As it was, he'd agreed not to press for more information on the blackmailer. Right now he needed to quietly observe, investigate, and protect. And hope she'd break down and ask for his help.

He also needed to telegraph *Fox* as this might take longer than he'd anticipated. Hell, he hadn't even broached the subject of the widowed Garrett with Emily. All he had was the man's word she was fond of him and his kids. He knew straight-out she was infatuated with Rome. His own feelings couldn't enter into this. He'd given his word. And truth told, out of the three of them, she was best off with Athens. Like Rome, Seth didn't have it in him to remain faithful to one woman. He didn't figure being in love would change that. After all, he was his father's son.

They walked side by side toward the mercantile, Seth wrestling with the absurdity of his situation. The difference one day, one person, could make in a man's life. With every step, he shoved his troubling affection for Emily deeper into the crevices of his heart. Denial was fast becoming his new best friend.

They entered the lively general store and Seth gave thanks for the absence of Mary Lee. He figured Emily had taken about all the upset she could handle for the day. She peeled off, heading toward the dry-good section and a cherubic saleswoman, probably the shopkeeper's wife.

He instantly recognized the owner, Ezekiel

Thompson, and the stick-up-his-ass cobbler, Frank someone-or-other. They stood in the hardware department, pouring over a newspaper with another man, a burly, ugly specimen chomping on an unlit cigar.

Thompson glanced up, bug-eyed. "You ain't gonna believe it, Emily. Wells Fargo suspended Rome and Boston. It's got something to do with I. M. Wilde's latest tale."

Seth registered her reaction with curiosity and confusion. She turned a whiter shade of pale, managed two shaky steps then promptly wilted, knocking over a display of canned beans.

CHAPTER *11*

*E*mily came to with a groan. She shoved a green glass bottle of smelling salts away from her nose, squinted up at the circle of blurry faces looking down at her. "What happened?"

"You fainted," Frank Biggins said.

At least she thought it was Mr. Biggins. She fingered the bridge of her nose. "Where are my spectacles?"

"Broke," another man said. "Went flying when you swooned."

"I'm afraid I stepped on them in my haste to get to you with the smelling salts," said Mrs. Thompson. "I'm sorry, Emily."

"Not your fault," she said, feeling increasingly foolish. She'd fainted. In the mercantile. More fuel for the gossip-mongers. Although Rome and Boston's suspensions would surely overshadow her spill. She couldn't believe it. She knew every one of Wilde's tales by heart and couldn't imagine what would cause the riff with Wells Fargo. Were specifics noted within that newspaper article? Woozy, she pushed herself up on her elbows. "Where's Mr. Pinkerton?"

"Right here." The sea of blurry faces parted as he crouched and maneuvered her into his arms. He pressed a cool, damp cloth to her throbbing forehead. "How are you feeling?"

Like she was burning up with fever. Like she had taffy limbs and apple butter for brains. She'd never been held by a man, not like this—all tender and protective. It riled her romantic nature, wrecked havoc with her chaste upbringing. She wondered if this was how Miss Sarah Smith had felt when Rome had revived her after the blow to her head. Had Pinkerton given her the kiss of life? Had she missed it? The notion made her plumb dizzy with regret. Surely being kissed by a friend was better than never being kissed at all. "What was the question?" She blinked up at the green-eyed poet, wondering how she could so clearly see the worry on his handsome face when all of the other hoverers were out of focus.

"Cracked her head good," Mr. Biggins said.

"Gonna have a goose egg," someone else piped in. Boris. Oh, no. Not Boris.

"Ezekiel's fetching Doc," Mrs. Thompson said, at

which point her husband and the wiry physician burst on the scene.

Doctor Kellogg squatted down, dragged his hand over his sparse white hair, and clucked his tongue. "I swan, you two are doing wonders for my practice."

"She fainted and hit her head," Pinkerton supplied without humor.

The older man peered under the folded cloth, whistled. "I can see that."

"Beaned by beans," Mr. Biggins joked.

She wished he'd disappear and take the bully owner of the Moonstruck Hotel with him.

As if reading her mind, Pinkerton addressed the gawkers. "I say, do you think you could afford Miss McBride some breathing space?"

"Fancy talkin', ain't he?" Boris said with disgust.

"Told you," Mr. Biggins said.

The innkeeper spoke around his fat cigar, nudged his skinny friend. "Why don't we finish readin' the newspaper? Leave the fussing to Doc and the women."

Emily wanted to come up swinging in Pinkerton's defense. Dang him for holding her down.

"Sticks and stones," he said close to her ear as the other men trailed off.

Meanwhile Doc pinned her with a chastising glare. "You haven't been eating properly, Emily. You're skinnier every time I see you, and that's a fact."

Mrs. Thompson nodded. "We've all noticed."

And no doubt speculated on the matter, she thought. "I . . . I haven't had much of an appetite."

"Awful thing what happened to your ma and pa, but you're mourning yourself sick."

"And crazy," someone mumbled from across the room.

She felt Pinkerton tense. "Sticks and stones," she whispered.

He squeezed her shoulder and *the bond* strengthened twofold. Again she likened their friendship to hers and Paris's. Sticking up for one another, sticking together. "I'm all right," she said, easing the compress from her forehead. She allowed Pinkerton and Mrs. Thompson to help her stand.

"I confess I skimped on the last few meals, missed lunch completely today," she told the doctor. "I'm weak is all. And now my head hurts. Oh, and I can't see very clearly." She managed a self-deprecating smile. "I'll take better care."

"See that you do. Best medicine I can offer is kindly advice. Get on with your life. Hitch yourself to a strapping, secure man like Cole Sawyer and have a few babies. It ain't too late to have a normal life."

A normal life had been the source of her mother's misery. Her blood boiled and this time it had nothing to do with the poet's touch. "I appreciate your concern, sir. As for your advice—"

"Miss McBride's spectacles," Pinkerton said to Mrs. Thompson, "might we be able to fix them?"

"Not unless you're a miracle worker. I not only bent the rims but crushed the lenses. Me and my big clodhoppers. I feel terrible, Emily. I think we have a few pair of spectacles locked in the display case with the silverware. I'd be pleased if you'd give them a try. No charge."

That solicited a grumble from Mr. Thompson, but his wife shushed him and moved in behind the counter.

"I've done my bit." Doc Kellogg shook his head and chuckled. "Be seein' one or the both of you soon, I reckon." Medical bag in hand, he lit for the door.

Before she could comment, Pinkerton steered her to Mrs. Thompson. A few pair of spectacles equaled *two* pair and neither suited her vision needs.

"Spectacle peddler should be passing this way in a week or two," Mrs. Thompson said.

Emily palmed her throbbing head. "Problem is, I need bifocals."

"You'll have to travel to Napa City for those. Zeke Karn's Jewelry and Optical Shop."

"Then that's what we'll do," Pinkerton said, pressing a firm hand to the small of her back.

Emily willed her knees and mind steady. A gentle-manly offer of support, she told herself, nothing more. Her skin flushed with awareness nonetheless. "Closed weekends," she croaked.

"Monday then."

"I work at the library on Monday."

"Difficult to catalog and such if the words are blurry," he said sensibly. "I'm sure Mrs. Frisbie will understand."

"I suppose." She squinted over her shoulder at the news-hound trio, wondering how she could get a peek at that article. Not that she could read it. She worried her lower lip as she mused. She knew Boston wasn't fond of the mounting attention he and his brother had been attracting due to being featured on several dime novel covers. Said it hampered their ability to circulate incognito. Rome didn't mind the fame, but he would mind something awful about a scandal. His work was his life. If Wilde had truly contributed to their suspension, there'd be the devil to pay.

"You best get Emily home, Mr. Pinkerton. She looks right peaked."

That brought her head around. "I'm all right."

Pinkerton looked as if he wanted to counter, but directed his attention to Mrs. Thompson. "Before we leave," he said with a friendly smile, "could I trouble you for a few skeins of yarn?"

"How many's a few? What color?"

Emily answered then listened in wonder as Pinkerton requested several food items. She tried to intervene more than once, but each time he gently hushed her. Nor would he allow her to put the total on her store credit. He settled in cash. Mr. Thompson, who turned right cheerful when Pinkerton paid his bill in full, insisted on fetching her buggy from the stable while Mrs. Thompson boxed their wares.

By the time they exited the store the sun was setting. Pinkerton loaded three boxes of supplies in the buggy and bid the storekeeper a pleasant farewell.

"I'll drive," he told Emily after helping her up and maneuvering her to the passenger side.

"Do you know the way?"

"I do."

Her head hurt something awful and her stomach felt all fluttery. No wonder, given the events of the day. "In that case I won't argue."

"Wouldn't matter if you did."

"Are you angry with me?"

"Why would you think that?"

"You sound sort of angry."

"I'm not angry." He released the brake and gently slapped the reins to Guinevere's rear.

Emily relaxed against the seat, grateful that traffic on the street and boardwalk was at a minimum as they exited town.

"Did I embarrass you? I caused an awful scene, I know. I'm not prone to the vapors. I just . . . it's been a trial of a day."

"That's a fact."

"So, did I?"

"What?"

"Embarrass you?"

Pinkerton glanced sideways. "Can't imagine that's possible."

She wasn't sure how to respond to that, so she didn't. She closed her eyes and tried to relax as they rolled further from town, closer to home. Nature's sounds came into play. The musical chirping of crickets. The sporadic hoot of an owl. Guinevere's hooves clopping gently on the well traveled path. She knew the sounds, the path, well. She'd traveled this way many a time with her parents. Church, socials, errands—personal and professional. Except for Sundays, once in town, the McBrides parted ways. Emily always ended up with Paris and the Garretts. Her parents didn't mind. Mostly she thought they were relieved.

So much for relaxing.

She shifted and focused on the colorful sunset in an effort to stave off dark thoughts. Pinkerton seemed lost in his own musings. She couldn't shake the feeling that he was irked. For all of his tenderness back at the mercantile, just now he was quiet and hard as a stone wall. Was he contemplating her breakdown in the library? Her collapse in the mercantile? She couldn't bear it if he contacted Paris with news that she was falling apart. The news would worry her friend ill.

"What Doc Kellogg said. It's not true," she said, grasping at straws. "I'm not mourning myself sick. I'm capable of accepting harsh truths."

He didn't comment so she rambled on, needing to fill the strained silence.

"I just . . . I don't want you to think I'm weak. Just because I fainted—"

"I don't think you're weak. I think your life's in turmoil. You lost your parents and gained a tormentor. Upheaval like that's bound to vex your appetite."

Her heart swelled at the depth of his understanding. Emotions and words jerked free of her tight rein. "Losing Mother, and soon after, Father, I confess, it was hard. And confusing. I felt so alone, and yet I felt free. I know that sounds awful. I just, they always, they wanted me to behave in a certain manner, to go against my nature. My mother went against her nature and I think she was one of the saddest people I've ever known."

"What was her name?"

"Alice McBride." The name scraped her throat raw.

He thumbed up the brim of his hat, angled her a look. Again, she marveled that she could so clearly see his expression when everything around them blurred. Or maybe she was sensing what she thought she saw in his eyes—interest.

He worked his jaw. "Favor her, do you?"

"I do."

"Then I reckon she was uniquely arresting."

Her skin burned head to toe. "You think I'm . . ." She couldn't say it.

"Inside and out."

Self-conscious, she looked away, tamed the curls that had escaped her braids, fingered the knot on her forehead. She wondered if it had purpled. "I don't remember ever being paid such a kindly compliment."

"That's a shame, and that's a fact."

He concentrated on the road and she grappled with what was happening between them. *The bond.* If his interests were that of a normal man, she might be concerned. After all, they were sleeping under the same roof. She reminded herself that she considered Athens Garrett attractive inside and out, but she didn't harbor lustful or longing thoughts about him. She considered Paris beautiful inside and out and she certainly didn't, well, she wasn't like Pinkerton. She was attracted to the opposite gender—specifically Rome Garrett. Trying to analyze the peculiar connection between herself and the poet was making her head throb harder, so she gave up and picked up the conversation a few sentences back.

"My mother, she's the one who opened my eyes to the wonder of words," she said, her nerves jangling like the buggy's rigging. "Whenever she could, she'd steal away to lose herself in a book. Once in awhile she'd read a passage aloud to me. In those moments, she sparkled. But then Father would interrupt with some need and her eyes and manner would dull." Emily embraced and shunned those memories. Mostly, she remembered the vibrancy in her mother's tone when she read about treasure hunts and jousts and damsels in distress.

"I wanted to sparkle like her. I wanted to feel what she felt when she escaped to those far off places, so I learned my letters early and advanced my skills with fervor. Read everything I could get my hands on. The more I practiced, the more it greased my imagination and soon I was spinning my own tales."

"That must have pleased your ma."

She never said, but Emily had hoped. "Maybe at first. But then I made the mistake of sharing one of my stories aloud one summer at the annual church picnic. It was about a twelfth-century knight shucking his armor to skinny dip in an enchanted lake."

Pinkerton's lips curved. "How old were you?"

"Ten."

He chuckled.

"The attending congregation failed to see the

charm or humor as did my father. Directly after he gave me a lecture on decorum and reminded me who I was—a preacher's daughter. That night Mother settled in with a copy of *Moby Dick* and sent me off to bed. Only before I went, she referred to the picnic scandal and advised me to channel my talents in a more respectable direction. Actually, it was more like an order." She massaged the tightness in her chest, blinked back tears. "From that day forth, I kept the stories of my heart tucked away, some in my head, some under my bed. The only person I shared them with was Paris. She and I have no secrets. We share a special bond." She paused, wet her dry lips. "Can I confess something?"

He reined Guinevere to the side of the road and gave Emily his full attention.

Maybe it was the knock to her head or maybe it was because she hadn't had anyone to confide in since Paris left. Or maybe she was plumb tired of squashing down her feelings. She didn't risk his gaze, but she did risk honesty. "I feel a similar bond with you, Poet. I know it sounds crazy. We've only known each other a couple of days, but . . . I . . . it's just that . . ." She blew out a breath. "Drat. I hate it when I babble."

"It's not crazy, what you're feeling," he said. "Sometimes people just get on. Don't waste your time trying to analyze what can't be put into words, Em."

Every time he called her that, her pulse skipped. So familiar, yet natural. As if they'd known each other forever. "Do you feel something? A connection of sorts?"

"I do."

She chanced his gaze, quirked a shy smile. "Must be an artistic thing."

"Life's full of surprises," he said gruffly.

"If one's lucky," she said, her mother's ghost hovering like a dark cloud. "Sometimes life's normal, too normal. Sometimes it plods along at a snail's pace. Every day the same. Nothing out of the ordinary. Sometimes a body so badly needs an adventure they'll risk judgment and condemnation to have one."

"Who are we talking about here? You or your ma?"

Both, although she wasn't willing to admit her part. As for her mother . . . No one knew the truth about Alice McBride's dreams, her disappointments, her death, aside from Paris. Her friend hadn't been around in months. Emily had suppressed thoughts and emotions since, and she was near bursting. "Her marriage was arranged. She married my father because he was a good match, according to her parents. She gave up her hopes and dreams and did what was expected. Became the wife and mother, the person society demanded. Meanwhile, she withered inside yearning for an adventure. *Everyone should have at least one grand adventure*, she once said."

"How did she die?"

His question was so blunt, she answered in kind. "In search of an adventure."

"Then I guess she went out of this world with a smile in her heart."

She'd never thought of it that way. Truth told, she'd been too bitter. Emily's Grand Design revolved around taking her mother on a once-in-a-lifetime adventure. The two of them. She saw it as a chance to bond with Alice McBride, a fanciful, bitter woman who had never been comfortable with her parental role. But before Emily had been able to make good on her plan, the woman had taken the issue on herself. Alone.

"You certainly have a way with words, Poet," she said by way of revealing the painful truth about her mother's death. "I'll try to keep that in mind."

Feeling awkward, she settled back against the seat. "Thank you for letting me ramble. Without Paris here, I sort of keep things bottled up."

"I'm pleased you feel comfortable enough to unburden yourself. Anything else you want to share?"

He was referring to the blackmailer, of course. The only thing left to tell was her secrets. She wasn't ready for that. She wasn't sure if she'd ever feel inclined. She squinted into the twilight. "We best get moving or we won't make it home before it turns pitch black. Mrs. Dunlap will be worried."

"I imagine she'll make a fuss when she sees the bump on your forehead," he said, clucking his tongue and setting the horse back on course.

"I suppose you're going to make sure I eat a big dinner."

"That's a fact."

They rode in silence for a stretch, both immersed in thought. The silhouette of the house came into view, lights flickering in the downstairs windows, and Pinkerton mused aloud. "Shame about Wells Fargo suspending the Garretts. From what Paris told me about her brothers, they're probably fit to be tied. Wouldn't want to be in I. M. Wilde's boots."

Emily's stomach flopped over and back, the thought of a big dinner enough to make her retch. "I confess, I'm a mite anxious about our fellow artist." She stole a look at the poet's strong form and profile. She was a mite anxious about a lot of things.

CHAPTER *12*

San Francisco, California

Rome Garrett fanned his cards, scowled at a losing hand, and folded. Shit luck had been dogging him for days. Even his lucky half eagle coin had lost its shine. Tonight he'd tried to dispel his black mood with a quart bottle and a poker game. But nothing could cut through the gloom of the suspension. "Screw Wells Fargo," he said to his little brother, the only man left at the table. "Screw Lancing." Their uptight supervisor had cut them loose to appease a blowhard politician. "Spineless bastard."

Boston smoothed his fingers over his moustache, collected his winnings with a mirthless smile. "That's the whiskey talking. You might want to slow up," he said when Rome poured another shot. "You've pert near polished off that entire bottle."

"Not on my own, I haven't. You've kept pace,

little brother."

"Difference is I'm an amiable drunk. You're an ass-hole." Boston waved off the barkeep coming their way, shuffled the cards. At this point, aside from Hoyt, a loyal employee and ten-year acquaintance, they were the only two left in the private salon of the Gilded Garrett Opera House. Boston didn't bother to curb his tongue but he did temper his volume. "Bert Lancing did what he had to do. Place blame where blame's due."

"When I get my hands on I. M. Wilde—"

"I was referring to you. You're the one who brought the wrath of a state senator down on our heads. Did-dling Osprey Smith's wife wasn't one of your brighter moves, Rome."

"She started it."

"That's a hell of a defense."

"Said she and her husband had an arrangement."

"Guess she wasn't clear on the boundaries. Or she was and ignored them. Or there was never an ar-rangement and you were just randy enough to swallow Sarah Smith's lies." Boston cocked a sardonic brow. "Knowing you like I do, I'm voting on the latter."

Rome rolled his half eagle coin over his knuckles, partly for calm, partly for luck. He refused to believe his had run out. "You're starting to irritate me."

"I've been downwind of your pissy mood for two days now. I'm well past irritated. You want me to back off?" He thunked the deck of cards in the center of the table. "Cut the deck and shut the hell up."

Rome pocketed his coin, reminding himself that Boston didn't deserve his ire. When it came down to it, the only reason his brother had been suspended was because he'd raised hell on Rome's behalf. When Lancing refused to listen to reason, Boston had retaliated with some disparaging remarks about the man's mother. Those colorful insults had earned him temporary walking papers as well.

As for sleeping with another man's wife, hell, no, it hadn't been one of his better moments. But Sarah had seduced him with hot, needy kisses and stories of a cold, cheating husband. He'd enjoyed her company, her insatiable appetite. Her casual attitude had backed up her claim that so long as she stayed out of her husband's affairs, he'd ignore hers. *The arrangement*. He didn't want to believe she'd made it up. Didn't want to believe he'd been that stupid.

"Sexual misconduct," he grumbled as Boston dealt. "If that don't beat all. Osprey Smith twisted the facts. Portrayed me as some sort of deviant. He wanted to punish me while salvaging Sarah's reputation."

"Can you blame him? He aims on running for governor. Last thing he needs is a tarnished wife."

"I've never taken advantage of a woman in my life. It's not in my character, and after eight years in Wells

Fargo's employ, if Lancing doesn't know—"

"He knows. But Smith's a powerful man and Wells Fargo can't afford to ruffle political feathers. Lancing said it straight up. Mrs. Smith was enamored with your fame. You're a hell of a lot more revered by her and the general populace than Osprey Smith. The double-talking, polecat resented that and gunned to make you pay. Public humiliation. Tit for tat."

Fed up with the insult to his integrity, Rome slapped his cards face down. "I," he growled, "was discreet. Wilde's the one who made the affair public by penning the kiss that launched the indiscretion. How did he know about Sarah's overzealous thank you? You were the only one alive on the scene other than us. I never discussed it with anyone aside from you."

"What are you implying?"

"Don't get your britches in a twist. I know you wouldn't speak out of turn. But someone did."

Boston rolled his eyes. "Obvious, don't you think?"

"Sarah wouldn't risk pissing off her husband."

"Where's the risk if they had an arrangement?" Boston looked disgusted. "Get your head out of your pants and see the light. Sarah Smith didn't take a shine to Rome Garrett, she took a shine to a dime novel hero. I'm telling you she bragged to someone about snaring you and it got back to Wilde who has elephant-sized ears when it comes to you and me."

"Add elephant-sized balls for scandalizing a state senator's wife."

"Maybe he didn't know. Smith's a common enough name."

"You sticking up for that piss-ant, Wilde?"

"Hell, no. Got my own bones to pick with that scribe. Some of that stuff he writes, it's like he knows my mind." Boston scowled, poured the last of the whiskey. "Downright creepy. Makes me feel, I don't know, violated."

"Good name for it. Violated." Rome drained his glass then motioned to Hoyt for another bottle.

"Never mind that. Take yourself on home, Hoyt." London Garrett, the eldest of the Garrett clan and chief proprietor of the inherited opera house, flipped a chair around and straddled it. Between his substantial height and confidence, he took up more space than Rome and Boston put together.

Boston collected the cards, stacked the chips. "Time to call it a night."

Rome glanced at his pocket watch. "It's just past midnight. Night's young."

"Two hours past midnight. Fun's over." London got that look, the one that said he was preparing to lecture them blue. "You've been drinking my whiskey, screwing my chorus girls, and generally irritating me with your bitchin' for two days. This ends now. We've got family business to attend."

As far as lectures went it was short but powerful. Rome sobered up right quick. Family was everything. "What kind of business?"

"I want to cut loose the Gilded Garrett. Relocate to Phoenix. Any objections?"

"To moving closer to Athens and the kids? Paris and her new one? To dumping this place?" Rome held up his hands in defense. "Not that the Gilded isn't a money-maker."

London had fashioned the family inheritance into a premier theater. In addition to this private salon, the three-story Victorian splendor featured a classy saloon, elegant conversation rooms, and a thousand-seat auditorium. The Gilded Garrett was popular and prosperous, the permanent home of London, sometimes home of Rome and Boston. Still, the establishment reeked of their father, and William Garrett was a bastard of the first water. Rome had no qualms about kissing the Gilded and the lingering spirit of his pa goodbye.

"There's more." The well-dressed, dark-haired, dark-eyed Garrett regarded his brothers with a steady gaze. "I want free of the family estate."

Boston shifted in his chair. "You want to sell our home."

"Yours if you want it. I'm moving on. Like Athens."

"Athens hasn't exactly moved on," Rome said.

"He's yet to get over Jocelyn. As for shucking his political aspirations, can't say I'm displeased, given my current opinion of government officials."

"Your troubles are of your own making, Rome. Always have been. You stuck your pecker where it didn't belong. Way I see it, you're lucky Smith didn't shoot it off."

No matter how old they all grew, London would always be the eldest of the Garrett clan. Having to provide for four younger siblings at the age of twenty-three had fashioned him into a force to be reckoned with.

Half booze-blind, Rome wasn't up for the challenge. He dragged both hands down his face, tamped down his annoyance. "Let's stick to the subject at hand."

Boston took up the reins of sensibility. "The only ones who lived there fulltime were Athens and Paris, Zach and Zoe. Now that they're gone, can't say I enjoy being there too often for too long. House ain't a home without family."

"You sure about this, London?" Rome asked. "The family business *and* home?"

"Break with the past. Start clean." He glanced around the salon, rolled back his shoulders. "I'm sure."

"I'm throwing in with London," said Boston. "I vote to bail."

The two men focused on Rome. "Don't look at

me. You know how I feel about the Gilded. As for home, I couldn't wait to get out of Heaven."

London grinned at that. "It's settled then." He stood, strode toward the bar, and nabbed a bottle of his best whiskey. "I cleared my belongings out of the house years ago and I've got my hands full with negotiations for the theater."

Boston glanced at Rome then London. "Guess that means we're traveling to Heaven."

"Guess it does." London settled back in the chair, poured drinks. "I want you to check in on Emily while you're there. Athens mentioned she canceled her trip to visit Paris. That doesn't sit right with me. Make sure she's not hurting for anything. See if you can offer her some of our better furnishings without it seeming like charity. She's proud."

She was also a pain in Rome's ass. A harmless pain, but an annoyance no less. She'd been mooning after him for years. His little sister's shy friend. The preacher's daughter. A bookish and backward innocent. Far and away from the type of woman Rome was attracted to. Still, Emily was part of the family and it pained him she'd suffered consecutive losses. Her ma and pa dying, and then Paris moving away.

He thought about his own ill luck as of late. He could do with some cheering up. Some social discourse. Maybe he'd do a kind turn and escort Emily to the Blossom Dance. The annual event was only a few days off, but he couldn't imagine she'd already been asked. If anyone was destined for spinsterhood, it was Emily McBride.

CHAPTER *13*

Napa Valley, California

He dreamt about her and that was a damned shame, because she was naked in his dreams. The vision would haunt him.

He'd had his way with her, too. He'd unwound those long braids and set her pale curls free. He'd suckled her lips, her breasts. He'd smoothed his hands over her slight figure, pleasured her with his fingers, his tongue. He'd scandalized her, thrilled her.

Touch me, Poet. I'm eager to learn.

She had no idea what effect those innocent words had wrought. Her innocence and fighting spirit unhinged his heart and fired up John Thomas. A powerful, unsettling combination.

In his dreams, Seth had mounted Emily's quivering, pliant body and claimed her as his own.

Only she wasn't his. She belonged to Athens

Garrett. At least she would as soon as he delivered the damned proposal.

Two full days since his arrival. He should have at least brought up the man's name by now. The opportunity to casually do so had not arisen. Or maybe it had and he'd missed it. "Or ignored it," he grumbled to the warped and cracked ceiling.

Mood dark, he swung out of bed, the unsteady frame creaking with his weight, and pulled on a pair of trousers. His left arm ached with the effort. He thought about the person who'd taken a shot at him, wondered at his motive. It was a hell of a lot more productive than pining after a woman claimed by another man. A woman deserving of a faithful husband.

Unlike tracking criminals, fidelity did not run in Seth's blood. His pa had been an upstanding lawman, but he'd fallen down on his role as husband. Even though he claimed to love Seth's ma, Lacey, and even though they had an agreeable marriage, Hershel Wright craved variety and frequently bedded the local doves. Lacey turned a blind eye, finding solace in denial. But Seth knew his pa's infidelity injured her feelings. At least his pa had been discreet.

Still, Seth had sworn long ago never to put a woman through that. The day he recognized his thirst for variety is the day he vowed to live out his days as a bachelor.

He hadn't counted on Emily.

Barefoot, he moved to the sole window of the small guestroom, peered outside. The morning sun hovered on the horizon. Barely dawn. Muted hues of red and orange spilled over the surrounding hills and valleys. Again, he was struck by all the green. So different from what he was used to. He was used to stark. Sparse, brown, and stark. The vivid landscape reminded him of Emily. She brought color to his world. Color and unrest.

He focused on the ominous rain clouds hovering over a distant hill, willed them to blow in and burst. He'd benefit from a dose of gloom, something to make this land less appealing. Something to make him ache for home.

He turned away, poured water from a large-mouthed pitcher into a matching chipped basin, and splashed his face to clear the mental cobwebs. His brain was full of Emily. Her shaky relationship with her mother. Her passionate views on hypocrites and intolerance. Her obsession with adventurous literature.

Her infatuation with Rome Garrett.

He'd worked every angle and still he couldn't work out her secret.

AS LONG AS YOU REAP BENEFITS, YOU WILL PAY THE PRICE.

What benefits? Not financial. Her property was

falling apart and the furnishings in this house, though dust-free from Mrs. Dunlap's incessant cleaning, were cheaply made and old to boot. Preacher McBride's earnings had been meager. Or maybe he'd been a miser. Emily had said the blackmailer had depleted her savings. To his knowledge, librarians earned paltry salaries. The blackmailer wasn't getting rich off of this scheme. He had an ulterior motive. His signature line had religious connotations. Was her *Savior* a member of her father's congregation? Someone who'd discovered something tawdry in Emily's background? Or perhaps her parents' background? Protecting someone else fit the woman's profile. Had her ma or pa been drinkers? How had she accumulated the wine bottles she used as targets? Her neighbor did run a winery and, according to Emily, Bellamont had been a close friend of her father's. Maybe the winemaker had simply offered used or flawed bottles as ready targets.

Dammit. There were too many missing pieces to this puzzle and the pieces he had didn't fit together in a way that made a lick of sense.

It would make his investigation easier if the shooter and the blackmailer were one in the same. Only the letters had originated in San Francisco. Emily claimed she'd never been out of Napa Valley, yet the black-mailer knew she worked at the library. He knew an intimate secret. Either he was acquainted with Emily or with someone close to her.

Like the Garretts.

Seth reached for a bar of soap and continued his morning ablutions as his mind traversed new and unsettling territory. Could the Garrett brothers somehow be connected with Emily's troubles, whether by accident or design? London owned an opera house in San Francisco. Rome and Boston worked for Wells Fargo. Home office: San Francisco. Seth had only met them once. They'd struck him as arrogant, but not ruthless. Certainly not the sort to terrorize a woman. Although he *had* witnessed Rome shooting a defenseless man. Granted, the cur had manhandled his sister. He'd also committed arson and murder. Still, there'd been no need to shatter the man's kneecap after Josh had nearly choked the life out of him.

Seth had recognized a dangerous edge to Rome Garrett that day. Now he wondered what he'd done to earn Wells Fargo's censure. Apparently, the offense was noted in an I. M. Wilde tale. But which one?

His gut told him the Garretts weren't directly responsible for Emily's troubles, but he suspected they figured in somehow and the niggling thought had him itching to read the newspaper article. That meant a visit to Thompson's Mercantile. A trip into town. Then he remembered it was Sunday. Maybe he could talk Thompson into opening the store after church—

he assumed Emily and Mrs. Dunlap would want to attend service. At the least, he'd engage the shopkeeper in conversation, encouraging him to relay the details behind the Garretts' suspension. Any clue to shed light on the mystery revolving around Emily would be welcome. He needed to deal with her current dilemma before addressing her future.

His chest tightened as he plucked Athens's sealed letter from his valise. He wondered at the manner in which the proposal of marriage was penned. Had his boss asked Emily reasonably or had he waxed poetic? In Seth's vast experience, women preferred flowery declarations of adoration as opposed to direct, logical statements.

My children need a mother and you need a protector, marry me didn't pack the same punch as *I'm bewitched by your sad blue eyes and sensitive heart, put me out of my misery and say you'll be mine.*

Athens struck Seth as direct and logical. That wouldn't cut it with Emily. Emily who equated an arranged marriage with sacrificing one's dreams. He didn't figure a marriage of convenience would rate much better in her eyes. A hopeful romantic likened practicality and convention with shackles. A hopeful romantic married for love, not duty or protection.

He considered his arguments.

There are all kinds of love.

Trust and respect are a strong seed. In time love will blossom.

He could quote Ralph Waldo Emerson, a fellow—*ahem*—poet. *Love and you shall be loved.* If nothing else it would verify his knowledge of his—*cough*—contemporaries.

So how did he convince her that Athens, and not Rome, was her knight in shining armor?

Rumor has it you can talk any woman into anything.

When his heart was in it, hell, yeah. Manipulating Emily and her feelings brought him no joy.

Frustrated, he slipped the letter back into his traveling bag. He donned his best suit, blocking graphic thoughts of Emily washing and dressing two doors down.

"Don't think about your boss's lady naked," he mumbled as he slipped into a clean white shirt. "You're a government agent, Wright. This is a mission." The sooner he delivered Emily from her troubles and into Athens's safe haven, the sooner he could kick miscreant ass.

Oddly, the prospect didn't hold the same thrill as it did before.

He contemplated the matter while stepping into his socks and boots.

Emily's talk of a grand adventure coupled with a tale of a man attempting to circumvent the world in eighty days had infected Seth with an irksome bug. Last night he'd entertained the ladies by reading aloud from Verne's *Around the World in Eighty Days*. He'd recited Phileas Fogg's escapades with dramatic inflection, glancing up now and again to revel in the sparkle in Emily's sky-blue eyes. His own life had been far from boring, but after experiencing her infectious anticipation and imagining Fogg's excitement as he raced across exotic foreign lands, suddenly Seth felt as if he hadn't lived at all.

He'd never second guessed his career. Wrangling criminals came as naturally as romancing the ladies. Like his pa, he excelled at both. He'd never yearned for more because he felt like he had it all. Sensing otherwise was annoying.

Emily had winged him like that renegade bullet with her sad blue eyes and sorrowful talk of her mother. Clearly, she'd bewitched him. Why else had he fallen in love? How else to account for this burst of discontent? He had to shake this, her. He had to suppress the affectionate and desirous feelings mangling his heart and good sense.

Today. He'd start singing Athens's praises today.

CHAPTER *14*

*E*mily spent the night alternating between insomnia, inappropriate dreams, and anguished nightmares. Awakening pre-dawn in a tangle of sheets, her chemise plastered to her sweat drenched body, had been the final straw. A nightmare was not to blame for her frenzied heart rate, but a passionate dream. Intent on weaving intimate aspects into the swashbuckling tale she'd been toiling over for months, she lit the kerosene lamp sitting on the table next to her bed and reached for her spectacles.

Only her spectacles weren't there. They'd died an ugly death under the heel of Mrs. Thompson's boot.

She penned her thoughts all the same. She couldn't read the scribbled pages, but at least she'd gotten the scenes out of her head and onto paper. Maybe it would help her to remember what she felt in the dream, for surely she'd never experienced such sweet torture. And she never would.

The shirtless hero in her dream had been Pinkerton.

She stood less of a chance with him than with Rome. At least Rome fancied girls.

Maybe she had an unconscious desire to be a spinster. At least she'd be assured her independence. Her Grand Design wouldn't be at risk. Unfortunately, her Savior had robbed her of her means to finance that adventure. If he had his way, she'd never utilize that talent to earn another penny.

"You're in a heck of a pickle, Emily McBride. You're also talking to yourself. Again." Sighing, she shoved out of bed and squinted at the clock on her bedside table. It was later than she thought.

She padded to her window, pushed open the curtains. Storm clouds blotted out the morning sun. Thunder rumbled in the distance. Thankfully, last night after unhitching and brushing down Guinevere, Pinkerton had fed and stowed the horse in the stall instead of turning her out in the pasture. Guinevere hated thunderstorms. Emily loved them. Rainy days meant extended time for reading and writing.

She needed her spectacles for that.

Drat.

Mrs. Dunlap would spend the day knitting.

Pinkerton could tinker with his poems and short story. What was *she* supposed to do? Mood worsening, she hurriedly washed and dressed. The least she could do was make breakfast. She could see well enough to hustle up some eggs. Anything of substantial size was simply fuzzy around the edges. Mostly she was far-sighted. So long as she didn't have to consult a recipe she'd do fine.

A few minutes later, she tip-toed down the stairs so as not to disturb anyone, locked away her journal in her desk, and commenced to preparing a hearty morning meal. Her own appetite was still weak, but she refused to succumb to more swooning. Doc Kellogg had been right about one thing. She needed to get on with her life. She couldn't let her Savior rob her of her health as well as her money and peace of mind. Mostly it was Pinkerton's heartfelt concern and the possibility he might alarm Paris that prompted her to take more care.

She cracked an egg into a bowl, her mind flashing on the way he had held her in his arms after she'd faint-ed in the mercantile. If he were Rome, he would've pressed his lips against hers and breathed life into her. If she were Miss Sarah Smith she would've thanked him by pressing her breasts against him and thrusting her tongue into his mouth. Rome had described it as a goddamned hot and wet, boner-inducing kiss. She wasn't sure what that was. But he'd been smiling like a cat that ate the mouse when he relayed specifics to Boston. She assumed a kiss like that brought immense pleasure.

He'd gone on to describe a few of the things he'd like to do to the lush-figured woman, using words that made Emily's cheeks burn. She'd quickly slinked away, not that they knew she was within earshot to begin with. Without Paris around, where the Garrett brothers were concerned, Emily was as good as invisible.

She wondered if Pinkerton knew anything about hot and wet, boner-inducing kisses.

"You're thinking about him, aren't you?"

Emily jumped at the sound of Mrs. Dunlap's voice. "I didn't hear you come in."

The woman sidled in beside her, filling a copper kettle with Arbuckles and water. "That's because you were daydreaming about him."

She cracked another egg into the bowl, refusing to look Mrs. Dunlap in the eye. How could she possibly know someone else's mind when she barely knew her own?

"I know a woman in love when I see one," she continued. "I still get that dreamy feeling whenever I think about my Harold. Doesn't matter he's been dead and gone for five years, or is it six? True love is forever."

Emily dabbed the cuff of her shirt to her perspiring

brow. The incoming storm had pumped the summer air full of humidity. "Part of me believes that. Part of me hopes it's romanticized cow flop," she said in a quiet voice. "If true love is forever, then I'm doomed to live life alone. Rome doesn't care two figs for me."

"Rome Garrett?" Mrs. Dunlap snorted. "You don't love him."

"I don't?"

"Not in a grown woman way, no. You're in love with Mr. Pinkerton."

Emily's mouth fell open. Thunder shook the panes like an unsubtle foreshadow.

Mrs. Dunlap smiled while setting the kettle on the stove to boil.

Shaking off her daze, Emily cracked open another egg, and lowered her voice to a self-conscious whisper. "I am not in love with Phineas Pinkerton. Even if I were, which I'm not, I would be just as doomed. He doesn't like . . . that is to say . . . I'm not his type."

"Nonsense."

"You don't know the particulars."

"You don't know your own heart."

"What are you lovely ladies arguing about?"

Pinkerton stepped into the kitchen, sucking up all the air. Emily couldn't breathe. Even blurred around the edges, he looked dashing and handsome, just like in her dream, only he was wearing clothes.

Mrs. Dunlap eyed him up and down while forking bacon into a cast-iron skillet. "My, aren't you dapper this morning?"

Emily thought he dressed impeccably every day. He'd probably look stylish wearing a potato sack. She concentrated on the eggs.

"You're fetching as always, Mrs. Dunlap."

"You're kind to say so, Mr. Pinkerton. You removed the bandage from your forehead, I see. Barely a scratch, as you said. You fared much better than poor Emily."

"I'm fine." But she knew she looked a fright. The bump on her noggin was swollen and discolored. She hadn't bled like Pinkerton, yet her head wound looked five times worse.

"How's your arm?" she asked. Even though the bullet had grazed, he'd still been shot.

"I'll live."

She heard the smile in his voice, looked over her shoulder and caught him staring at her. He did that a lot. Her heart constricted along with her lungs. She squirmed under his appraisal. She hadn't dressed in her Sunday best. She'd dressed hastily and in honor of Calamity Jane. She'd dressed, not for vanity or propriety, but confidence. "Didn't figure you for a practicing Christian, Mr. Pinkerton."

"I'm not, but I assumed you and Mrs. Dunlap were."

The older woman busied herself setting the table. "I keep faith in my own way."

"As do I," Pinkerton said, pulling three mugs from the cupboard.

Emily bristled. What? Because she was a preacher's daughter she was expected to act more traditionally? She stabbed the yolks, whipping up scrambled eggs as her scrambled brain whipped up her defense. Surely he understood that she couldn't, in good conscience, enter the house of the Lord with this blackmail issue hanging over her head. Not only that, but her faith had been sorely tested this past year.

"I've read the bible front to back, not once, but several times," she said, pouring the eggs into a second frying pan. "I suspect my father's sermons will ring in my mind for eternity. I know what's expected of a decent soul. I've done my best to abide. Attending church for the sake of attending is not going to make me a better person." There. That sounded logical. Didn't it?

"You're fine just the way you are, dear," said Mrs. Dunlap. "They don't come any finer."

"I'm inclined to agree," Pinkerton said, moving in, hovering.

Her skin sizzled. Or maybe that was the bacon. Her senses whirled.

He placed one hand on her hip as if sensing a dizzy

spell, reached around her with a fork, and flipped over the strips of frying meat.

She stood frozen, her mind replaying that sensual dream. She imagined him kissing her neck, her shoulder . . .

"Are we expecting company?" he asked, breaking in on her thoughts.

"No." She cleared the gruffness from her voice. "Why?

"That's an almighty serving of eggs, Em."

She squinted at the griddle, then at the counter littered with, was it, yes, *twelve* shells. My, but she'd been distracted.

"Thanks to you," Mrs. Dunlap said, "our girl's got her appetite back."

A knock at the door saved Emily from having to comment. "Who could that be?"

"I suspect it's Mr. Bellamont," said Mrs. Dunlap. "He mentioned he'd be stopping by."

She sidestepped the poet and whirled to face her boarder. "When?"

"Now, obviously. On his way to church."

"No. I mean when did he tell you he'd be stopping?"

"Yesterday."

"Yesterday, when?" Pinkerton asked in a voice much calmer than Emily's.

"Just after you two went off for target practice."

"Did you tell him where we were?" This again from Pinkerton.

"I believe I did, yes." The woman, who'd been polishing the silverware, scrunched her nose. "What's all the fuss?"

Emily refrained from looking over her shoulder at Pinkerton. She knew what he was thinking and it was ludicrous. Still, she was painfully uncomfortable with a visit from Mr. Bellamont. "I wish you would have told me." She could've figured out a reason not to be here.

"I did," the woman said, then frowned. "Didn't I?"

Another knock, louder this time.

"You go ahead, dear. See what he wants." Mrs. Dunlap nabbed the spatula from Emily and shooed her toward the hall. "I'll mind the bacon and eggs. If he wants to stay for breakfast, we have plenty."

She didn't aim on inviting him, although he had a way of inviting himself now and then. It's not that she didn't like Mr. Bellamont. He always seemed to have her best interests at heart, even going so far as to offering marriage when she'd been abandoned so abruptly in this world. He'd been a good, if not misguided, friend to her father. He'd seen her through a horrific night and for that she was grateful. Except it meant he was privy to her darkest secret. In her mind it was far worse than what her Savior held over her head. Though he'd sworn to carry the secret to his grave, and though she believed him, each time she saw Mr. Bellamont she felt panic and shame.

"I'll only be a moment," she said to Pinkerton, adding a silent *stay here* with her eyes.

She skedaddled before the man could counter, walked briskly down the hall. With any luck she wouldn't have to invite her father's friend inside. Hopefully, he'd say his piece and hurry toward town in an effort to beat the storm. She smoothed her sweaty palms down her trousers and opened the door. "Mr. Bellamont."

"Emily."

He swept off his bowler revealing a full head of silver hair. In contrast, his moustache was black with only a sprinkling of grey. He wore a tailor-made suit, dove-grey, expensive. He'd tucked the ends of his black silk cravat under the tips of his turned-down collar. Gold cufflinks glittered from the cuffs of his starched white shirt. A watch fob dangled from his vest pocket. Whenever on business and always on Sundays, Claude Bellamont dressed like the wealthy wine baron he was. He reminded Emily of a rendering she'd seen in one of the dime novels of dandy lawman, Bat Masterson. Only Mr. Bellamont was shorter and older. Maybe it was the cool, sophisticated air more than an actual likeness. Maybe it was her blurry vision.

"To what do I owe this honor?" she asked, loitering on the threshold.

He didn't answer and she realized with a start that he was staring. Self-conscious, she lifted a hand to the bruised bump on her forehead. "Clumsy accident."

"Last evening in the mercantile. I heard."

Of course.

"Are you all right, my dear?"

She quirked a nervous smile. "Perfectly fine."

"I also heard you took on a male boarder."

"Phineas Pinkerton."

"People are talking."

"They always do."

"Your father—"

"—wouldn't have approved. I know." She thought about the fateful night that had allied her and Mr. Bellamont. Standing over her father's body, he'd described the circumstances of the preacher's death and why they should twist the truth. She felt ill. "In all honesty, my head aches something fierce, sir. Forgive me, but I'm not up to company just now." What was one more lie on her list of many?

He stroked his moustache, nodded. "I'll make this quick. I understand Cole Sawyer invited you to the Blossom Dance."

"Yes."

"You turned him down."

"I'm not comfortable with socials." Or with Cole Sawyer.

"I understand, child. But I feel you should make the effort. There's talk as to your . . ." His eyes flitted over her attire. ". . . state of mind. Allow me to escort you to the dance. Drink, eat, and make merry. Prove to the town you're just like any one of them."

She looked away, over his shoulder toward turbulent skies. "But I'm not."

"Indeed, *mademoiselle*. You are quite special." He stepped forward causing her to step back. "I've never seen you without your eyeglasses, Emily." He surprised her by skimming his fingers along her jaw. "*Vous êtes charmante.*"

She jerked back and smacked into something solid.

Mr. Pinkerton.

"I don't believe we've met." He casually finessed Emily to his side. It reminded her of the first day they met, when he'd shielded her from Cole. Ever polite, he extended a hand to Mr. Bellamont. "Phineas Pinkerton, poet."

"Claude Bellamont, winemaker." The older man smiled easily, though his eyes lacked warmth. "I'm an avid reader, though I can't say I'm a fan of poetry."

"I prefer whiskey to wine."

"To each his own," Bellamont said. *People are talking.*

"Indeed. Although to enjoy life to its fullest one should sample all life has to offer," Pinkerton said.

"Do you not agree?"

Emily blinked up at him. It occurred to her, not for the first time, that he adopted a more formal manner of speech when in the company of others. Was it deliberate? Unconscious? His duality fascinated her. She realized in that instant she knew next to nothing about Phineas Pinkerton. Maybe they'd bonded because they were, in truth, very much the same. Perhaps he too lived a double life.

Bellamont ignored the question and focused on Emily. "About the dance—"

"How awkward," Pinkerton said, placing a hand over his heart. "Miss McBride has already accepted my invitation to the Blossom Dance."

"But—"

"I confess, I pressured her. I do so love a gay affair."

"I couldn't let him attend alone," Emily said, snagging the lifeline he'd just thrown. "He's a guest. A friend of the family."

"Gracious! Where does the time go?" Mrs. Dunlap rushed down the hall, securing a straw bonnet on her head. "Sorry to keep you waiting." She glanced at a confused Emily while wiggling her fingers into a pair of gloves. "Yesterday, Mr. Bellamont kindly agreed to escort me into town this morning. Don't tell me I forgot to mention it?"

The look on the winemaker's face indicated this

was news to him, though he was quick to recover. He inclined his head, repositioned his bowler. "I am happy to be of service."

A crack of thunder prompted the woman into action. She looped her arm through his and ushered him outdoors, preventing lengthy farewells. "We best hurry if we're to beat the worst of it," she said, gesturing to the ominous clouds. She glanced over her shoulder at Emily. "Breakfast is on the table, dear. Toodles."

Emily stood dumfounded as she watched her neighbor help her boarder into his fancy surrey. "Is she imagining things now as well as forgetting? I think she took Mr. Bellamont unaware."

"I think she knew exactly what she was doing."

Emily turned and faced Pinkerton, her breath catching when she noted the hard glint in his eyes. Once again he'd transformed from delicate poet to dangerous warrior. "And what do you think she was doing?"

He closed the door, shutting out the blustery winds and the rest of the world. "Affording us time alone."

If Seth had to guess, he'd say Mrs. Dunlap acted on a spontaneous urge to play matchmaker. Or maybe she had it planned. She'd questioned him about his marital status and had bragged about Emily's numerous glowing qualities over the past two days. She had her forgetful moments, but the rest of the time she was pretty sharp. She probably hoped her absence would inspire a little chaste romance.

Seth was too fired-up about what he'd just witnessed to indulge in handholding and sweet talk. He could tell by the wary look in Emily's eyes she sensed his agitation, so he came right out with it. "Bellamont makes you nervous."

"No, he doesn't."

"Yes, he does. Why?" Seth's thread-thin patience snapped the moment the weasel winemaker touched her. Even from a distance, he'd seen lust in the smooth-talking devil's eyes. Maybe she didn't recognize it for what it was, but she sure as hell didn't welcome his familiarity. Neither did Seth. He couldn't give in to his feelings for Emily but, by God, he didn't have to stand by while other men, namely Bellamont, Sawyer, and her Savior, tried to have their way with her.

"Our breakfast is getting cold."

"You don't have an appetite. Especially after that exercise in forced cordiality. You know it and I know it."

"You don't know anything."

"I think I do. I think your discomfort has something to do with those wine bottles you used as targets."

She paled and he knew he was dead on. She tried to sidestep him but he blocked her way, trapping her between his body and the front door. Frustration flashed in her eyes. "Would you please move?"

"Not until you answer my question."

"You promised you wouldn't pry."

"I didn't promise anything."

"You agreed—"

"That was pertaining to your blackmailer. Is Bellamont *Your Savior*?"

"Don't be silly. He's a wealthy man. He doesn't need my money. Besides, if I *knew* the identity of my Savior, I'd . . ."

"What?"

"I'd . . . confront him."

It was all he could do not to shake sense into her. "Then what? He's a criminal, Emily. A man with little to no conscience."

"You agreed not to press me on the subject of—"

"*Your Savior*. Who you're certain is not Bellamont. So, let's talk about him."

Eyes bright, she balled her fists at her sides. He couldn't tell if she was going to burst into tears or throw a punch. She could do both for all he cared. He wanted some damned answers, and he'd play dirty to get them.

"Why are you so persistent?" she asked in a choked voice.

"Because I care." He jammed a hand through his hair to keep from touching her. If he touched her, he'd pull her into his arms. Comfort would lead to a kiss. It sure as hell wouldn't be chaste. "Friends confide in one another. Help one another. You said you and Paris have no secrets. That you share a special bond. You said you feel a similar bond with me."

Her eyes glittered with unshed tears. "I do."

If he pressed, she'd crack. He pressed. "Why does Bellamont make you nervous?"

"Because he knows something ugly about me, about my father!" she blurted. "Now please let me pass!"

She shoved at his shoulder and, though he easily could have held his ground, he moved.

She stalked past him, clenching and unclenching her fists, muttering to herself.

He followed her into the kitchen, his mind sifting through bits of information. His bad temper simmered toward boil when he saw her scoop her plate off the table and toss the food out the back door. *Hold it in, Wright. Let loose and your cover's blown. Channel Pinkerton. The gentle soul. The intuitive detective.*

"Those bottles carried the Bellamont Winery seal," he said evenly, as she discarded her plate in the sink. "By your admission, your father and the winemaker were good friends. Did your father have a fondness for liquor? Did he drink with Bellamont? Drink to excess? Did he do something inappropriate while under the influence? Is Bellamont holding that over your head,

threatening to ruin your father's good name unless you
. . . what? Marry him? Sell him your land?"

"Stop." She gripped the counter for support. Her
body trembled, and he knew she'd cracked. He braced
himself for a tearful, incoherent rant, but when she
turned to face him her eyes were dry, her color heightened by anger.

"Paris was right," she said, her voice steady and
tinged with resentment. "You're intuitive and clever.
You have observed and deduced and mostly you are
correct, Mr. Pinkerton. My father appreciated fine
wine. Yes, he partook in a glass now and then with his
friend, Mr. Bellamont. But it was not until after my
mother died that he drank to excess.

"Yes, he did something wrong. He gave up on
the living. He drowned his sorrows in alcohol. He
passed out at night. Woke up with hangovers. He forgot to write sermons, so I wrote them for him. He slept
through appointments, so I showed up in his stead and
made his excuses. Only I was always nervous and I
babbled, and when the person eventually questioned
my father, he'd rattle off his own explanation and chalk
up my ramblings to my overactive imagination.

"Yes, Mr. Bellamont enabled him by supplying wine,
but only after my father threatened to purchase his drinks
at Percy's Poker Palace if his friend cut him off. Mr. Bellamont may have been wrong to feed my father's thirst

for numbness, but his heart was in the right place. He was trying to keep Preacher Walt McBride from making a public spectacle of himself. Trying to keep his sickness a secret, as was I. *"Walt will come around,"* he kept telling me. *"Just give him time."* Only time ran out.

"Mr. Bellamont found my father dead in his wine cellar. He snuck in and drank himself to death. Actually, he tripped and hit his head, but he did so because he was falling down drunk, so it's all the same." At last her voice wobbled. "Mr. Bellamont didn't tell anyone. Not even his sons. Only me. He said we needed to alert Sheriff McDonald, but in order to avoid a scandal we should leave out the part about him being intoxicated. He said he'd fault a loose stair. He told me he'd take care of it. Told me to put it out of my head. So I did."

She looked Seth dead in the eye and he felt his heart break. "I couldn't handle it, Poet. So I put it out of my mind. Only every time I see Mr. Bellamont, it all rushes back. The guilt. The shame. Mr. Bellamont didn't do anything wrong. It's just that he knows my darkest secret. And now so do you."

Thunder boomed and the heavens opened. Rain pelted the kitchen window as Emily hastened to leave the room. "Happy now?"

He sank into a chair as she disappeared into the hall. "Delirious."

CHAPTER *15*

Territory of Arizona

*A*thens wondered if she'd want a fancy wedding.
Emily wasn't materialistic or pretentious, but
she was a woman and this *was* her first marriage. She'd
want a traditional ceremony, a special dress, flowers,
and music at the very least. He could envision his sister and her friend pouring over a mail order catalogue,
eyes and voices bright as they considered china and
flatware for Emily's new home.

Athens could easily imagine her sitting around the
dining room table, enjoying a meal and conversation
with him and the children. What he couldn't imagine
was Emily in his bed. Partly because he'd never considered her in a sexual way. Mostly because his heart
and mind were full of Kaila Dillingham.

He had no business lusting after the sensual for-
eigner. He'd penned a proposal of marriage to a demure

librarian—a respectable choice for a government official. A sensible choice for his children. Zach and Zoe
knew and trusted Emily. They loved her. His children's
comfort and happiness took precedence over his physical needs and desires.

Since he didn't aim on being celibate or unfaithful,
he needed to warm to the idea of Emily warming his
bed. There was no turning back as he assumed Seth
had extended his proposal. By his calculations, the
man had been in Heaven two or three days. He'd expected a wired update by now. The silence intimated
that Emily had hesitated and Seth was in the midst of
wooing her on Athens's behalf. If talk was true about
Wright's reputation with the ladies, then his engagement was set in stone.

"*She's the sensible choice*," he reminded himself.
Up until Kaila had fallen in his arms, he'd never sec-
ond-guessed that decision. He'd known Emily most of
her life, even if only as his sister's best friend. Unlike
Kaila, he knew her background and temperament. She
didn't intrude upon his thoughts every five seconds.
She didn't distract him from business. He had a personal stake in the Peacemaker Alliance and it chafed
that the Englishwoman had impeded on his almost
manic determination to get the agency up and running.
But even as he strived to reconcile their powerful love-
making as a one-time affair, he yearned for more. The

devil of it was, like Emily, he suspected Kaila might be fascinated with one of his famous brothers. Unlike with Emily, he'd felt a flicker of jealously.

"Step right up! Buy your tickets for the wildest show in the west!"

Athens jerked out of his reverie as the crush of people inched forward. Zach and Zoe flanked him, their expressions exuberant as there were now only three people between them and the raspy-voiced barker. They'd been waiting in line for twenty minutes. Seemed everyone in the county had turned out for the opening performance of J.P. Fishburn's Circus.

Zach had wanted to skip church in order to spend the entire day on the grounds watching the entertainers prepare for this afternoon's performance. He'd sulked when Athens refused, fidgeting in his Sunday-go-to-meeting clothes like they were a size too small. "You don't go to church. Why do we have to?" he'd complained.

"Because I'm your father and I say so." Usually he was capable of a more eloquent argument, but his quarrel with the Maker was bone-deep personal. When he came to terms, he'd return to the flock. He'd been a wayward lamb for three years now.

"I heard tell they've got people who fly through the air," Zach told Zoe, his mood considerably brighter than this morning.

"You mean they have wings?"

"Don't be silly, stupid."

Athens squeezed his son's shoulder. "Don't call your sister stupid."

"People don't have wings," he grumbled to Zoe.

"Sparkles has wings."

"She ain't a real person."

"She isn't a real person," Athens corrected as they moved forward another two inches.

"Course she ain't," Zoe countered with a roll of her big blue eyes, "she's a fairy." She pushed back the brim of her bonnet. "Are there fairies in the circus, Papa?"

She smiled up at him in a manner reminiscent of Jocelyn—trusting and innocent. He swallowed hard, crouched to readjust her hat. His daughter's pale skin had darkened a shade since moving to Phoenix. He tried to shield her from the intense heat, but, like Zach, she often disregarded his advice. Bonnets, she'd told him in her little girl voice, were bothersome. "*Sparkles said tree dwellers don't wear hats.*"

He'd been at a loss to argue otherwise. He imagined the ribbon secured beneath her chin snagging on a branch, imagined his daughter slipping and choking, and that was that. "*You worry too much,*" he could hear Jocelyn saying. She used to say that a lot. In fact, it was one of the last things she said before he helped her onto that ill-fated train.

"You look sad, Papa."

Athens blinked away the moment, conjured a smile. "Just pensive."

Zoe itched at the ribbon he'd just tightened. "What's that mean?"

"Means his thoughts are fixed on something sorrowful," Zach said. "Don't worry. The clowns will cheer him up."

"Step right up! Buy your tickets for the wildest show in the west!"

"Come on, Papa. We're almost next!"

The excitement in his son's voice fixed his thoughts in the present. Festive music filled the air along with the smell of fried pastries. The area was staked out with several smaller tents and a massive tent known as The Big Top. Painted wagons housed wild animals. Assorted novelty acts teased the onlookers with glimpses of their skills. The smells were pungent and the sights spectacularly gaudy.

He flashed on Kaila's beautiful face, remembered her eagerness to attend the circus. The thought of running into her filled him with anticipation and dread. She'd professed the ability to pretend that their lustful coupling never transpired. If she succeeded, he'd be wounded. That realization cemented his decision to steer clear of the woman. She breathed life into his long dead heart. That scared the devil out of him. The last thing he wanted was to feel.

"Sorry I'm late," Parker said, coming from out of nowhere as was his practice. "Bailey nabbed my ear and wouldn't let go."

"That must've hurt," Zoe said.

The men grinned. "Did he mention anything about a telegram while he was flapping his gums?" Athens asked.

His assistant handed him a folded paper. "Another from London. Nothing from Wright."

"Guess you've got business to attend," Zach said, his voice laced with anger and disappointment.

Athens flushed with guilt. He'd stepped out of the political limelight to devote more time to his children. He'd yet to strike a balance. "Not tonight." He pocketed the note to read later.

"Step right up!"

Athens bellied up to the brightly painted booth, placed his fingers over Zoe's mouth before she could comment on the barker's dramatic appearance. He was pretty sure she'd never seen a man sporting a pompadour, waxed moustache, hoop earring, and enough face paint to rival a dove's. Growing up in the theater business, he'd seen it all. He smiled at the man, indicated himself, Parker, and the kids. "Four tickets, please."

Zoe nudged away his hand. "Five."

"Sparkles doesn't need a ticket, baby."

"Course not. But Miss Kaila does."

Heart pounding, Athens looked to where his daughter pointed. Sure enough, Mrs. Dillingham had joined the long, winding line.

Zach craned his head around. "She the cookie maker you told me about?"

Zoe nodded. "Best cookies ever."

"Sure dressed fancy for the circus."

"She'll be standing in line for some time," Parker noted. "It's a scorcher today."

"What'd she wear so many frills for?" Zach asked.

"Be a real shame if a fine lady like that wilted from the heat."

Athens frowned at Parker. Was he playing matchmaker or did he, himself, have designs on the lady?

Zoe tugged at his shirt sleeve. "Papa."

He suppressed a sigh, plunked more money in the barker's hand. "Five."

CHAPTER 16

Napa Valley, California

Seth had just finished patching a leak in his bed-room ceiling. Before that he'd tended to two leaks in the kitchen. Temporary, but the best he could do. All the while he lamented the way he'd bullied Emily. He'd played the friendship card. Manipulated her. This was only the beginning. He still had a black-mail scheme to bust and a marriage to arrange.

She'd kept to herself while he patched and hammered. He'd welcomed the silent treatment as he processed all the information regarding her father. But now he was tending a cracked window pane in the sitting room and she was staring through a window on the adjacent wall. He couldn't tell if she was angry or depressed. The possibility he'd driven a wedge between them chafed. "A penny for your thoughts."

Emily addressed his question without turning.

"I'm thinking they've been gone a long time."

They being Bellamont and Mrs. Dunlap. "Only two hours."

"Seems longer."

"A watched pot never boils."

"What?"

Seth set aside his tools, took off his spectacles, and sleeved his moist brow. He'd changed out of his good suit into loose brown trousers and a comfortable shirt. She still wore her tomboy get-up and braids. This was the first time he'd ever fancied an ass in trousers over an ass in a skirt. Not that he'd ever jump over to Pinkerton's side of the tracks. This was a unique situation. A doomed attraction. Now was as good a time as any to bring up Athens. But first he needed to smooth things over regarding suitor number one—the weasel winemaker.

"Bellamont would be a fool to travel in this storm." The northwestern tempest made a desert monsoon look like a sun shower. "He didn't strike me as a fool."

He struck him as shady. She was deluding herself if she thought he offered marriage out of the goodness of his heart. Even if his efforts to protect her father had been sincere, his intentions toward Emily stemmed from lust. There was no mistaking his desire. That didn't make him a bad man, Seth conceded, just a man.

He set his spectacles on her writing desk as he

crossed the room and moved in behind her at the west window. A hard blowing rain pummeled the glass pane. The roads would be flooded by now, thick with sucking mud and he'd venture lightning had cut down a tree or two. At this rate, Bellamont and Mrs. Dunlap might be stuck in town until tomorrow.

Alone with Emily all night. His dick twitched at the thought. *Nuns and puppies. Nuns and puppies.*

"You're hovering."

"I am."

"I don't mind."

A pleasant surprise.

"You don't make me nervous anymore. I'm not mad anymore either."

Hot damn.

"I know you meant well. You're right. Friends confide in one another. What happened with my father, it's difficult . . . I don't like to talk about it."

"You know you're not to blame. For his drinking. His death."

"I know. I just wish . . . I wish he could have loved me half as much as he loved her."

Well, hell.

"I wish we wouldn't have fought the night he died. I wish . . ."

He wanted her to turn around so he could pull her into his arms and show her the affection denied to her by Walt and Alice McBride. Even though his own home situation had been less than perfect, he'd never doubted his parents' love for their only son. "You have to let this go, Em."

"I said something similar to him about my mother." She shook her head. "It's hard. But I'm going to try. I think it helped, talking to you about it. It's not the awful secret that it was. The awful burden. Mr. Bellamont has offered a sympathetic ear time and again, but I just, I wanted to forget it ever happened. Now I'm thinking maybe it's better to accept it and move on. Thank you, Poet."

"For upsetting you?"

"For being my friend. It's nice to have someone to talk to. Someone I can trust. I do feel that bond, I do."

He should've felt good about that. Instead he felt like an ass. She didn't trust *him*. She trusted Phineas Pinkerton, a man who'd prefer wearing her drawers as opposed to getting in them.

She rolled back her shoulders, sighed. "You've probably sensed that I'm a little . . . preoccupied."

"That the same thing as tense?"

She'd yet to turn around, but he could see her reflection in the window pane. Her mouth lifted in a slight smile, but then she closed her eyes and scrunched her brow. "I need to talk to you about something very important."

Thank you, Jesus.

She turned abruptly, knocking into him.

He steadied her and stepped back to give her space.

She surprised him by closing the distance. "Remember that pesky plot problem I mentioned yesterday?"

He rubbed the back of his neck, trying to jockey his thoughts. This was out of the blue and not what he'd hoped for. But at least she was talking. Maybe he could steer the conversation around to her blackmailer once he grabbed hold. "You wanted to run it by me."

"Right. Well, I thought it was a plot problem, because I was stuck on a certain scene. But I've been giving it a lot of thought and I think it's more of a sensory problem."

"Sensory."

"The sense of touch, to be exact."

"You've lost me."

"I've been working on this story about a man and a woman, mostly this woman, but there's this man. A pirate."

"A pirate."

"Yes. You know. A swashbuckler, a treasure hunter, a rogue and a rake."

"Got it."

"The woman, well, she's an explorer, an adventuress. He's never met anyone like her and he's fascinated. Not only that, he thinks she's . . ."

"Pretty?"

She blushed. "Well, yes. But more than that. He's, well, entranced. He wants to . . . May I be blunt?"

God, no. "Sure."

"He wants to ravish her."

She was wringing her hands. Nervous. Just now he wasn't all that at ease himself. "I can't imagine," he said, tongue in cheek.

"That's too bad. I was hoping . . ."

He took an unconscious step back.

"It's flat," she said, coming toe to toe.

Like hell. "Excuse me?"

"The scene, every scene between Constance and Antonio that's supposed to be . . . passionate. It reads flat. I didn't understand that until this morning. I knew something was wrong, but I didn't know what. Music publishers once told Paris that her lyrics lacked depth. I told her it was because she was writing about things she had no personal connection to. She was writing about love but she'd never been in love. I told her she had to get out there and live, take chances. Life experience inspires passionate prose."

He backed into the bookshelves.

"I'm trying to write about soul-searing kisses and I've never been kissed."

"Ever?" Damn. Had his voice cracked?

"Surely, you're not surprised. Look at me."

What the hell was that supposed to mean? "I see a beautiful woman."

She smirked. "Yes, but you're not wearing your spectacles."

"Talk like that pisses me off, Emily."

She pursed her lips. "I don't understand you, Poet. One minute you're soft, the next you're hard."

Christ.

"I don't understand your . . . kind."

"You surely don't."

"We're friends, right?"

"Right."

"Friends help each other out."

Please, God, bring up your blackmailer. "Yes."

"I'm just going to come out and ask."

"Go ahead."

"Have you always been . . . that is . . . Was there ever a time . . ."

"Spit it out, Em."

"Have you ever been with a woman?"

He'd never been amused and scared shitless at the same time. Interesting. "Yes."

"Did you find it . . . disgusting?"

He bit back a smile. "No."

She leaned in. "So, it wouldn't disgust you to . . ."

He put his hands on her shoulders, keeping her from pressing up against him. Never in his life had he resisted a woman's advances. At least he thought that's what was going on here. He couldn't be sure. She'd shocked and seduced him at the same time, an odd combination that left him befuddled. Another first. "You don't know what you're asking of me, Em."

"I know it's a huge favor to ask of a . . . friend, but I'm desperate, Poet. I've been working on this story for more than a year. It's the story of my heart. Even if another soul never reads it, I have to know that it's my best effort. That it reads sincere. I'm asking you, from one writer to another, in the name of research and artistic integrity . . . Kiss me."

He raised an eyebrow, an almighty effort since his body had seized up. "Just a kiss?"

She bit her lower lip then licked it. "Well, I was hoping . . . that is . . ."

"Spit it out."

"I was hoping for a specific kiss. A hot and wet, boner-inducing kiss."

He laughed. Swear to God, he couldn't help it.

Her face crumpled. "What?"

"I'm sorry." He flattened his smile, smoothed his hand over wavy locks that had escaped her braids. He adored those messy braids. "Do you know what a boner is, hon?"

"No."

"It's a slang word for a man's erection. When a

man gets aroused, he gets a boner."

"Oh. So you can't give me one."

"No."

"I'd have to give one to you."

"Yes." No. *Shit*.

She stood on her tip-toes, leaned into him, her breasts against his chest, her lips against his mouth. Nice, but . . .

"I think I'm supposed to put my tongue in your mouth," she whispered. "Don't be alarmed."

Holy hell.

The moment he felt the flick of the velvety tip, he lost control, took control. He flipped her around so that her back was pressed against the bookshelves, framed her face, and plundered her mouth. Slow and sweet, hot and wet. And, hell yeah, boner-inducing.

She whimpered, soft, sexy sounds as he tasted her, sampled her, tutored her. She wrapped her arms around his neck, splayed her fingers through his hair.

An earsplitting crack of thunder coincided with his heart slamming against his ribs. He tightened his embrace, swept his lips over her brow, her cheeks. He nipped her chin, her lower lip. He prompted her to open her mouth wider, allowing his tongue free rein. She melted against him and followed his lead, oblivious to the storm raging outdoors, stirring the storm within. Again, his heart expanded. His body throbbed, ached. He knew lust. This was lust, and beyond. *Love.* The force of it, the pureness, damn near brought him to his knees.

He took liberties, gliding his hands over her trembling body, memorizing every slight but feminine curve. One kiss. One time. He cupped her sweet ass. She moaned and wiggled against him, deepened the kiss of her own accord.

His mind blanked, his breath stalled. It was the single hottest moment in his life.

Soul-searing.

Emily pulled back, blue eyes clouded with passion and curiosity. "Is it working?"

His mind scrambled.

"Am I giving you one?"

Ah. *Don't do it, Wright.* "In the name of research?"

The nod was barely perceptible, but all he needed. He clasped her hand and pressed it against his arousal. He expected her to jerk back. The fabric of his trousers was the only thing between her palm and his hard and heavy shaft. She didn't flinch. She looked at him with a sense of awe, and he thought, if she applied any pressure in the least, one squeeze, one stroke—*in the name of research*—he'd lose it.

"It's much bigger than the ones I've seen," she whispered.

He blinked down at her. "You've seen—"

"In books. Art books. Sketches. Sculptures."

"Research?"

"The skinny-dipping knight. I didn't know what a naked man looked like. I needed a visual reference. I thought Michael Angelo's *David* was impressive, even though his, you know, is much smaller than yours."

And still she palmed John Thomas.

"It's very . . . hard. Like a statue's." She furrowed her brow. "I'm surprised they don't call it a stoner."

The thought of her studying classic nudes . . . This conversation . . . Innocent, yet erotic. He'd never been more aroused, and they were both fully clothed.

Then she did it, a slight brush of her thumb.

He sucked in a breath.

"Did that hurt?"

"In a good way." He placed her hands around his neck. He kissed her, because he couldn't stand another word, another stroke. Because this moment had to last him forever. He poured his heart into a slow, deep kiss, pulling away only when he could no longer trust himself not to go farther.

She splayed a hand over her heart, fought for an even breath. "Mercy."

At least she was capable of speech. He couldn't think straight enough to form a coherent thought, let alone word.

"That was . . ."

Incredible? Amazing? Earth rocking?

"Inspiring." She brushed past him, hurried toward her desk. "I have to write this down." She fumbled with a locket around her neck, took out a tiny key and unlocked the drawer. "Now I know how to handle that scene. I know what Antonio would do." She grabbed her journal, a pencil. "Drat! I can't write. I can't see. I . . ." She picked up his spectacles, examined them. "May I try these, please?"

He held up his hands as if to say *be my guest* because, although his brain had kicked in, he didn't trust himself to speak. *I just silently, lovingly bared my soul and you're thinking about Antonio?*

"I can't believe it!"

She took the words right out of his mouth.

"I can see!" She adjusted the spectacles, beamed at him. "Not perfectly, but well enough to read and write. May I borrow these for awhile?"

"Sure."

"I'm going to grab a couple of biscuits and work in my room. Feel free to use my desk."

"For?"

"Writing. Yesterday you said that manual labor spurs your creative process. With all the repair work you did this afternoon, and I do appreciate it, I imagine you're bursting at the seams."

He shifted. "You could say that."

"Have fun polishing your short story."

"On the long side just now."

"Need any help?"

"I think I can handle it."

Clutching the journal to her chest, she turned to leave then turned back. Her grateful expression made him want to shoot himself. "Given your . . . preferences, you really went above and beyond with that kiss, Poet. You don't know what it meant to me."

Apparently, nothing near what it to meant to him. "Anything for art."

Smiling, she disappeared into the hall.

He imagined her in her room, sitting on her bed, writing about Constance and Antonio, and boner-inducing kisses. He imagined himself . . . alone.

He prayed for the storm to break. For Mrs. Dunlap to come home.

He cursed the day he met Athens Garrett.

CHAPTER *17*

Territory of Arizona

The American circus was as vibrant, raucous, and thrilling as she'd imagined. For two hours Kaila sat breathless and bedazzled by clowns, jugglers, acrobats, and various animal acts. The kaleidoscope of fun was heightened by Zach and Zoe. Their excitement and wonder was infectious. The man introduced to her as Mr. Parker appeared equally entranced.

The only fly in the ointment, if that was the correct usage of the American cliché, was Athens Garrett.

With the exception of the few times she caught him smiling at his children's animated reactions, he looked decidedly unimpressed. She worried that she'd spoiled the experience for him. Although he purchased her ticket, a very thoughtful gesture, she had the distinct feeling he'd done so at Zoe's urging. Mr. Parker was quite amiable and Zach, though guarded, didn't seem to mind her joining the family outing.

Athens was aloof. Cordial, but aloof. It bothered her immensely, even though he'd warned her they had no future, intimating their coupling was a one-time affair. She'd assured him she'd be able to pretend as if no intimacies had transpired between them. So far, she'd kept her word. The moment she'd seen him and his beautiful family coming toward her, she'd shut down her emotions. It was second nature. But the longer they sat next to each other, shoulder to shoulder, thigh to thigh, in the crushing midday heat, the more her resolve melted.

She ached to touch him, to kiss him. Wanton desires pulsed through her body. She yearned not only for sex, but for affection, and companionship. A relationship. Not with just any man, but with Athens. How was it she'd lost her heart to a man she barely knew? A man who'd made it clear they had no future. "Bloody hell," she whispered.

Athens glanced over. "What's wrong?"

"Nothing." In truth, she felt faint.

He studied her for a moment then turned to his right, mumbled something to his assistant and son. Mr. Parker nodded. Zach rolled his eyes then focused back on the hosiery and bloomer-clad man walking the tight wire. Next, Athens leaned across Kaila, touched Zoe's shoulder. "Baby, I need to take Mrs. Dillingham home. She's not feeling well."

Embarrassed, Kaila frowned. "I told you, I'm quite well."

"Don't look it. Your face is grey," Zoe shouted over a fanfare of music. "And you're all sweaty."

She flushed at the unattractive description, gasped as her stomach cramped.

"Looks like she's gonna puke, Papa."

Athens motioned to Zoe. "Come over here. Sit next to Zach. Mind Mr. Parker and I'll see you after awhile."

Packed as they were into the wooden stands, people grumbled at the shifting of bodies, especially since a bear just danced into the second ring wearing a bright red tutu. Kaila grumbled the loudest.

"Don't make me carry you out of here, Mrs. Dillingham."

"You wouldn't."

"I would."

She excused herself when she stepped on a myriad of toes in her efforts to escape the big top on her own two feet. She expected a dose of bracing fresh air when they exited the tent. Instead she was hit with a stifling wave of heat. It didn't help that she'd been sitting in tight confines for so long. Her knees wobbled, the music garbled, and the scenery blurred. "Blast."

Athens swept her off of her feet.

"Put me down."

"So you can fall on you face? How'd you get here?"

"I walked. It's not so far," she added when he frowned.

"It is on a ninety-degree day. It is when you're wearing layers of petticoats and a high-necked gown buttoned up to your chin." He carried her across the grounds, toward a man leaning against a two-seater buckboard. "You're not in the English countryside anymore, Mrs. Dillingham."

"I know where I am, Mr. Garrett. I'm faint, not delirious."

"You wouldn't be faint if you dressed appropriately."

"I dressed for a special event."

"It's a circus, not an opera."

"I know what it is," she snapped. "Cease talking to me as though I were one of your children."

"My children have more sense."

Her cheeks stung as though he'd slapped her. Her entire body tingled. She would've retaliated but her mind went blank. The heat radiating from Athens rivaled that of the desert sun.

"You're Herb Miller, aren't you?" she heard him ask over the buzzing in her ears.

"You got a memory for faces and names, Mr. Garrett. We only met once. A few weeks back at the general store."

"You remembered *my* name."

"Yeah, but that's cuz you're famous by way of your brothers."

Kaila smiled to herself. She knew it. He *was* related to Rome and Boston Garrett.

"Ain't that the limey baker lady?"

"Mrs. Kaila Dillingham," she said, extending a limp hand.

He shook her fingertips, addressed Athens. "What's wrong with her?"

"Overheated."

"Yeah, well, she looks the delicate sort and it is hot as a whorehouse on nickel night." He scratched his whiskered jaw, tipped his hat. "Pardon my language."

"Can you give us a lift, Mr. Miller?"

"Sure enough."

Once she was settled in the rear seat, she pushed off of Athens and forced her spine straight. "I'm trying to fit in here," she whispered through clenched teeth, "and you're not helping by making me seem like a namby-pamby tenderfoot."

He raised an eyebrow. "Where'd you hear talk like that?"

She hiked her chin a notch. "I read it somewhere."

"Like a dime novel maybe?"

She pulled a laced kerchief from her sleeve, dabbed at her perspiring brow. What made him ask that? Did he find out about her obsession with the American tales? Did he think, as she'd first worried, that she was only interested in him because he was related to the famous Garrett Brothers? Is that why he'd been so standoffish today?

They fell silent for the rest of the short ride. She felt more ill by the moment.

"Thank you for seeing me home, Mr. Garrett," she said as he helped her down from the buckboard. "Please express my apologies to Zach and Zoe for ruining your family outing."

"You didn't ruin anything, and I'm seeing you inside." He thanked Mr. Miller, waving goodbye as the man steered the horses back toward the circus grounds.

"Are you certain I didn't spoil your special day?" she said weakly as he helped her up the front steps. "You didn't look as though you enjoyed the performance."

"I enjoyed it fine. It's just that I've seen one or another variation of most of those acts multiple times over the years. My mother was a musical actress. My father owned an opera house. I grew up around theater people. Novelty acts, variety acts, singers, dancers, actors, musicians."

"How exciting."

He shrugged as if to say *not really*, opened the door and guided her inside.

"I'll be fine now," she said forcing a smile and offering her hand in a farewell gesture. "Thank you again for your assistance."

"You're welcome." He ignored her hand, tossed his hat on the corner chair, and shrugged out of his jacket. "Take off your clothes."

"I beg your pardon?"

"We have to lower your body temperature before you succumb to a heat stroke. Can you undress yourself or do you need my help?"

"I can do it."

"Then do it." He brushed past her and into the kitchen. Just now he had the compassion of a crooked barrister. Her temper flared. Why was he being so controlling? So rude? She didn't recognize or like this side of him. She thought she'd escaped this sort of treatment when her husband's heart had ceased to beat.

She wanted to stomp into the kitchen and vent, but she didn't have the strength. She sank down on her sofa and loosened the top buttons of her bodice. Quite the accomplishment since her fingertips were numb.

Athens reentered the room with a glass of water and a folded cloth. "For the love of . . . " He set aside the glass and cloth, sat down, and brushed away her fumbling fingers.

"I can do it," she protested.

"I can do it faster." He unhooked her bodice and

unlaced her whalebone corset just as quickly as he'd done the day before, only this time the effort lacked unbridled heat.

Her mind clouded over as he stripped her to her undergarments. She should've breathed easier, but her chest tightened with anger and grief. Where was the gentle, passionate man who'd shown her the stars?

"Drink this."

She lamented her shaking hands, blessed the refreshing liquid trickling down her parched throat, and cursed the stern-faced man sitting at her side.

When she set down the glass, he pressed the cool, damp cloth to her forehead, her cheeks, and lastly on the back of her neck. His tender ministrations reminded her of the man she'd fallen for. Tears pricked her eyes, so she closed them.

"I want to know one thing, English. Were you distant today because you were pretending, as we agreed, that yesterday never happened? Are you that accomplished at hiding your feelings? Or did you lose interest when you discovered I'm a diplomat, a boring lawyer and father, nothing like my flamboyant, crime fighting brothers."

Were it not for his ragged tone, she might have slapped him for having so little faith in her. In himself. "I'm that accomplished at hiding my feelings." She lifted her chin, opened her eyes, and allowed him to see her heart. "Usually."

"Well, damn." He stroked away her tears with his thumb, rested his forehead against hers. "Don't cry, honey."

"Is that why you acted so abominably today? Because you thought I was a . . . I don't know the American term."

"You did say you were keen on an adventure, so, yes, the thought crossed my mind. Let me explain," he said when she tensed. He eased her around so she was lying longwise on the sofa, her head in his lap. Then he lifted a copy of Harper Bazaar from the mahogany end table and fanned her face and body. "Feeling better?"

"Getting there."

He smiled down at her. "Explanation for abominable behavior forthcoming."

Though she was not yet in the mood to return the smile, her heart was indeed lighter and breathing no longer a chore.

"Yesterday, in my haste to ravish you, I knocked over a stack of your books and periodicals. When we were rolling around on the carpet, I noticed several dime novels in the mix. When I left by way of your back door, I saw one of them lying on your kitchen table, opened to a story featuring my brothers."

"*Showdown in Sintown*. I. M. Wilde's latest."

"Wilde's a bit of a sore spot with me, Kaila."

"Wilde's the reason I am here. In America."

He furrowed his brow. "How's that?"

"My life in Kent was very structured. Sterile. I was expected to behave in a certain manner. Though I was a woman of title and wealth, I felt trapped, enslaved. A friend who often traveled abroad gifted me with several American dime novels. They all called to me, but specifically Wilde's tales. So full of intrigue, justice, and romance. So full of . . . life. Were I ever presented the chance, I vowed I'd move to the land of opportunity. When Charles died, I acted upon that vow."

"You're a woman of title?"

"*Was* a woman of title." She grasped his hand. "I beg you to keep that knowledge in your confidence."

He studied her face, brushed his thumb across her palm. "All right."

"I only revealed as such because I want you to know that I am well acquainted with people wanting to befriend me simply because of who I was and who I knew. I am not so shallow. Or devious. I care not that you are related to Rome and Boston. Nor do I think you boring."

He said nothing, but he did smile. His smile conjured all sorts of feelings stemming from tender to lustful. Indeed, he was the man she'd been waiting for all her life. How could fate be so cruel?

"So, what do have against Mr. Wilde?"

"He's turned my brothers into larger-than-life heroes."

"Are you saying he exaggerates their adventures?"

"A little, yes."

"Are they displeased?"

"Yes and no."

"But you are displeased."

"For multiple reasons, yes." He set aside the magazine. "How do you feel?"

"Much better, thank you." She pushed herself up. "You are right. I dressed inappropriately. I dressed like a duchess."

"You're a *duchess*?"

"Was." She drew on ingrained dignity, even though she was clad only in a thin chemise. "I need to examine my life. Make adjustments. I must know . . ."

"Yes?"

"Do you—"

"Yes. But I can't."

"Why?"

"I've asked another woman to be my wife."

CHAPTER 18

Napa Valley California

Seth's mood was as foul as yesterday's weather.
Bellamont had returned Mrs. Dunlap safely home
late evening, saving him from a night alone with Emily.
Not that she came out of her room. Mrs. Dunlap even
carried up her supper. Reportedly, she was on a writing streak, burning the midnight oil with Antonio and
Constance.

Meanwhile, he'd spent a sleepless night burning
for Emily.

Frustrated, sexually and otherwise, he rose at
dawn, washed and dressed. He'd fought an almighty
desire to search the barn. He couldn't shake the feeling that she'd stashed something in there, something
she didn't want anyone to see. But he had no idea what
that something was and he worried she'd catch him in
the act. He wanted to hang on to her trust for as long

as he could because, for sure and for certain, he could kiss it goodbye when she learned his true identity. An inevitability that turned his gut.

So he resisted the urge to poke around. He saddled Guinevere, vacated the barn with haste, and set off for an early ride. The mare was too docile for his taste, but, damn, it felt good to be back in the saddle. It reminded him of who he was, where he came from, and where he belonged. A hard-riding, hard-living lawman, policing the raw and restless southwest.

He'd been detoured by a bedeviling librarian, but he'd get back to business, and he'd feel better, whole. Just now his mind was scattered to the four winds. He blamed the star-crossed situation, the Garretts. Mostly because it felt good to curse someone other than himself. Then he turned his ire on the weasel winemaker, simply because he didn't like him.

The storm had long since subsided. The ground was soft, the roads muddy, but the sky was cloudless, and the sun bright. Too early to hit town so he rode for Bellamont Winery. He didn't venture too close, just rode the perimeter, perused the vineyards and the rambling estate. Noted several Chinese workers. Cheap labor. Not uncommon, but it galled him. A person deserved appropriate pay for his work, no matter his race, gender, or religion. He'd bet his Stetson Emily shared the same view. He couldn't imagine her living here, couldn't picture her in Bellamont's bed.

Or Sawyer's, or Rome's, or his goddamned boss's.

Well, he could, but it took its toll on his temper.

He was in a hell of a fix.

Jaw set, he swung Guinevere around and spurred her toward Heaven.

Time to speed up this investigation.

Time to rid Emily of her blackmailer and to deliver Athens's proposal. He had promises to keep, outlaws to wrangle, and a fierce need to distance himself from the woman who'd roped his heart.

Emily woke sprawled on her bed with her journal lying open on her stomach. Her heart pounded and her nightshirt was drenched with sweat. She'd fallen asleep writing about Constance and Antonio. She dreamt about them, too. Only, when they embraced, when he framed her face with his strong but gentle hands, Antonio transformed into Pinkerton. Constance faded away and Emily melted in his arms.

The kiss.

She'd dreamt about it over and over.

Her body tingled and ached in intimate, scandalous places. Just as it had when Pinkerton swept his tongue into her mouth and moved his hands over her body. The sensations were intense and exhilarating. She knew there was more to lovemaking. She'd read explicit novels in her attempt to understand physical relations between men and women. If she was going to write about seduction and romance without the benefit of experience, she needed to learn about intimacy *somewhere*. Certainly her parents had never spoken of such things. She knew the words, the motions.

Desire. Lust. Naked flesh. Entwined limbs. Intimate body parts joined in a primal dance. Giving, taking. Harder, faster. A moment when mind and body reach an earth-shuddering climax.

Given last night's encounter, she was as curious about the earth-shuddering climax as she was about the boner-inducing kiss. Her fondest *desire* was to ask Pinkerton for a demonstration. She was pretty sure what she'd felt for him was *lust*. But asking was impossible. Not because it would be inappropriate, although it would, but because it was Pinkerton. He'd already been so generous. She'd made a mad dash, escaped to her room, before branding herself a selfish, wanton fool. How could she ask him to appease her curiosity, knowing he wasn't attracted to the female form?

Although he had been aroused. Enormously aroused. She couldn't make sense of that part. And she'd given it plenty of thought.

Smiling, she stretched and squinted at her bedside

clock. Ten o'clock a.m. That couldn't be right. But then she realized her room was bursting with mid-morning sunlight. She also realized there was no need to squint. She could see fine.

She palmed her face and sure enough, she'd fallen asleep wearing Pinkerton's spectacles. She fingered the rims and sighed. With or without his eyeglasses he was a striking man. She thought him even more handsome than Rome.

When had *that* happened?

It probably had something to do with his attractive inner qualities, she mused. Kind, generous, courageous. Yes, there were occasional spells when he turned cool and commanding. But mostly he was smart, and funny, and tenderhearted. He was sensitive to her feelings whereas Rome, as Cole had so rudely stated, barely knew she was alive. If the rakish Garrett had the choice between playing poker and reading a book, he'd flip cards, not pages. Pinkerton shared her love of literature. That was a powerful connection.

Uniquely arresting. Inside and out.

His description of her applied to him as well.

Mutual appreciation.

Mutual interests.

The bond.

Similar to what she felt with Paris with one big difference. She didn't want to experience an earth-shuddering climax with her best friend.

"You've got to stop thinking about that kiss, Emily McBride. You have no future with Poet."

Unless . . .

She bolted upright in bed, her brain sparking with an unconventional idea.

Could she? Would he? It's not like it hadn't been done before. She'd overheard Paris's brothers talking about it. Common in the theater, they'd said.

Pinkerton's in the theater.

Suddenly, she envisioned a way of being with Pinkerton as well as another way to utilize her talent. A way of cutting loose her *Savior*, Mr. Bellamont, Cole . . . this town. There was hope for her Grand Design. All she had to do was find someone to take in Mrs. Dunlap. Oh, and convince Phineas Pinkerton of the brilliance of her plan.

"No worries," she told herself as she bounced out of bed. "You can argue a gopher into climbing a tree." Today they were riding to Napa City in order to visit Zeke Karn's Jewelry and Optical Shop. She'd have plenty of time to concoct a perfectly-worded, rational proposal. Then all she had to do was spit it out.

Mind churning, she padded to her chamber set, her breath catching when she noticed a letter slipped beneath her door. For a paralyzing second she feared it was from her blackmailer, but then she saw the handwritten script.

Lovely penmanship for a man. Foolishly, she hoped for a poem. Instead it was a short note advising her that he'd ridden into town to handle errands.

I'll alert Mrs. Frisbie of your dilemma and will return shortly to escort you to Napa City. I hope life experience inspired passionate prose and that you slept peacefully. Eat breakfast.

Yours, P

His direct note charmed her as surely as a flowery poem. Perhaps he was incapable of loving her as a man loved a woman, but he cared for her all the same.

For what she had in mind, that was more than enough.

His first stop had been the mercantile, but he'd peered through the window and noticed a gaggle of ladies stocking up on their weekly wares and decided to drop back later. He wanted private time with Ezekiel Thompson, so he continued on to the livery.

Given the state of the roads, it would take considerably longer to journey by buggy to Napa City. The less time spent alone with Emily, the better. Physical distance was preferable as well. Riding horseback would be quicker, not to mention easier on John Thomas, who, along with Seth, was almighty fond of the pretty lady.

He introduced himself as Phineas Pinkerton to the liveryman who said, "Ah, the poet," and then tried to sell him a sway-backed mare. Seth opted for a spirited gelding, a Palomino by the name of Streak. He purchased suitable tack and said he'd return within the hour.

After that, he visited the telegraph office and wired Phoenix, attention: Fox

MISSION IN PROGRESS. S.W.

He figured that about summed it up. Parker collected all correspondence for Mr. Fox, a *client* of the law offices of Athens Garrett. At least his boss would know he was in place and working on the *venture of national importance.*

He sent similar updates to Paris and Josh, though separately.

Next, Seth swung by the library to let Mrs. Frisbie know her assistant would not be reporting to work due to compromised vision. Turns out she'd heard about the fainting spell. She'd also heard that he was escorting Emily to the Blossom Dance, and he'd said,

"News travels fast." Then she sang Emily's praises, which made him think she'd spoken to Mrs. Dunlap and agreed, for whatever odd reason, that a Nancy boy poet made a good match for a good-girl librarian. God help him. Although he did garner some interesting background on Em. Like the fact she didn't charge Mrs. Dunlap rent, although they did barter her knitted goods for food supplies at the mercantile. Apparently the widow's afghans sold fairly well.

Thirty minutes later, he hit the mercantile. Mrs. Thompson was in deep discussion with a woman over a bolt of fabric and a basket of trimmings. Other than that, the store was empty except for Mr. Thompson who had his nose in a newspaper.

"Just the man I wanted to see. Good morning to you, sir."

Thompson looked up and greeted Seth with a face-splitting smile. "How can I help you, Mr. Pinkerton?"

Seth hitched back his frock coat, stuffed his hands in his pockets. Deep pockets, by Thompson's way of thinking. Hence, the overly-friendly grin. "Let's begin with writing paper."

The request wouldn't strike the store owner as strange seeing the man asking was a poet. He wouldn't know that Seth was trying to locate the kind of paper used by Emily's blackmailer. The letter had been mailed from San Francisco. Didn't mean it had been written there. Seth's gut said he was looking for a local.

"I've got patriotic stationary and some fine writing paper with various figureheads and symbols. Couple of different shades. Blue, cream, white."

"No ordinary writing paper?"

He shook his head. "Plumb out. Reordered last week."

Huh. Not wanting to arouse suspicion, he decided on several sheets of the fine writing paper, cream-colored and embossed with a leaf in the upper left hand corner.

"Quills? Ink? Pencils?" Thompson asked eagerly.

"Typewriter?"

"Not too much call for those new fangled contraptions. Too pricey to stock. I could order you one!"

"Won't be here that long." Remembering Emily favored pencils over quill pens, he asked for a half dozen. While the man gathered the merchandise, Seth inquired about today's news.

Thompson rattled off a few highlights, ending with, "Nothing near as interesting as yesterday's scandal."

"You mean the Garrett brothers."

"The whole town's talking. Not that we're surprised. Rome always was a ladies' man. Still, you'd think he'd know better. Athens, that's one of his older brothers, being a politician and all."

"Hard to believe," Seth said.

"Believe it." Thompson slapped yesterday's paper on the counter, pointed. "Right there. Read it for yourself."

Since he was without his spectacles, Seth had to squint and adjust the distance, but at last the words came into focus enough to read. Unbelievable. The stupid ass skirt-chaser had seduced a state senator's wife. I. M. Wilde had tipped off anyone who had coin and the ability to read. Did Wilde have a death wish? Osprey Smith would kill his career (if not the man) as surely as he'd crippled the Garretts'. For that matter the dime novelist should be watching over his shoulder for Rome. Guaran-damn-teed he was mad as a peeled rattler.

"Carrying on with another man's woman." The mercantile owner shook his head. "Just ain't right."

Seth pressed two fingers to his temples, massaged.

"Head paining you, Mr. Pinkerton? Medical peddler came through a few weeks ago. Bought a few bottles of Dr. Daylight's Healing Bitters. Doc Kellogg don't approve, but the ladies swear by it."

"What about revolvers?"

He snapped his suspenders, frowned. "Shooting yourself seems a mite extreme."

That lured a smile out of him. "I'm interested in

purchasing a gun for protection."

Thompson glanced at the arm Doc had patched. "Been hassled, have you?"

The man reminded him of a big-eared innkeeper he knew back in Florence. A Nosey-Nate and a gossip. "It's for Miss McBride."

"She been hassled?"

"If someone were to threaten her, I'd like to ensure she has the means to protect herself."

Seth chose his words carefully, wanting them to get around. "I'll be purchasing a firearm for Mrs. Dunlap, too."

"Two women living alone, aways from town. I see what you mean. Mighty thoughtful of you." Dollar signs shone in his eyes as he motioned Seth to the opposite side of the mercantile. "Don't sell a lot of hardware, but I keep the store stocked. You never know."

"No, you don't." He inspected a .32 Derringer revolver and Remington Single-Barrel Shotgun. "These will do."

"I can dictate specifications—"

"No need. How much?"

Thompson stated a price, including ammunition, and a special holster.

Seth paid in cash. "Miss McBride won't be coming into town today," he said matter-of-factly as Thompson stowed the money in his register. "We'll be riding for

Napa City to replace her spectacles."

The older man winced. "Mrs. Thompson was real sorry about the mishap."

"Accidents happen," he said with a pleasant smile. "As long as I'm here, I thought I'd check and see if any packages arrived for the ladies. I believe Mrs. Dunlap ordered a new pair of knitting needles." His real interest was the mail in general and any insight Thompson could give him regarding the letters from San Francisco. Not so much the ones Emily had received from the blackmailer, but the ones she'd written in return. Where had she sent the money?

"Mail won't arrive until later this afternoon. Don't expect the needles for another few weeks, but there's bound to be something for Emily. Between Paris Garrett, or whatever her married name is, and her special friend in San Francisco, letters and packages are always a comin' and a goin' for Emily."

Seth's mouth went dry. "Special friend?"

"Mr. Herman Beeslow."

CHAPTER 19

*E*mily bathed, dressed, and ate breakfast, and still Pinkerton had not returned. What was taking him so long? Had he snooped in the barn, discovered her chest? Had he ridden into town to wire the Napa County Reporter with her juicy secret? Not that she thought he'd do such a thing, but *someone* had pried into her affairs at some point. Specifically, her *Savior*. Paranoid, she ventured outside and into the barn. To her relief, her treasure chest was exactly where she'd hidden it, lock intact.

She'd hoisted the small chest into the hayloft the day after she received the first blackmail letter. Then she'd filled it with every journal, every manuscript page, every draft of every story she'd ever written and saved. In his first letter, her *Savior* had included an original page from *The Downfall of Dutch McCree*. Proof that he knew her secret. There were no drafts of that particular story. She'd written the tale in one sitting and mailed it directly to Mr. Beeslow. Only he never received it. That had been almost two months ago.

Once she realized her Savior had intercepted the package, she refrained from mailing more tales. She did, however, correspond with Mr. Beeslow via two brief letters. She didn't mention she was being blackmailed, simply that she needed a break. She'd been writing adventure yarns non-stop for a full year. He'd promised to break the news to the publisher, but encouraged her to continue work on her historical romance.

Like Paris, he believed she was destined to write novels in addition to her short pulp tales.

"*Your yarns are fun,*" her musical friend had said, "*but think of the lives you could touch with a novel-length adventure.*"

"*You've only tapped the surface of your talent,*" Mr. Beeslow often wrote.

If only her parents could have recognized her storytelling as a gift.

Emily unlocked the trunk and pushed open the lid. Beneath an art book and two research books on human sexuality, lay drafts of her swashbuckling tale, trial love scenes between Antonio and Constance. Scenes that read like a scientific breakdown of lovemaking. Scenes lacking the benefit of personal experience. She rolled her eyes at her attempts at eroticism. The scene she'd written after Pinkerton's kiss gushed with twice the passion and yet the language was tame. Proving that the power is not in the word, but in the feelings it evokes.

Beneath those pages were tales from her youth, and beneath those, her adventure yarns. She lovingly touched the stories she used to hide under her bed. Stories unbefitting a preacher's daughter. Stories her mother should have adored and encouraged because they were very much in the vein of the books she loved. They weren't novel-length, but they were packed with romantic intrigue. Dashing, courageous heroes, and heroines of all manner—blushing, daring, in distress, in command. Bigger-than-life characters embracing over-the-top adventures.

Her tales weren't scandalous. They were entertaining. Lots of people liked them, and the more she wrote, the higher her income had become. That money was supposed to finance her Grand Design. At first it had been about sharing one great adventure with her mother. Then it had been about surviving.

Now, she thought as she closed and locked the lid, it was about letting go and moving on.

Before Pinkerton, she'd felt stuck. Stuck in Heaven. Stuck living a lie. His friendship had yanked her out of the darkness, into the light. His kiss had inspired passionate prose and a new outlook on life. He'd touched and stirred something deep inside, something she dare not examine too closely. Instinctively, she knew she needed to detach emotionally for her plan to succeed.

"I can do this," she mumbled to herself as she descended the ladder.

Hands encircled her waist as she neared the bottom rungs. "Do what?"

Pinkerton.

Drat!

A consummate gentleman, he helped her down. When she turned, he released her, but held his ground. They stood very close. Her heart beat very hard. Part of her wanted to rush him out of the barn, away from her stories. Part of her wanted to read her favorites aloud and see the approval in his eyes. Still another part of her wanted to ravish him where he stood. Her body thrummed with the memory of that kiss. Mercy.

"I was just . . . there were . . . rats."

"Rats?"

"I've had a problem with rats."

"In the hayloft?"

"Precisely. Where were you?"

"In town. Didn't you get my note?"

"Yes, but . . ." She cleared her throat. "You were gone so long and I worried that maybe—"

"What?"

"I'd scared you off."

His Stetson shadowed his eyes, but she felt his keen regard.

Nervous, she focused on a horseshoe nailed to the wall for good fortune. Unfortunately, it had swung upside down, allowing the luck to run out. "You know," she said, throat tight. "The kiss."

He remained silent and her discomfort intensified.

"Are you sorry?" she asked.

"No."

"Did you hate it?"

"Wish I could say I did."

She wasn't sure what that meant, but it didn't sound bad. She'd definitely broach her proposal today. She chanced his intense gaze. Maybe.

She swallowed, took off his spectacles. "Thank you for sharing these with me."

"Keep them. You need them more than I do."

"But . . . aren't we going to Napa City?"

"We are. When we replace your spectacles you can return mine." He looked up at the hayloft.

Her pulse skipped. "Well then." She breezed past him and out of the barn, hoping he'd follow. He did.

She stopped short of an unfamiliar horse. A beautiful Palomino. Taller and broader than Guinevere. "Where'd she come from?"

"She's a he. His name is Streak and he's mine for a spell. Roads are too muddy to travel by buggy."

"So we're going to ride?"

"That a problem?"

"No." It's just that she'd imagined them in the buggy, thigh to thigh, a lazy ride enabling easy conversation.

"Good." He reached into Streak's saddlebag, produced a small holster and gun.

"What's that?"

"A Derringer."

"What's it for?"

"Protection."

"Kind of puny compared to your Colt."

"Deadly if you use it right."

She thought back on her shooting lesson. "Strong stance. Tight grip. Focus. Fire—slow and smooth."

He didn't smile, but his eyes sparkled with approval. "Lift your skirt."

She blinked.

"The revolver's for you, Em. It's a leg holster. You're better off concealing your piece."

"You bought me a revolver?" Her heart fluttered as though he'd presented her with flowers.

"And a shotgun." He crouched and she hiked up the fabric of her split skirt. He worked swiftly, attaching the holster around her stockinged leg with detached expertise. "I'll leave the Remington with Mrs. Dunlap. She ought to have more protection against an intruder than your busted shotgun."

"She could always stab him with her knitting needles," she joked.

He didn't laugh.

It occurred to her that Phineas Pinkerton was moody. Then again so was she. Paris had always been a tad dramatic. Must be an artistic thing.

His hands lingered at her ankle as he lowered her skirt into place. She imagined him unhooking her boots, rolling down stockings. His fingers gliding up her bare leg and touching her womanly center.

She sighed, thinking, she could live with moody.

He cursed under his breath then rose and withdrew the shotgun from its scabbard. "Wait here. I'll have a word with Mrs. Dunlap then we'll set off."

He turned for the house, shotgun in hand, and she shivered. Her infatuation with his actions finally turned to the reality of them. "You're expecting trouble."

"Always."

"See that stained glass front window? New. The mirror in the back bar? New. I'd be mighty peeved if they got shattered because a bottle or body smashed into them."

Rome considered the barkeep of Percy's Poker Palace with a raised brow. "That's a hell of a welcome home, Tom."

"Welcome home." He slid two mugs of beer into the brothers' hands. "Don't bust up my place."

"You'd think we get into a tussle every time we visit Percy's."

"Sounds about right," Boston said.

Rome grinned. "Guess it does."

They drank their beers, scanned the premises. Small and gaudy compared to the Gilded Garrett. Then again it wasn't an upscale opera house. It was a gambling hall with a stage. A place to drink, play poker, ogle dancing girls, and get laid.

Late afternoon. Hardly a body in the place. Percy's didn't come alive until early evening. The few souls in attendance had noted the Garrett brothers' entrance with nods and smiles. Old timers who wiled away the afternoons drinking coffee and playing cards. Poker and faro dealers. A house pianist and a few doves. Rome and Boston knew them all. They'd been frequenting Percy's since they were barely young men. They'd raised a lot of hell in this bawdy. Tom had reason for concern.

It didn't help that they were trail weary and wound tight. Just in from San Francisco, they'd decided to stop for drinks and a meal before heading home. They weren't looking forward to the domestic task at hand. They'd rather be tracking I. M. Wilde.

Rome's mood soured every time he thought about

the bastard. How had he learned about that kiss? What else did he know about the Garretts? Tipping off the public to an adulterous indiscretion had earned him a suspension. Betraying an industry secret could cost him and his brother their careers.

As much as he enjoyed the perks of being portrayed as a legendary hero, he despised the thought of someone infringing on his integrity. The possibility that Wilde had trailed them and listened in on private conversations made him want to pummel the man. No doubt part of the reason London had sent him and Boston to handle the sale of the estate. He wanted them to cool off before they confronted the writer or his publisher and made a bad situation worse.

Still and all, Wilde needed to be silenced before he wrote them into retirement. Or their graves. London was right. He was damn lucky Osprey Smith hadn't shot him in the balls. That's what he would've done were the situation reversed.

Rome set his empty mug on the bar. Tom refilled it. "Guess you boys will be cooling your heels here in Heaven for awhile," he said with a knowing smile.

"Guess you heard about our suspension," Boston said outright.

"Story ran in the Napa County Reporter yesterday."

"Considering how fast news travels in this town," Boston said, "stands to reason most everyone's privy."

"Yup."

"What's the word?"

Tom topped off Boston's beer, slid a jar of pickled eggs their way. "They're applauding you for sticking up for your brother." He jerked a thumb at Rome. "It's his behavior they're questioning."

"Can't fall too far from grace," Rome said. "I've never been an angel."

"No," Tom said. "But you never screwed another man's wife neither."

"That we know of," Boston joked while helping himself to an egg.

Rome cast him a sidelong glare.

"I wouldn't worry about it," Tom said. "Your reputation ain't taken nearly the beating as Miss McBride's."

"Emily?" the brothers said as one.

Tom spent the next few minutes filling them in on one Phineas Pinkerton, poet. It didn't surprise Rome that she'd taken a writer under her wing. Emily had been cooking up stories since she was a kid. Part of the reason she got on so well with Paris. Vivid imaginations. Artistic sensibilities. He could imagine her sticking up for the scribe when folks called him names like Nancy boy and Fancy Pants, even though Tom was certain the names fit. Emily used to stick up for his sister when they called her Goofy Garrett. He'd always liked that about her. Shy until you insulted a loved one, then she said her piece. Didn't look the offender in the eye, but gave them hell all the same.

"So she took in a male boarder," Boston said. "From what you're saying, Pinkerton's harmless. Plus, she's got a constant chaperone. Mrs. Dunlap."

"Not so constant." Tom braced his forearms on the bar, leaned forward and lowered his voice. "Yesterday, Mr. Bellamont escorted Mrs. Dunlap into town. First we've seen of her in months. Far as we can tell Miss McBride and Mr. Pinkerton were alone in that house for hours. Day before that they went off to Weaver's Meadow. Together. Without Mrs. Dunlap," he added in case they weren't catching on.

"You hear that from Mrs. Dunlap?" Rome asked.

"Doc Kellogg. Later that day he treated the poet for a gunshot wound. Apparently he was giving Miss McBride shooting lessons."

Boston scratched his forehead. "Are you saying Emily accidentally shot him?"

"Why in the hell is she handling a gun?" Rome added.

Tom shrugged. "Some folks think it might have been Cole Sawyer and that it might have been on purpose. He had words with Pinkerton at the Lemonade and Storytelling meeting."

Rome inclined his head. "About?"

"Emily."

He and Boston looked at one another then back at Tom.

"Sawyer asked her to marry him. She said, no, but he hasn't given up. Doesn't like that Pinkerton's sleeping under the same roof as Miss McBride. Doesn't like the way he touches her. All familiar like," he added when Rome raised a questioning brow.

He then went on to describe how she fainted in the mercantile and how the poet had fussed over her. He'd gotten the lowdown from Boris Shultz and Frank Biggins. Being a barkeep and proprietor of the town's only saloon, he heard all of the gossip. Want to know something about someone in Heaven? Ask Tom Percy or Ezekiel Thompson.

Rome didn't know what to think of Phineas Pinkerton. The name sounded familiar. Possible he'd seen him on stage. Maybe even at the Gilded Garrett. If not him, his type. For that reason he wasn't overly concerned about the man making inappropriate advances. Cole on the other hand . . . He and Rome were the same age. They grew up together, had the same taste in women. "What's Cole see in Emily?"

"Same thing as Bellamont, I guess. An available young woman. Ain't many around, you know. Least wise of the virginal nature."

Boston held up his palm. "Hold up. Claude Bellamont

proposed to Emily?"

Tom nodded.

"He's old enough to be her father," Rome said.

"So what? He's rich. She'd be set. Instead, she's scraping by and taking in forgetful widows and swishy poets. I don't know if she's pining for her folks or skimping on meals, but she's a skinny thing now. Folks say she's gone . . ." He twirled a finger next to his ear.

The brothers pushed away their mugs and straightened.

Tom held up his hands in surrender. "Sorry. Forgot some used to say that about your sister. No offense intended."

Rome dragged his fingers over his hair, braced his hands on his hips. "Did she turn down Bellamont, too?"

"Yup."

"That's something," Boston said. He wiped his hands on a towel, smoothed his moustache. "London said he was worried."

"Guess he had cause," Rome said.

"Same for the Blossom Dance," Tom continued, clearly absorbed in Emily's saga. "Refused Cole and Bellamont's invitations. But she accepted Pinkerton's. Attend the dance this weekend and you'll get to meet the poet yourself."

Rome set his hat on his head, tugged down the brim. "I'm thinking we should ride out there now."

"You read my mind." Boston paid for their drinks and pushed off of the bar.

"Won't do you any good," Tom said. "They ain't home. Rode to Napa City. Got that from Cole who got it from Mrs. Dunlap when he stopped by to call on Emily. "Speaking of. . ."

He glanced up at the doves' private rooms.

Rome looked that way, too. Cole was descending the stairs, tucking in his shirt. He looked spent and drunk, and Rome got pissed when he thought about him trying to seduce sweet Emily McBride.

Cole hit the last step and caught sight of him. "You son of a bitch."

Rome unbuckled his holster, passed it to Tom. "You best hold on to this."

Boston passed his hardware over the bar as well. "Just in case."

"I knew it," Tom complained.

Patrons who'd witnessed many a bar brawl cleared a path as Cole staggered toward the Garretts.

"If it weren't for you," he said to Rome, "I'd be married by now."

"Fail to see how I'm standing in your way, Cole."

"Emily's smitten with you. Always has been. If you'd had the decency to tell her you weren't interested, she'd have purged you from her heart by now. But, no. You led her on."

"The hell I did."

"The hell you didn't."

Even though Boston held silent, Rome knew his mind. He was siding with Cole on this one. Not that he'd ever say. And, dammit, he was right. He knew Emily had a crush on him and he'd never addressed it. He hadn't taken her seriously. He'd even winked at her a time or two, just to see her blush. Shit.

Cole clenched his fists. "You ruined Emily as sure as you ruined that politician's wife."

"Take it outside," Tom said.

Nobody moved.

"You look pissed, Rome." Cole swayed a little, flashed a cocky smile. "Have a change of heart? Interested in Emily now that she's tainted?"

Rome shrugged out of his duster.

"I'd shut up if I were you, Cole," Boston warned.

"You can have her." The booze blind rancher swiped his hands together as if wiping them clean of Emily. "I'm through with the crazy slut."

"Hell," Tom grumbled. "There goes my mirror."

CHAPTER 20

The ride to Napa City didn't go the way Emily had planned. She'd intended to ease her way into her proposal by learning more about Pinkerton and his past. She knew nothing of his family, his friends, his work, while he knew a good deal about her world. She wanted to know about his parents, his life as a traveling poet, his experiences as an intuitive detective. But every time she asked a question, he maneuvered the focus back on her.

After awhile she got miffed. "If you don't want to talk about your life, just say so."

"I don't want to talk about my life."

"Why not?"

"It's not as interesting as yours."

"Surely that's a matter of perspective."

"From where I'm sitting, your life is infinitely

more intriguing." He leaned forward, flicked away a fly from Streak's twitching ear. "Any chance Herman Beeslow's *Your Savior*?"

She started and slipped sideways, her left foot jerking out of the stirrup. The question was out of the blue and packed an almighty punch. "How do you know about Mr. Beeslow?"

"I offered to pick up mail for you and Mrs. Dunlap when I was at the mercantile." He urged Streak closer, reached over and helped her realign her foot as she struggled for balance and composure. "Nothing as of this morning, but Thompson said there might be something later today. Mentioned the steady flow of packages exchanged between you and Herman Beeslow."

Ezekiel talked too much. Why was her correspondence anyone's business? "Did Mr. Thompson also mention Mr. Beeslow's a bookseller?"

"He did. And that his bookstore is in San Francisco."

"So?"

"Those blackmail letters were postmarked—"

"I know. But he didn't send them." She bit her lower lip, looked at the trees, the flowers, anything but Pinkerton. "The library does not fill all of my needs. What I can't find there, be it fiction or nonfiction, I get from Mr. Beeslow. I can't afford to purchase every book, so we established a borrowing system."

"What does he get out of it?"

"That's awfully cynical."

"Realistic."

Careful not to look him in the eye, she relayed their concocted tale. "Mr. Beeslow is writing a children's book. I'm critiquing his work." There. That sounded plausible. Didn't it?

"Is he returning the favor? Critiquing your pirate story? The love scenes between Constance and Antonio? Did he send you those art books you were telling me about, the ones with nude sketches?"

Her face burned red. "It's not like that. Those were legitimate art books. You make it sound so—"

"Tawdry?"

Flustered, she jerked her gaze to his. "Mr. Beeslow is not blackmailing me."

"You sure?"

"Yes." Her stomach turned and she realized, no, she was not sure. How could she be sure? She'd never met Mr. Beeslow in person. But he was so kind. So accommodating. She hated that Pinkerton had planted a seed of suspicion. *I know your secret.* Mr. Beeslow certainly did.

"I'm only trying to help, Em."

"I know."

"I'd like to rid you of your blackmailer, so you can get on with your life."

"I'm thinking along the same lines."

"You're not going to tell me what this person has on you, are you?"

Her heart raced, her brow beaded with sweat. It felt so huge, so complicated. Her reputation was at stake along with cherished friendships. She couldn't say it. She couldn't breathe. The reins fell away as she clasped her hands to her chest and bent forward, gasping for air.

"What the hell?" Pinkerton lifted her off of her horse and settled her on his lap. "Relax," he said, smoothing a hand down her back. "You're panicking, honey. Take it easy. Breathe slow."

He pulled her against his chest, rested her head on his shoulder. "You don't have to tell me, Em. I don't need particulars."

It took a minute, but the panic eased. Her lungs contracted and expanded and her heart thumped hard but slower. "I'm sorry," she rasped. "That's never happened before." Tears pricked at her eyes. "I'm so embarrassed."

He shushed her and held her close.

She melted against him, grateful for his comfort, his strength. She felt foolish, but she also felt cherished. It was a first. Overwhelmed, hot tears flowed. The more she tried to hold them in, the greater her sobs.

"Oh, hell, Em. Don't cry." His voice sounded gruff, but his touch was gentle. He brushed away tears with the pad of his thumb.

She fought for control. She wasn't a crier. This wasn't like her at all. She sucked in a hiccupping breath, pushed off of his shoulder, and swiped her wet cheeks with the heel of her hand. She gazed into his soft green eyes, so full of compassion. "No one's ever . . . you're the only one . . . I don't want you to think ill of me."

"Not possible." He took her face in his hands, studied her expression. He cursed softly then leaned in and kissed her.

It was different from their first kiss. Softer. Sweeter. Yet her body tingled and ached in response. The heart-melting moment ended too soon.

He eased away, struggled for words. "This is complicated."

"Yes."

"You're going to hate me when this is over."

She managed a small smile. "Not possible."

They took their time in Napa City. After fitting her with new spectacles, they strolled the boardwalk, stopping to peruse the occasional shop. She had the feeling Pinkerton was trying to take her mind off of her embarrassing breakdown. Maybe he needed the distraction as well. He'd been troubled by her tears. Or maybe he'd been shaken by the kiss. Maybe she'd reawakened his interest in women. Wouldn't that be wonderful? One thing was certain, her breakdown had triggered a pensive Pinkerton.

He surprised her by treating her to lunch at a fine cafe. She'd never dined out with a man, not like this. It felt so . . . intimate, and her heart fluttered throughout. Conversation was light and minimal. She had no way of knowing his thoughts, but her mind settled back on her plan. Never had she had such an intense desire to be with a man. Her infatuation with Rome paled in comparison. Where he was concerned, she'd imagined a fairytale marriage, perpetual hearts and flowers. Since meeting Pinkerton, her views on a blissful relationship had broadened. She understood now about respect and companionship. Sharing and trust.

By late afternoon, they were back on the road. As soon as they cleared town, Emily kicked Guinevere into a gallop. She reveled in the sun and wind on her face, in the possibilities of the future. Racing across open fields, her inhibitions fell away.

She smiled over at Pinkerton, enjoying the crystal clear vision as he raced his mount alongside hers. His strong and handsome profile, the menacing tilt of his Stetson, the way his frock coat billowed behind him, revealing his holster and gun. *A warrior of God.* Streak

was a handful, but the enigmatic poet handled the spirited horse with easy expertise, making it seem as though
he'd spent more time in the saddle than on stage.

Phineas Pinkerton was a puzzle. Quite possibly
a person with more secrets than she. She didn't care.
She knew at heart he was a good man. Although it
was fanciful, she felt they were destined to share an
adventure. All she had to do was ask. All he had to
do was say yes.

Garnering her courage, she pulled back on the
reins, easing Guinevere to a walk. Pinkerton followed
suit and she urged her horse closer. This was it. Time
to state her argument. *Spit it out, Em.*

But he spoke first. "Met Paris's niece and nephew
when I was in Phoenix. A little on the wild side."

It took a second to focus on what he said. Not
the discussion she had in mind, but maybe she could
swing the subject around. Besides, she missed her
friends. If she couldn't be with them just now at least
she could reminisce. "Zach and Zoe are good kids.
They just need boundaries. Athens is lax in that area.
He's afraid of alienating them. Thinks they blame him
for their mother's death."

"Do they?"

"The only person who blames Athens for Jocelyn's death is Athens. I do think Zach and Zoe resent
him for not being around very much. He stepped away

from politics to amend that."

Pinkerton looked thoughtful. "How did his wife die?"

She shivered remembering that awful day, three years past. The Garretts never spoke of it. Athens never spoke of it. She felt a little funny discussing something with Pinkerton that was so painfully personal to a man he barely knew. Still, the words tumbled out.

"Shot and killed during a train robbery. She was on her way to Calistoga to visit her sister who'd fallen ill. Nothing life threatening, but Jocelyn insisted on visiting right away. Athens wanted to cancel business meetings to accompany her, but she wouldn't hear of it. The issues being discussed were too important, she said, plus he needed to stay with the children."

"He thinks he could have saved her if he'd been there."

She could hear his intuitive detective wheels turning. "Probably. Or that he shouldn't have let her go, period. She was sweet tempered and he was very protective of her."

"Were the outlaws apprehended?"

"Not by the local authorities," she said, unable to keep the disgusted tone from her voice. "Don't get me wrong, they tried. But the outlaws outsmarted them."

"Let me guess. They didn't outsmart Rome and Boston Garrett."

"Very intuitive."

"Not really. She was family. They're expert track-ers. My guess is Jocelyn's killers never made it to trial."

"They made the mistake of drawing on Rome and Boston. I know it's not Christian of me," Emily said, "but I think they got what they deserved."

He glanced at her. "How did Athens feel about his brothers avenging his wife's death?"

She shrugged. "I assumed he was relieved. I don't think he could have . . . that is to say, he's not like his brothers. He's a gentler man."

He looked thoughtful again, as if he were drawing conclusions about Athens. She was curious as to why, but they were nearing home and she wanted to pose her question out of Mrs. Dunlap's earshot.

"Zach and Zoe," he said, again beating her out. "I guess you knew them pretty well."

"I looked after them quite a bit after Jocelyn passed on. Athens focused on work more than ever. To keep his mind occupied and off of Jocelyn, I suspect."

"You got on with them? Even though they're ornery?"

"I'm quite fond of them." She smiled. "Especially because they're ornery."

"What about Athens?"

"Athens is not ornery. He's," she pursed her lips, "stable."

"Do you like him?"

"What's not to like?" Why was he so focused on Athens and his kids? She spotted the house. She told herself, *now*. "He's a nice man, a good man, and I sincerely hope that he marries again. He deserves someone special and any woman would be lucky to have him."

He opened his mouth to say something, but she kept rolling. "Just like any woman would be lucky to have you."

He pulled up short.

She reined Guinevere around so they were facing one another, moved in close so that her knee brushed against his. She forced herself to look him in the eye. *Just say it.* "I think we'd make a good match."

He remained silent.

"You and I," she added, lest his mind was still on Athens.

"I'm not the marrying kind, Em."

"I know what you are."

"No. You don't."

"I know you prefer the company of men to women." There. That was direct. "I want you to know I'm all right with that. I don't understand it precisely, but, well, I don't condemn it. We can't choose who we're attracted to."

"Christ." Frowning, he rubbed the back of his neck.

"I don't want to shock you."

"Too late."

"But I know about some things. Like how sometimes a man . . . like you . . . will take up with a girl . . . like me . . . so that people don't talk. She's like a pretend wife, or fiancé, or . . ." she swallowed hard, "girlfriend."

He looked like he wanted to run for the hills.

"We'd make a good match. We could travel the theater circuit together. You could write and perform poetry. I could write plays, hopefully sell them. People wouldn't shoot at you or make fun of you for being . . . different. Because you wouldn't appear to be different. We'd be . . . a couple."

He shifted in the saddle. He was definitely uncomfortable. "This is insane."

"No, its not. It's advantageous. You like me, don't you?"

"Yes."

"Care about me?"

He nodded.

"You want to help me, right?"

"Yes, but . . ."

"I want to leave this town. Travel to Arizona Territory. I want to be there when Paris's baby is born and then I want to go anywhere and everywhere. Wherever the theater circuit takes us. I want to wake up not knowing what to expect of the day. I want an adventure." Her heart thumped against her ribs. "With you."

He swiped off his hat, sleeved sweat from his brow. He looked at her and her heart bumped up to her throat. "Em—"

"I know I goaded you into that boner-inducing kiss and that I was . . . overzealous. If my behavior concerns you, I want you to know you don't have to worry about me conducting research with anyone else. I'm not promiscuous."

"I am."

She bit her bottom lip, dug deep. *He's your friend, not your lover.* "As long as you're discreet—"

"That doesn't make it right! Jesus, hon." He jammed his fingers through his hair. Clearly, she'd hit a sore spot. He tugged on his hat, pinned her with those striking green eyes. "Promise me you'll never settle for less than a fully committed relationship."

He truly did care. She smiled. "You're a good man, Poet."

"Not good enough. Now listen to me."

"No. Don't say it. Don't say anything. Think about it. Sleep on it. Tell me you'll at least consider it." She didn't wait for him to answer. "Good," she said, then turned Guinevere and raced toward the barn.

CHAPTER 21

He was screwed. This mission was a disaster. His only course was to accomplish his objective and to accept that the woman he loved was lost to another man.

Together they unsaddled and fed the horses. Twice he tried to speak. Twice she shushed him. "Sleep on it."

She had to be joshing. She'd just proposed they take up as a couple. She hadn't mentioned marriage, but she was all for an adventure. Of course, she probably wasn't thinking about sex because she thought he favored men.

Together, they walked to the house. There was a bounce in her step and she was smiling. Her good humor unsettled him as surely as her tears.

Seth tried to focus on Emily's blackmailer, but all he could think about was her proposal. *"We'd make a good match*." Except she thought he was a poet, a writer, a like-minded artist. She wouldn't want anything to do with him when she learned he'd been lying to her all this time. He'd be lucky if she ever spoke to him again.

He'd never given due thought to the consequences of his ruse. He simply assumed it would all work out. He'd rid her of the blackmailer, marry her off to Athens, and return to fighting crime. He hadn't counted on falling in love. Even so, he still thought he could rope his tender feelings and wrestle them into submission. He'd work hard and play hard and forget he ever loved Emily McBride.

Now he wasn't so sure.

"*We'd make a good match*."

Except, in the end, he'd cheat on her. Wouldn't he?

Watching her hop up the porch stairs, her blond braids swaying, cheeks flushed from the long ride, or perhaps from sexy thoughts about Constance and Antonio, he couldn't imagine ever tiring of this woman. Ever wanting another woman.

Come to think of it, he hadn't thought about another woman since he'd gotten to know Emily.

Yup. *Screwed.*

He held the door open, stepped in behind her, and followed her down the hall. "That must be them," he heard Mrs. Dunlap say.

Emily entered the sitting room first. "Oh. I . . . This is a . . . surprise."

That was an understatement.

From the looks on their faces, Rome and Boston Garrett shared a like thought.

A surreal pause stretched on as they took stock of one another.

Boston sat on the sofa next to Mrs. Dunlap, held his hands wide as she wrapped pink yarn around them. Rome hulked by the bookshelves. He snapped shut the novel in his hands, breaking the awkward silence.

"Good heavens, Emily," Mrs. Dunlap said. "Sit down before you fall down."

She did look unsteady and Seth bristled, thinking she'd gone weak in the knees at the sight of Rome.

"I'm fine," she said, though she was flushed and breathless. "It's just that . . . we've been . . . riding hard, that is . . . for a long time. Mr. Pinkerton and I."

Christ.

"Mr. Pinkerton," Boston said, his voiced laced with sarcasm.

"Phineas Pinkerton," offered Mrs. Dunlap, the only smiling person in the room. "He's the man I told you about. The poet."

"Poet." This again from Boston, who looked less menacing than Rome. Probably due to Mrs. Dunlap using him as a human spool.

"How are you, Emily?" Rome asked.

"Never better," she said, though she looked like she was going to keel over.

Seth battled the green-eyed monster.

"And you?" she squeaked.

"Been better. You probably heard about the suspension." He glanced at Seth.

"Where are my manners?" she said, her voice unnaturally bright. She gestured to the Wells Fargo agents. "Boston Garrett. Rome Garrett. This is . . . my friend. Phineas Pinkerton."

Rome crossed the room and they shook hands. "Pleasure to meet you," Seth said, intimating it was the first time.

Rome tightened his grip, his eyes saying, "*What are you up to?*"

Seth telegraphed, "*Play along.*"

"You look familiar, *Mr. Pinkerton.*"

"You might know me from your sister and brother-in-law's opera house." In truth, they'd worked side by side, saving The Desert Moon from a fiery demise.

"He's a friend of Paris. Athens, too," Emily said, trying to ease the tension.

Rome crossed his arms over his chest. "Been awhile since I've seen my sister. How is Paris?"

"Feisty. Adjusting to impending motherhood."

"My brother? Zach and Zoe?"

"Adjusting to life in Phoenix."

"Where are my manners?" Emily said for the second time in as many minutes. "Would any one like lemonade?"

"I would," the three men said.

Mrs. Dunlap eased the yarn from Boston's hands, set the bundle in a basket. "I'll help you, dear."

The younger brother joined Rome. One dark, one fair. Both tall and fit. Both smart and tough. Both dedicated to wrangling outlaws, like Seth. Unlike Seth, a former sheriff of Pinal County, they played loose with the law. As a Peacemaker he'd be swimming those same risky waters. *A license to bend the law.* The notion had been more appealing when he'd been fired up and fed up. Now it chafed.

Boston withdrew a cheroot from his coat pocket. "Care to join us outside for a smoke, Mr. Pinkerton?"

"He doesn't smoke," Emily said.

Actually, he did although he'd refrained since taking on the poet's persona.

"Keep us company, then," Rome said. "I'd like to hear more about my sister."

Clearly, Emily didn't want him to be alone with the brothers. He appreciated her protection, though he didn't need it. "We won't be long," he said, trying to console her with a smile.

Seconds later, he was standing on the vast green

lawn facing off two seething Garretts. Most men would take flight. They didn't intimidate Seth. They pissed him off.

Keeping up pretences, the brothers struck casual poses and lit their cheroots.

Seth, being Pinkerton, waved off the smoke.

"What the hell are you doing here, Wright?" Rome said with a fake smile.

"Athens sent me."

"Why?"

"To propose marriage to Emily on his behalf."

Boston's mouth fell open. The smoldering cheroot dangled from his lower lip.

"She's in a financial bind. Zach and Zoe need a mother. He figured they'd both benefit from the union."

Rome shifted his weight. "Athens wants to marry Emily?"

"He thinks they'd make a good match." He nearly choked on the words

"I'll be damned," Boston said.

The fair-haired Garrett didn't comment on the nuptials. He blew out a stream of smoke. "Why the charade?"

"Long story involving your sister."

"Figures," they said.

"Emily was expecting Paris's friend. She wasn't expecting me. She assumed I was Pinkerton and introduced me as such to a passel of folk. The ruse became convenient. I needed to be close to her, and her reputation would suffer less if folks thought I was . . . otherwise inclined."

Boston shook his head, grinned. "You've got balls, Wright."

"Did what I had to do to protect Emily."

"We know about Cole." Rome flexed his fingers. "He won't be bothering her anymore."

"Cole's not her only problem," Seth said, hoping he loosened a few teeth when he sent the bastard flying.

"Know about Bellamont, too." Boston whistled. "Three men courting the shy bookworm. Who would've thought?"

Rome snuffed his smoke. "She's changed. I'm not just referring to her shucking her prim gowns for rugged wear. There's fire in her spirit." He narrowed suspicious eyes on Seth. "That because she's excited about moving to Phoenix?"

"Haven't delivered Athens's proposal yet." He held up a hand, warding off whatever they planned to let loose. He spit out a condensed explanation, trying not to revel in knowing he'd ignited that fire. "Emily's biggest problem is that she's being blackmailed. Can't tell you the reason, only that he's bleeding her dry, and the letters originate in San Francisco. She doesn't know the identity of the man. Neither do I, not for lack of trying. I can't address her future, can't involve your brother, until I nail the scheming bastard."

Though their expressions betrayed nothing, he knew he'd poleaxed them. What could someone have on a preacher's daughter? Two days ago, Seth wondered the same thing.

The front door creaked open and the two ladies stepped onto the porch with a pitcher and five glasses. "We thought we'd have refreshments outside," Emily called. "Shame to waste a pretty sunset."

"Be right there," Rome called.

Seth watched Emily in domestic mode. Arranging a weather-beaten table and mismatched chairs, serving up lemonade. He imagined her in the kitchen cooking up too many eggs. Curled up on the sofa absorbed in a book. Sitting at her desk scribbling stories about swashbuckling pirates and skinny-dipping knights.

He thought about the feel of her, the taste of her, her insane proposal, and wished like hell that she could write them a happy ending.

"Got a personal stake in this, Wright?" Rome growled as they moved closer.

He flashed on his job with PMA, his promises to Athens, Paris, and Josh. He fantasized about Emily.

He didn't answer Rome.

"Emily's family," Boston said in a low voice. "Do what you have to do, Seth. We've got your back."

CHAPTER 22

*I*nstead of dreaming sweet dreams about a future with Pinkerton, Emily endured nightmares regarding her past. Why hadn't she mattered more to her parents? Why had she been a disappointment? An embarrassment? Buried feelings of unworthiness, loneliness, and resentment resurfaced and ravaged her spirit.

Because of them, she'd assumed another identity. For the money. For the creative freedom. And now, she realized, for validation. As her work gained favor, she grew more confident. More bold. To her current shame, more reckless. She'd compromised good people in the name of sensational storytelling. Maybe even broken up a marriage and damaged a man's chance at being voted governor.

Maybe her *Savior* was Osprey Smith. He'd certainly made Rome pay for his sins. Why not the scribe who made his wife's affair public?

Rome and Boston's surprise visit had pushed Emily beyond her physical and emotional limit. She'd wanted to sink with the sun when talk turned to their suspension. They mentioned Wilde and his exaggerated tales. Tales that often included their personal quirks and interests. They'd cited invasion of privacy and how they'd felt violated.

Violated.

Emily had felt sick, but she'd held strong. Or rather she'd lapsed to the old Emily, the socially backward bookworm. When she'd first laid eyes on Rome and Boston in her sitting room, she feared that they'd uncovered her secret and come to give her the devil. She'd braced herself for their disappointment and outrage. But the call had been social. They'd returned home, heard about Pinkerton, and wanted to make sure she was all right. They were worried.

It only made her feel worse.

To her dismay, Mrs. Dunlap invited them to stay for supper. It had been the longest evening of her life.

The first hint of dawn filtered in through the partially drawn curtains.

Exhausted, Emily stared at the ceiling, analyzing her life just as she analyzed plot problems and character faults. Her knees had buckled at the sight of Rome, but it had nothing to do with moony-eyed adoration. She'd looked at him and felt nothing resembling desire.

When had she fallen out of love with Rome Garrett?

Unless Mrs. Dunlap had been right. Unless what she felt for Rome hadn't been love at all, but a girlish infatuation.

"You're in love with Mr. Pinkerton."

Certainly, she had all of the symptoms she'd read about in numerous romantic novels. The man didn't even have to be in the same room. All she had to do was think about him and her breath quickened, her heart skipped. Phrases like *floating on air* may be clichéd, but they had merit. Phineas Pinkerton had blown into her life like a tornado, whipping her emotions and values into a frenzy. Though she'd not mentioned sex in her proposal, it was certainly on her mind. Since he ravished her against the bookshelf, she'd thought of little else. She wasn't ashamed. She wanted more. With Pinkerton.

The bond strengthened by the day, the hour. She'd thought the connection artistic, yet he never shared his work. They'd never talked craft. His love of literature was apparent. He enjoyed her book collection, was familiar with authors of poetry and fiction. But he didn't commit time or thought to pad and pencil as she did. If she didn't bring her characters to life daily, she'd go mad.

Phineas Pinkerton was more obsessed with solving mysteries than creating poetry. *Intuitive detective.* Maybe he'd applied for a job as a lawman, but had been rejected because of his sexual preferences. Or maybe he just assumed he'd be rejected and never tried. As an artist she understood how scary rejection could be. More than ever she was convinced he wasn't living the life of his choosing.

She could relate.

Her body pulsed with self-directed anger. She pushed out of bed and rushed through her morning ritual. Since her parents' deaths, she'd been so focused on not giving over control of her life that she'd never really taken control herself. By asking Pinkerton to take her away, wasn't she really asking him to save her?

"What would Calamity Jane do?" She'd show some backbone, handle her own mess. She'd make things right.

Emily tied off her braids then reached under her riding skirt and strapped her new holster and gun to her leg. "Whether Pinkerton accepts or declines your proposal, your life starts today."

In order for Emily McBride to live, I. M. Wilde needed to die.

For the second morning in a row, Seth woke in a lousy mood. Something had shifted in Emily with the arrival of the Garretts. She'd grown distant. Even Mrs. Dunlap voiced concern when Emily had begged off joining them in the sitting room for more chapters of *Around the World in Eighty Days*. She'd claimed exhaustion, blaming the long journey to Napa City.

He knew a lie when he heard one.

He'd checked in on her an hour later, a soft rap on the door, a gentle inquiry. She didn't open the door, but she answered. Again, she claimed to be fine, merely spent. Were that so, he'd thought, she'd be asleep by now. He didn't press, but he did ponder her sudden taciturnity. The pondering affected his own sleep, making him surly.

This morning she was just as pensive. Seth figured she was either fretting over his decision regarding her proposal or regretting that she ever asked. Fact of the matter was she'd had a life-long crush on Rome Garrett. Was laying eyes on the man all she needed to deem Pinkerton a passing fancy? The thought chafed, making him pensive as well.

Breakfast was a somber affair.

Sensitive to the tension, Mrs. Dunlap ate quickly then excused herself. She mumbled something about spring cleaning despite being well into summer.

Once alone, he attempted conversation. "You look

tired, Emily. Maybe you should beg off work. I'm sure Mrs. Frisbie would understand."

"I wouldn't dream of missing two days in a row. I'm fine. Honest." She stood and rinsed her plate.

So much for conversation.

A half an hour later they were on their way to town. He'd opted for the buggy, forcing Emily to sit next to him. Mentally, she was miles away. Was she thinking of Rome? Jealousy snaked through Seth and sank its fangs into his heart. How the hell was he going to feel when she was wearing Athens's ring? Sleeping in his bed?

Her continued silence pricked his temper. He gritted his teeth against the vibrating tension, kept waiting for her to bring up her proposal. He'd slept on it. They were alone. What was she waiting for?

He sighted the picturesque town of Heaven. Moments from now he'd drop Emily at the library. He'd be damned if he'd spend the next few hours stewing on the source of her quiet mood.

"I want you to know that I value your friendship, Em." He spoke from the heart even though his heart wasn't in it. "Your happiness, your welfare, is of fierce concern to me."

"You're turning down my proposal."

She didn't sound surprised or upset. More like resigned. "Though tempting," he said, carefully choosing his words, "a union, such as you suggested, is impossible for numerous reasons."

"I understand."

He didn't want her to understand. He wanted an argument, dammit. The fangs sank deeper. He cursed his venomous thoughts, refusing to let jealousy rule his actions. *"We can't choose who we're attracted to."* She couldn't help wanting Rome.

Seth wrestled with turbulent feelings as he pulled up in front of the library. *She's not rejecting you*, he told himself. *She's rejecting Phineas Pinkerton. She slept on it and she's taking your advice, holding out for that fully committed relationship.* Well, hell.

She surprised him by reaching over and squeezing his hand. "Your happiness and welfare are of fierce concern to me, too." Her voice was steady, her gaze bright with compassion. "You're not a poet at heart. You're a warrior. A man born to detect and protect. I don't know about you, but I'm tired of living a lie."

Had the Garretts betrayed him or had she drawn her own conclusions? He felt as though he'd been buffaloed.

She broke contact to take off the necklace she wore daily. "I want you to know the real me." Fingers trembling, she opened the locket and withdrew a small key. "This will unlock my desk. You'll find my journal in there. It's actually the latest draft of my swashbuckling story. You'll also find another key. It will unlock a chest I hid in the hayloft. That chest contains my life's work. I want to set things right and I'm starting with you."

She pressed the key into his hand, kissed his cheek, and whispered into his ear, "Love isn't always perfect, but it's never wrong. I love you, Poet."

He stared at her, heart hammering. Of all the things she could have said, that was the one thing which rendered him speechless.

She scrambled out of the buggy and into the library, while he sat like an idiot trying to regain use of his mind and body. She loved him. How in the hell was he supposed to ignore that?

"I'm tired of living a lie."

The statement resonated with him. Like her, he aimed on setting things right.

He pocketed the key, a revised mission in mind as he steered Guinevere toward the Garrett estate. Still concerned for Emily's safety, someone needed to watch over her while he did her bidding. He was eager to read what she'd felt compelled to lock away. Beyond the thrill of getting to know the real Emily McBride was the anticipation of discovering the blackmailer's fodder. Surely the two were connected.

Purpose surged through his body, intensifying his focus. He was going to track and squash that bastard like a bug.

Next step: The proposal.

CHAPTER 23

*E*mily may as well have missed another day for all the good she was to Mrs. Frisbie. It took twice as long to re-shelve newly returned books because her mind kept drifting. He would arrive back at her house any minute. What would he think when he read her work? Would he be more shocked by her attempts at writing erotic scenes or by learning that she was I. M. Wilde?

She'd wanted him to know the truth first, but she couldn't be there when he read it. She also wanted him to know her heart. The new Emily didn't repress anymore. She attacked life with honesty and courage. That's why she'd blurted her feelings. Knowing they didn't have a chance at a normal man/woman relationship didn't diminish them. She was in love with the man. She could only wonder how he would feel about her after he read her secrets.

Nervous energy made her clumsy. The third time she knocked something over, causing a ruckus and disturbing the patrons, Mrs. Frisbie interceded. "Emily, dear, I'm wondering if you'd mind walking over to the mercantile and collecting our mail. I never made it yesterday."

She gave Mrs. Frisbie a sheepish smile. "I'm sorry about. . .everything. I'm distracted."

"Maybe some fresh air will help." The woman patted her on the shoulder and steered her to the door. "Take your time."

She appreciated the break, a chance to walk off her anxiety. Eventually, she'd confide in Mrs. Frisbee. First she needed to make amends with Rome and Boston. Directly after work, she told herself. Surely she'd summon up the nerve by then.

Deep in thought, she nearly plowed into Mary Lee Dobbs when the woman stepped in her path.

"Well, if it isn't Bookworm McBride. Surprised to see you out and about alone. I was beginning to think you and Mr. Pinkerton were joined at the hip. From what I've seen and heard, well . . ." She laughed, a mean-spirited laugh that implied she had dirt on Emily. "I'm impressed, truly. Turning the head of a Nancy boy. Who would have thought you had it in you?"

Steam formed between Emily's ears. "I don't think—"

"Question is, how far have you gone? Kissing? Fondling? How convenient that he's staying at your house. Even if Dotty Dunlap witnessed anything inappropriate, she'd forget three seconds later."

Emily balled her fists at her side. *Sticks and stones*, she told herself. Only it wasn't the attack on her reputation that burned. It was the attack on her friends. "Name calling is cruel, Mary Lee," she said, heedless of the gathering crowd. "I can think of a dozen names befitting you, such as spiteful shrew or scheming slut, but I would never address you as such as it would be insensitive."

Some gasped. Some chuckled. Mr. and Mrs. Thompson stepped outside, no doubt curious why the mob gathered in front of their store.

Mary Lee glowered. "How dare you speak to me like that!"

"How dare you judge others?" Once Emily's words were out, protecting her friends, she began to feel more in control. As though the words she spoke had been waiting there all along.

"You're carrying on with a . . . a degenerate!"

"Let him who is without sin cast the first stone."

Mary Lee's eyes bugged.

Words like adulterer and gold-digger emerged from the whispering crowd. Emily wasn't the only one wise to Mary Lee's sinful behavior and now Mary Lee knew it. Her face turned purple. "You crazy, spiteful bitch!"

Emily cocked a brow at the woman dressed in her frou-frou finery. A gown bought by her loving husband. A man she constantly cheated on. *This is for you Mr. Dobbs.* "Never speak in the heat of anger, Mary Lee. Let me help you cool off." With the aid of frustrated years behind her, she shoved the woman into a horse trough.

Water splashed the closest gawkers, who whooped and applauded while Mary Lee flailed. She came up sputtering and spewing unladylike curses. "You're going to regret that," she shrieked as Emily shouldered her way through the crowd.

"Neither do I condemn thee," she said, quoting the bible as she entered the mercantile. "Go and sin no more."

Her pulse raced as she approached the counter. She readjusted her spectacles. She'd never acted out like that in her life, but Mary Lee had pushed her beyond her limits.

"That's been a long time in coming," Mr. Thompson said rounding the counter.

"I feel kind of bad," Emily said. Though not bad enough to apologize.

"Don't," Mrs. Thompson said. "Only reason folks put up with that witch is because they like Mr. Dobbs. Maybe you did her a favor," the woman said as she reorganized a shelf of pots and pans. "Maybe she'll think twice before taking up with another cowhand. Oh, yes," she added. "Most everyone knows."

"She thinks she's being discreet," Mr. Thompson said, "but a couple of those boys kissed and bragged. A few beers over at Percy's and their jaws start flappin'"

Emily swallowed. "Do you think Mr. Dobbs knows?"

Mr. Thompson sighed. "Don't see how he can't. I'm thinking he turns a blind eye. Part pride. Part not wanting to lose her."

Yesterday, she'd told Pinkerton that as long as he was discreet she could endure his seeing other people. Today, she knew that to be false. She didn't need a wedding ring, but she did need a full commitment. He'd been right to decline her proposal, though the knowledge didn't soothe her broken heart.

"What can I do for you, Emily?"

She blinked at Mr. Thompson. "Oh. The mail. For the library."

"Nothing today."

"Anything for me?" She braced herself for another threatening letter.

"Nope."

She nearly sagged with relief. She exited the mercantile, also relieved to find the crowd had dispersed and Mary Lee was gone. A trail of soggy footprints suggested she'd marched home. Smiling, Emily turned for the library pondering the townsfolk's reaction to the scene. They'd actually been on Emily's side. It stupefied her.

"Miss McBride!" Sheriff McDonald waved her down. "Just heading over to see you. I was going through my mail, which tends to pile up, and I came across this." He passed her a letter. "Got mixed with mine. McBride. McDonald. Easy mistake." He scratched his forehead. "Don't know how long it's been there. Hope it ain't important."

The red seal filled her with dread. "Thank you, Sheriff."

"Sure thing." He tipped his hat and ambled away.

She tore open the letter.

MEET ME IN SAN FRANCISCO.

BEESLOW'S LIFE IS AT STAKE.

YOUR SAVIOR.

He included an address and a time to meet. She readjusted her spectacles, heart pounding, thinking she'd misread. She hadn't.

"Oh, no. I'm late." She sprinted toward the bank.

"This is bad."

"Maybe not." Rome saddled his horse. They'd been watching Emily all morning at the request of Seth Wright. He'd knocked heads with the man when they first met, months back. They had different ideas on justice. Still, he respected Seth's reputation and he *was* his brother-in-law's best friend. He felt obliged to give him some leeway. If he were anyone else, he would've cold cocked him last night. He may not have touched Emily, but he sure as hell seduced her. He himself had seen that look in many a woman's eye.

"You saw her expression when she read that letter. She withdrew money from the bank then hightailed it to the livery and talked Chet into loaning her a horse that *he* has to make arrangements to pick up in Napa." Boston tightened the cinch on his Mustang. "Still can't believe how she sold him on that notion."

"She told Paris how to elude us when she ran away from home," Rome reminded him. "She's a bright girl."

"She's reckless. Heading for San Francisco on her own. You know damn well she's meeting her black-mailer. How is that good?"

"As soon as she makes contact, we'll kick his ass." Rome swung into the saddle. "Ride out and let Seth know. I'll track her. You know where we're headed."

Boston mounted, shot his brother a thoughtful look. "He's sweet on her, you know."

Rome raised a sardonic brow. "Ya think?"

He'd meant only to glance at her journal, a leather binder stuffed with fifty or so handwritten pages. But once he started reading, he couldn't put it down. Constance and Antonio grabbed him and didn't let go. He'd suspected that Emily had talent, but he never imagined this.

With carefully chosen words, she swept him away to the Caribbean islands. She wrote as though she'd been there herself. Weaving the reader along the glittering coastline in a creaking schooner. The tropical sun beating down on a bared, tanned shoulder, begging to be kissed.

He'd dropped into a chair when he came to that love scene. Antonio and Constance's first kiss. Only two paragraphs with fairly tame wording, but he'd broken into a sweat. She'd skillfully described a boner-inducing kiss.

Christ. This is what he'd inspired?

He could feel the couple's passion, and because he cared about them, related to them, he kept reading. He was disappointed when he reached the end, because it wasn't the end. This was only the beginning of their adventure.

In awe of Emily's storytelling, he carefully replaced the pages into the binder and returned the journal to the desk. He found the second key and hastened to the barn, assuring Mrs. Dunlap for the third time that he was fine. Better than fine, he was intrigued. He couldn't wait to read more.

Once he climbed into the hayloft, he easily located the chest. His palms were slick with sweat when he unlocked it and opened the lid. His heart pounded with anticipation when he noted a few books and several journals. Her life's work.

First he skimmed the books. The first two were explicit, though scientific, studies on human sexuality. The third, an art book, probably supplied by that bastard Herman Beeslow. Some of the sketches dated back several centuries and depicted graphic, creative sexual positions.

"Holy shit."

What kind of a man supplied a reputable, young woman with graphic material? Had Beeslow no scruples? At the same time he admired Emily's conviction to her art. She didn't know the particulars of man/ woman relations, so she'd researched the facts. Had she been shocked? Titillated? Given her passionate response to his kiss, probably a little of both.

Smiling, he set aside the books and examined the first layer of manuscript pages. Different versions of the story he'd just read and—whoa—extreme versions of the love scene. Explicit words. But the more he read, he realized there was no . . . passion. There were pages and pages of erotic passages. Her research showed, but Constance and Antonio lacked a real connection. Regardless, the material was pretty damned scandalous.

This is what the blackmailer had on her.

This constituted tawdry.

He dug deeper and found several different stories, much tamer, but all full of adventure and romance. The handwriting differed at times. These, he assumed, were written when she was younger. Curious, he flipped through pages looking for the story on the skinny-dipping knight.

He dug deeper. What he found were stories about Rome and Boston Garrett. Handwritten drafts of stories he'd read in dime novels. Adventures written by—

Son of a bitch.

The erotica was tame compared to this explosive revelation.

The sounds of an approaching horse and the shout of his name punched through the haze of his paralyzing shock. He shoved everything back into the chest, locked it, and pocketed the key. He hustled down the ladder. "In here!"

Outside the open barn doors, chunks of grass and dirt flew as Boston Garrett reined in his horse. He'd been riding fast and hard. "Mount up," he said, expression grave. "Emily's taken things into her own hands."

CHAPTER 24

Territory of Arizona

Athens glanced from the telegram about his marriage to the article about his brothers. Toss up as to which irritated him more. He wasn't surprised Rome had seduced another man's wife, just that he hadn't been smarter about it. Athens had faced off against Osprey Smith over legislation in the past. The senator was a ruthless blowhard with full pockets and an uncanny ability to get his way. Rome had gotten off easy with the suspension.

Still, it was a devil of a thing to see his little brothers' names dragged through the mud.

He cursed I. M. Wilde.

He could spend the morning concocting ways to bring down the dime novelist who catapulted his brothers to fame then compromised their careers in the space of a year. But he dropped the article to his desk and returned his attention to the telegram. He'd received the wire yesterday. MISSION IN PROGRESS. He'd read the one line countless times, trying to accept that he'd set a future in motion that he could not change. His future with Emily, not Kaila.

It didn't feel real. It didn't feel right. Yet he couldn't retract the proposal. He couldn't, wouldn't do that to Emily. At the same time, she deserved better than a husband who spent every hour of his existence aching for another woman.

Mission in progress. Seth couldn't have been more specific? Obviously, Emily hadn't jumped at the chance to become Mrs. Athens Garrett. Of course, in her mind he was the wrong Mr. Garrett. He'd known her infatuation with Rome would be a barrier, but he'd expected Seth to find a way around it. He took the message to mean he was doing just that. Explaining the advantages of a practical, amiable marriage. Persuading her to marry a man she didn't love. A man who didn't love her.

He should've hired another nanny, or a live-in housekeeper who cooked and cleaned every day, but, unlike Maria, did not go home every night. He should've just been more selective in his hiring. Someone Zach and Zoe could not run off. But, deep down, he didn't want someone too tough or rough. After all, their mother had been sweet and fun loving. Was it so wrong to want them to be raised with that similar care? Kaila flashed in his mind. Her white bloomers flashing from a tree on Washington Street.

He shook his head and instead thought of Emily. They loved Emily.

It was then that Athens acknowledged the sick truth. The union he'd claimed to be mutually beneficial was mostly beneficial to him. He wanted not only a mother for his children but also someone to ease his guilt so he could focus on PMA.

He dropped his head in his hands. "You are an ass."

"If you say so, sir."

Parker.

Athens straightened and focused on the newspaper on his desk. "I thought you had business at the general store."

"I did. Got back a minute ago. You were absorbed in the newspaper. Probably why you didn't hear me come in."

"Uh, huh. I think you like practicing your stealth skills on me."

The man's lip twitched.

The door slammed open and Sammy Kirk burst in, wide-eyed and winded, for the second time in less than a week. "Mr. Garrett, come quick!"

Parker groaned.

Athens stood, realizing he did not feel his usual

frustration at the interruption. It occurred to him that it was time to care for his children himself. Not just keeping them in line and providing food, clothes, and shelter. But offering the affection of a parent, which he had not since Jocelyn's death. He'd pulled away from Zach and Zoe, and no doubt they were confused and angry. It made him angry at himself. He'd been throwing up barriers between himself and his children for too long. Afraid to get too close again. Afraid what he might do if he lost someone else he loved.

PMA allowed him to protect them without getting close.

He'd been fooling himself. He couldn't protect his heart. It was too late for that. He'd already lost his heart to them long ago.

He'd also, more recently, lost it to Kaila.

He could admit it now, which gave him a sense of relief. He was growing tired of holding up the dam against his emotions. Still, he had no idea how to untangle this web he had spun and that left him more than a little miserable.

He shrugged into his frock coat. "Where are my children?"

Kaila hesitated when Zach and Zoe pounded on her

front door, asking to come inside. She and Athens had agreed to keep their distance. Visiting with his children, delightful as they were, seemed ill advised.

Then she saw the boy's swollen eye. Someone had socked him good.

She studied Zach's disheveled clothes, his hair sticking up every which way, his freckled face, and the chipped tooth when he spoke. "Zoe says you make good cookies."

"The best!" Unlike her brother, the little girl didn't bear markings of a tussle. She looked sunny and cute as the dickens in her yellow gingham dress. Instead of wearing her bonnet, she carried it. Hence the wind-blown curls and sunburned cheeks.

Kaila wanted to hug them, instead, she invited them in and ushered them into her kitchen. After serving them iced tea and a plate of cookies she asked why they weren't in school.

They spewed their story at the same time, stepping on each others' sentences, but she got the gist.

"I don't understand why you didn't defend yourself," she said after Zach described the pummeling.

"Papa said words are more powerful than fists. Said I should use my head and reason my way outta fixes."

"Yes, well, one should avoid violence when possible. I agree. But if the other boy failed to see reason—"

"He called our uncles graces," Zoe piped in.

"Disgraces," Zach corrected.

Kaila handed the boy a used tea bag. "Press this to your eye and hold it there."

"Why?"

"It will ease the swelling."

"Papa just slaps a piece of raw beef on it."

She frowned. "How many black eyes have you had?"

"Lots," said Zoe.

"It occurs to me that your reasoning skills are not up to par, Zach."

Zoe swiped crumbs from her mouth. "His fightin' stinks worse."

Kaila handed her a napkin. "Perhaps you should ask your father for some tips," she said to the boy, "for defense purposes only."

He snorted. "Like he'd know how to throw a punch." He gulped the remnants of his iced tea, bit into another cookie. "Now, if my uncles were here, *they'd* show me how to fight. They're heroes."

She understood why he admired Rome and Boston Garrett, but not at the expense of his own father. "There are all kinds of heroes. Teachers. Lawyers."

"Papa's a lawyer," Zoe said.

Kaila nodded. "As such he defends people's rights. When he was a state senator, he helped create laws, also for the good of the common man. He's fought many battles, and won."

Zoe scrunched her nose. "So, he's like a soldier?"

She smiled. "In a manner of speaking."

Zach looked unimpressed. "You don't know my uncles."

"Not personally, no, but I've read about their adventures."

"You have?"

"Yes, well . . ." She hurried into the living room and brought back three dime novels, each featuring a tale about the Garrett brothers.

"I can't believe it," Zach said, fingering the pages. "Zoe was right. You *are* a pistol."

She didn't know if that was a compliment. A knock on the door kept her from asking. "I'll be right back."

She smoothed her skirt as she left the kitchen, anticipation and dread coursing through her veins. She opened the door, not surprised that Athens Garrett looked unhappy, wishing she could kiss away his frown.

"Someone saw my kids knocking on your door."

She motioned him inside. "They're in the kitchen." Belatedly she remembered the dime novels. *Oh, no.*

He saw the children leafing through the pages but didn't comment. "How'd you get the shiner, son?"

Zach glanced up, tossed the tea bag on the table.

"Trying to reason with a bully."

"Miss Kaila says he shoulda used his fists," Zoe said.

Her cheeks flushed. "Not exactly."

He hitched back his coat, slid his hands in his pockets. "Thank Mrs. Dillingham for the refreshments and go on home. We'll talk about this later."

"Talk, talk, talk," Zach complained as he scooted back his chair.

Kaila bit her tongue.

"Come on, Zoe." The sullen boy took his sister's hand.

"Aren't you coming, Papa?" the girl asked.

"Later. I want to have a word with Mrs. Dillingham."

She looked up at Kaila, her brow scrunched. "Uh oh."

Her thought exactly.

The children moved into the living room.

"Hey," Athens called over his shoulder.

"Thank you for the cookies," they droned in unison then hurried outside.

Her kitchen suddenly seemed quite small, and warm. "I can explain the dime novels."

"Explain the tea bag."

She blinked. "Excuse me?"

He turned and faced her. "Why was my son holding a tea bag over his eye?"

"To reduce the swelling."

"That actually helps?"

"It certainly doesn't hurt." She bristled. She didn't have children, but she'd been young once. She'd experienced bumps and bruises and she distinctly remembered the tea leaf remedy.

He rocked back on his heels, narrowed his eyes. "Why do you suppose, after getting into a scrape, Zach and Zoe sought refuge here?"

She hadn't the slightest idea. "Because Zoe likes my cookies?"

"Because Zoe likes *you*. She talked about you all day yesterday." He indicated the dime novels. "And now you've won over my son."

She scraped her teeth over her lower lip. "I know you don't approve of I. M. Wilde."

"Because of him, my brothers are on suspension."

"I know. I read the article. As did the boy who hassled Zach. Or perhaps he heard about it from his father. I don't know, but that brute of a child called Zach's uncles a disgrace. Your son was trying to defend their honor."

"I know."

Agitated, she started to pace. "You can't blame him for that."

"I don't."

"He tried to reason with that bully even after the boy knocked him to the ground. I don't encourage violence, but really, Athens, a boy should know how to defend himself."

"I agree."

"Sometimes action is the best course. Take your best shot and consequences be damned!"

"You're sexy when you're fired up, English." He snagged her wrist and yanked her flush against him.

"What are you doing?" she squeaked.

"Taking action." He caressed her cheeks and ravished her mouth.

She melted against him, matched his ardor. Her brain screamed, *He's promised to another*, while her body strained against him asking for more. Asking for everything.

They groped, kneaded, and stroked, their actions frantic. He hiked her skirt and dropped his pants.

She wrapped her legs around him, guided him in and . . . *"Yes!"*

He backed her against the wall, slammed inside of her, hard, deep. She would have cried *More*, but her tongue was tangled with his. He sensed her needs, met her demands, again and again, until she cried her release.

He was right behind her. His body shuddered, and long after they continued to kiss.

She was certain she'd died and gone to heaven.

Or maybe this was hell.

He eased her to her feet and they quietly dressed, each deep in thought.

"This is insane," she said, tears pricking at her eyes.

"I know." He dragged his fingers through his hair, studied her a long, torturous minute then headed for her front door.

Her heart burst with affection and need. "Where are you going?"

"To take my best shot."

CHAPTER 25

San Francisco, California

For the first time in a long time, Emily was glad for Mr. Bellamont's company. She'd been surprised when he sat next to her on the train. Shame and guilt reared, but this time she immediately slew those demons. Pinkerton was right. She was not to blame for her father's death.

Neither was Mr. Bellamont.

He's not the enemy, she thought, forcing herself to relax. Indeed, this moment he was a blessing. He was traveling to San Francisco on business, and, unlike her, he'd taken the train and ferry many times. When he inquired as to why she was traveling to the city, she'd answered, "Library business." Thankfully, he hadn't commented other than to say Mrs. Frisbie was fortunate to have her as a liaison.

Over the hours, the winemaker told her about

areas of interest in the booming city and attempted casual conversation. Though polite, Emily proved lousy company. She kept imagining Mrs. Frisbie and Mrs. Dunlap sick with worry. And what about Pinkerton? By now he knew her secrets. Would he leave her to face her fate alone or join her for the showdown?

She'd asked Chet to get word to the poet and to her boss that she'd been summoned to San Francisco. Mrs. Frisbie would be at a loss, but Pinkerton would know she'd gone to confront the blackmailer.

Part of her wanted his help. Part of her needed to handle this alone. Another part worried that if he was with her, he might get hurt. She couldn't bear that. She loved him deeply. As a friend. As the man she could never have. Putting him at risk was beyond her limits. So she'd left the decision to fate. Or, rather, Pinkerton.

Admit it, Emily. You want him to follow you. You want him by your side when you face down the man who's terrorizing you.

It was true. She'd made a big stink about wanting to handle her own trouble, but she wasn't an idiot. Clearly, she was in over her head. Pinkerton was right. Her *Savior* was a criminal. A scalawag with no conscience. In addition to threatening to expose her alias, he was now threatening the life of a helpless bookseller.

At least she had the Derringer. She wouldn't hesitate pulling the revolver in defense, but, if need be, would she be able to fire? Big difference between shooting a bottle and shooting a man.

Hopefully, it wouldn't come to that.

She had no idea what was in store, only that Mr. Beeslow was in danger. She couldn't allow another person to suffer because of I. M. Wilde.

She thought about Rome and Boston. She'd meant to come clean with them tonight. To admit she was I. M. Wilde, to apologize, and to make amends in whatever way they saw fit. Now it would have to wait until tomorrow. Her double life weighed heavily on her conscience. It would be easier to write them a letter, but she needed to tell them face to face. She owed them that. The new Emily demanded nothing less.

Honesty and courage.

She prayed the Garretts would forgive her, just as she prayed she hadn't alienated Pinkerton with her erotic interests and double life. She closed her eyes and prayed that, when she opened them, she'd see the poet racing Streak alongside the train.

She realized, as she drifted off, that it was the most she'd prayed in a long time.

They arrived in San Francisco late that evening. Emily was overwhelmed by the enormity of the city, the silhouetted buildings, the endless gas street lamps, the burgeoning traffic of humanity—even at this late hour. Were she here for any other reason, she would have delighted in the chaos. This was not the adventure for which she'd hoped.

As if sensing her trepidation, Mr. Bellamont grasped her elbow and guided her though the crush of travelers. "How is it you're traveling with no luggage, my dear?"

"I won't be staying long."

"But surely you'll be staying overnight. It's late."

"I . . . um . . ."

"I assume you are going straight to your hotel and handling business tomorrow?"

Hotel? Good Lord, she hadn't thought about staying overnight. But, of course, she must. This was her first trip outside of Napa Valley. Except for the nights she spent with Paris at the Garrett estate, she'd never slept anywhere but in her own bed. Her pulse raced and her breath quickened. *Get a grip, Emily. You can do this.*

She licked dry lips. "Those are my plans, yes."

"I'd be happy to escort you to your hotel."

"Thank you, but that's not necessary."

"As you can see, this is a big city. It isn't safe for a young woman to mill about alone after dark."

"I'll be okay." Frantic to be on her way, she looked

around for a mode of transportation. "You mentioned something about cabs for hire?"

"Hansom cabs. I'll acquire one for you if you're sure—"

"I'm sure." She forced a confident smile. The letter with the address and time of the meeting burned a hole in her reticule.

"Very well." He raised his hand and, with a flick of his wrist, a fancy horse-drawn coach approached.

She noted with interest that the driver sat on a high seat behind the cab. She wondered if he'd wait for her until after her meeting and at what cost. Her funds were limited and God only knew what the blackmailer wanted from her.

Mr. Bellamont cleared his throat, reclaiming her attention. He took off his bowler, fingered the brim. "May I speak frankly?"

After his hours of kindness, it seemed rude to say no. She nodded.

"I know you declined my offer of marriage, Emily. I respect your decision. But I want you to know, should you ever change your mind . . . I want you to know you can rely on me. For anything. Protection. Money. I will not lie. I am quite fond of you."

She swallowed hard, willed herself not to back away. "I appreciate your honesty, Mr. Bellamont."

"I wish you'd do me the favor of calling me Claude."

He smiled kindly, pulled a note from his pocket and pressed it into her hand. "I'll be in San Francisco for the next two days. I've written down the name of my hotel. Should you be in need, please do not hesitate."

"Thank you." She placed the note in her reticule alongside the blackmailer's letter, allowed Mr. Bellamont to help her into the cab.

After he walked away, no doubt stopping in the shadows to make sure she got off all right, she provided the driver with the address.

"You sure about that, miss?"

Unsettled by his skeptical tone, she double checked the letter. "I'm sure."

Heart pounding, she leaned forward and scanned the crowd for one particular face. If this were one of her stories, the crowd would part and Pinkerton would be standing there in one of his stylish suits, holster slung low on his hip, Stetson set at a rakish tilt. Spurs would jangle as he strode toward her, a smile tugging at his lips.

The only jangling she heard was the harness as the driver snapped the reins.

The cab lurched forward.

He didn't come. If he really wanted to be here she was certain he'd find a way.

Emily massaged the ache in her chest. She never knew a heart could hurt so badly. Her eyes burned with tears, and that's when she took a deep breath. *You have to wait to cry, Emily. When you're home. Alone. You already know how to do that.*

She did know how to be alone. She could do this. She was Emily McBride and no one was going to hurt her or her friends anymore.

Vowing not to lose, she braced herself for a confrontation. "Hang on, Mr. Beeslow."

When the hansom cab stopped, Emily looked through the window and her heart sank.

Dark. Seedy. Dangerous.

"I can do this."

During the drive, she started thinking about herself as a heroine in one of her stories, mostly as a way to distract herself from the absence of her hero. A Calamity-Jane-like figure who wouldn't take guff from no one, no how. Emily had never smoked or chewed, but she tried to imagine the taste of tobacco. Imagined herself leaning forward and spitting a stream of brown juice into the street. It was disgusting and out of character for Emily but not for the woman she needed to be just now. A swaggering, tobacco-chewing, sharp-shooting, tough-as-nails mule skinner. She wished she hadn't bathed for a week.

She reached under her skirt and withdrew the Derringer. She checked the chamber. It was a single-shot revolver. One bullet. If she followed Pinkerton's instructions, she'd only need one. Instead of returning it to the holster, she dropped it into her reticule. Closer to her hand should she need to draw.

Steeling her spine, she jumped out of the cab and peered up at the driver. "How much do I owe you?"

"Already been paid, Miss."

"By who?"

"Your silver-haired friend."

"Oh. Well, I need you to wait for me."

He glanced around the undesirable neighborhood. "How long you gonna be?"

She pulled her father's pocket watch out of her reticule. Almost midnight. Her pulse kicked up, along with a heady dose of adrenaline. "Not long."

"It'll cost you."

"How much?"

He named a figure.

High, but worth it. "All right."

When she turned, she noticed the scantily clad women loitering in the doorways, sitting on the front steps, and posing under the street lamps. Painted ladies, she'd heard them called. Calico Queens. Doves. They were everywhere. She tried not to stare. Although she knew they were staring at her, along with a few questionable-looking men.

She ignored the rude comments, the whistles, and walked directly up the steps of the building marked 1182 Market Street. She knocked on the door. No answer. She tried the knob. It turned so she let herself in. She crept down the hall, toward a wash of light coming from an adjacent room. Surely, he must be in there. But the room was deserted, near as she could tell, save for a kerosene lamp sitting on a pickle barrel. She smelled mildew, rotting food and . . . body odor.

"Yer as pretty as he said. 'Cept for them specs."

She wanted to turn and run, but she straightened her spine. He was leaning against the wall, arms folded over his middle. His clothes were rumpled and worn. She couldn't make out his face. Shadows concealed him from the shoulders up. She imagined he was ugly. Really ugly, like his soul.

She swallowed hard. "I assume you're referring to Mr. Beeslow." Only Mr. Beeslow had never seen her.

"If you say so."

"Where is he?"

"Hell if I know."

She gritted her teeth. "Are you or are you not my *Savior*?"

"I'm anyone you want me to be, Sugar Tits."

He lurched forward, grabbed her up in his beefy arms.

"Let me go, you bastard!" The vehemence in her voice surprised her. Yes, she was scared, but more than that she was incensed. Had he lured her here under false pretenses?

Where was Mr. Beeslow?

"Feisty thing, ain't ya? This'll be fun." He pawed her breast, licked her ear.

She froze. Did he plan to rob her of her virginity as he'd robbed her of her savings? The thought sickened her. "Touch me and I'll kill you." Only her right arm was pinned. She couldn't draw her gun.

He laughed and slid his hand up her leg.

She swung out with her free arm and smashed him in the head with her reticule.

He dropped her and staggered back, dazed.

The Derringer. In her reticule. She must've clipped him in the temple. She turned to run but he nabbed her wrist, backhanded her across the face and sent her flying. The breath whooshed from her lungs when she slammed against the wall.

Bleary-eyed, she struggled to her feet. That's when she saw his gun. *Oh, my God.*

"I will have you," he said.

"I'd rather die." She charged, head-butted him in the stomach and knocked him into the pickle barrel. The kerosene lamp shattered and his shirt caught on fire.

He screamed and flailed, socking her hard in the process.

She saw stars, saw him aim the gun.

She heard the shot and blacked out.

CHAPTER 26

They'd ridden hard, and still Seth and Boston arrived in San Francisco two hours after Emily. Two hours too late.

Guilt and anger pummeled Seth. His knees wobbled. He sank down on the mattress next to her, smoothed pale curls from her face. He'd only seen her without her braids one other time, the morning she'd raced into the barn, into his arms. His heart ached as he inspected her injuries. Busted lip, swollen eye, and an angry bruise on her left cheekbone. "Bastard."

London squeezed his shoulder.

He knew he needed to let her rest, but he didn't want to leave her. He never wanted to let her out of his sight again. They'd both been living a lie, a hell of an obstacle to hurdle, but she loved him and he loved her. They were friends. Soulmates. *The bond.* He'd make sure they had a happy ending if he had to write it himself.

Seth brushed his lips over her forehead. "I'm here, honey." He tucked the quilt around her, doused the light then followed the senior Garrett out of the small bedroom into the hall.

They were in a private wing of the Gilded Garrett Opera House. Boston had led him straight here. "*Stop worrying*," he'd said repeatedly through the trip. "*Rome will protect her. Guaran-damn-teed they'll end up at the Gilded.*"

He'd been right about the last part.

London closed the door, leaving it open a crack. "I know she looks bad, but she'll be fine. The doctor gave her something to help her sleep. That's why she's out cold."

He heard the words, but they didn't sink in. His ears buzzed with a simmering rage.

"Come on." London led him into the next room, where they could still hear Emily if she needed them. A study with leather furniture and a mahogany desk. "Sit."

Seth didn't want to sit. He wanted to kill the son of a bitch who'd inflicted those injuries. Only, according to London, it had been Rome's pleasure. Why in the hell hadn't he shot the man *before* he hurt Em?

The rage burned hotter. He wanted to visit the morgue, wanted to see for himself the bastard was dead. But that would mean leaving Emily.

London poured them both a double. He handed a full glass to Seth. "Sit."

He sank down into a plush wing chair. Not because London told him to, but because it was wiser than punching a hole through the wall. He'd rather break his knuckles on Rome's jaw.

Boston joined them, poured his own drink. "Horses are taken care of." He swigged a shot of whiskey, poured another. "How's Emily?"

"Still sleeping." London looked at Seth who was imagining fifty ways to make Rome Garrett cry. "Listen, Wright. I know you're upset about Emily. Probably blaming yourself. I know you're blaming Rome. I'm telling you right now you can't say anything to him that will make him feel worse than he does. We've known Emily all her life. She's family."

Seth fixed his gaze on a poker near the ornate fireplace.

"Are you listening to me?"

"Yeah." He drank some whiskey.

"He was shaken when he brought her here. I can count on one hand the number of times I've seen Rome rattled."

"That's a fact." Boston dropped on the sofa next to his brother.

"I'm confused," London said, "and I'm counting

on you to clear things up, Wright. So drink up and stop fuming about Rome. This isn't about him or you. It's about Emily."

Seth's first impression when he'd met London Garrett months back was that he was a bossy son of a bitch. Time had not changed that opinion. But he was right. Seth needed to reach past his anger and focus on Em. He took another drink.

"Emily was being blackmailed," Boston told London. "Did you know that much?"

He fell back against the sofa, surprised as they'd all been. "No."

"Been going on for awhile," he added then looked at Seth. "Right?"

"A couple of months."

"What kind of dirt could anyone have on Emily?" London asked.

Boston shrugged. "Beats me."

They both looked at Seth. "Do you know?"

"I do."

London waited, sighed. "But you're not going to tell us."

"I'm not." He polished off the drink, welcomed the slow burn of the whiskey and its relaxing effects. "If she wants you to know, she'll tell you."

Boston picked up the tale. "Emily received a letter today, we're guessing from her blackmailer. She withdrew money from the bank and took off. Rome tracked her. I collected Seth, but we were already behind."

"I can take it from here," London said. "Rome had her in his sights for the entire trip. She sat with Claude Bellamont."

Seth's head snapped up. "The winemaker?"

"A Heaven local. He's in San Francisco on business. I have an appointment with him tomorrow." London sipped his drink. "You have a problem with Claude?"

Seth didn't mention his role in Preacher McBride's death. Emily didn't want people to know about her pa's drinking problem. No reason they should. "He makes Emily uncomfortable."

"He asked her to marry him," Boston said.

London raised a brow.

"Cole Sawyer asked her, too."

The other brow shot up.

"Athens—"

"Can we get back to what happened to Emily?" Seth snapped, interrupting Boston. He didn't want to talk about Athens. He didn't want to think about that damned proposal.

London spit out the rest of Rome's report right up to where Emily got into the cab and Bellamont went his way. "Rome unloaded his horse from the ferry, was set to trail her when he was detained by the local law. Osprey Smith is investing a fortune to make

Rome's life hell. By the time Rome broke free, Emily had a ten-minute head start."

"Goddamned corruption." Rome stalked into the room looking as though he'd been drug backward through the bushes. "I should have been out of that police station an hour ago. It was a clean kill. This is Smith's damned doing."

Seth glared at the man.

London glared at Seth. "I should've been with him to grease palms. He insisted I stay here to look after Emily."

The whiskey had numbed his rage just enough that he didn't come out of the chair swinging. He was weary of this conversation. He wanted to check in on Em. Bottom line: Her *Savior* was dead. He hated that he hadn't been the one to rid her of the menace, but he hadn't been there. Rome was. Better she suffer a few bruises, than . . . He didn't want to imagine worse because he'd witnessed worse.

"I'm sorry, Seth," Rome said. "Bone-deep sorry." Looking uncomfortable, he rounded the bar, nabbed a bottle.

Seth rose, set his glass on the bar.

Rome refilled it. "You gonna try to kick my ass?"

"Not tonight."

"Good call."

Seth bristled. "Tell me again about this bastard

who hurt Emily."

"He was a mess. He was on fire, for chrissake. There was a busted lamp. I don't know if she hit him with it, but she sure as hell put up a fight. I broke in just as he aimed his piece at her." Rome dragged his hands down his face. "Considering what he did to Emily, he's lucky I shot him in his black heart. Should've let him burn."

"You don't mean that," London said.

Rome didn't comment.

Seth didn't condone torture, but he wasn't sorry the bastard suffered before he turned up his toes. Besides, the way he saw it, the man would burn for eternity. "Did you get a name?

"Everett Finn." Rome threw back his whiskey, poured another. "Small-time thief. Thug for hire. Operates mostly in the red light district. That's where the son of a bitch lured her."

Seth hated that Emily had been subjected to such a gritty neighborhood. Yet she hadn't asked the cabbie to turn around. She'd confronted her blackmailer, just as she said she would. He cursed and admired her courage. He puzzled on Everett Finn.

None of this sat right with Seth. "I don't understand how a man like Finn could finesse Emily like he did. The blackmailer, a man who considered himself her Savior, seemed more sophisticated than that."

That's when it hit him.

Emily roused from a deep, painful sleep. She'd been shot. At least she thought so, given the pain in her heart and her last recollection.

Pinkerton hadn't raced to her rescue. No fairytale ending for her.

Except she kept hearing his voice. "*I'm here, honey.*"

She squinted into the dark, realized she was lying in a bed. She bolted upright, heart pounding. Where was she? Where was the man she'd set on fire? Bile rose in her throat at the memory of his shirt in flames, his panicked scream.

She shoved aside blankets, scrambled out of bed. She ran her hands over her body. No gun wound. Just bumps and scrapes. She was stiff and sore, but very much alive! She found her spectacles on the side table and shoved them on, heedless of her tender eye and the fierce pounding in her head. Light sliced through a partially opened door. She located her reticule, rooted inside, and breathed a sigh of relief when her fingers curled around the Derringer.

Gun in hand, she eased into the hall. She heard voices, male voices. Several men. She had only one bullet. She contemplated climbing out of the window at the end of the hall. Then she recognized two of the voices. London and Rome.

She breathed in masculine scents—tobacco, cologne. No rotting food or the stench of her attacker. She gazed at the carved gold ceiling, the fancy tapestry wallpaper. This must be the Gilded Garrett!

She bolted down the hall, froze on the threshold of a room full of men. She focused on one.

"Poet!" Heart racing, she flew across the room and into his arms.

"Whoa." Rome plucked the gun from her hands as she wrapped her arms around Pinkerton's neck and planted kisses on his cheek.

"You came," she whispered in his ear.

"I'm sorry I was late, Em." He hugged her close, smoothed a strong hand down her back.

"It was awful," she croaked.

"I know, honey. But you did good."

She nestled her face in his neck, reveled in the smell of him, the strength of him. Her prayers had been answered.

Someone cleared his throat.

"Poet?" said London.

She smiled, ignoring the sting of her split lip. "I never could get used to calling him Phineas."

"Why would you call him Phineas?"

Arms still locked around the poet's neck, she looked over his shoulder at London. "Because that's his name. Phineas Pinkerton."

Boston drew a hand over his moustache.

Rome scratched his forehead.

London looked perplexed.

She didn't understand their confusion.

Pinkerton eased her to her feet and took her hand. "We need to talk."

Her heart hammered against her ribs as he led her back to the room she'd just left. He lit a lamp and urged her to sit next to him on the bed.

"I want you to know that it wasn't my intention to mislead you. You assumed I was Pinkerton and the situation warranted that I play along."

She swallowed hard. "I don't understand."

"My number one concern was to protect you from whoever was terrorizing you. I needed to stay close, live under your roof. Pinkerton posed less of a threat to your reputation."

She couldn't believe her ears. "You're not Phineas Pinkerton?"

"No."

"You're not a poet?"

"No."

"You're not—"

"Hell, no."

She thought about the way he'd kissed her, the arousal. No wonder. He liked girls.

She felt a twinge of betrayal. He'd slept under her roof. She'd told him her most intimate secrets. She'd practiced kissing on him. Yet the thrill that rushed through her made her grip the mattress edge. "Who are you?"

"Seth Wright."

She scrunched her brow. "Josh's friend?"

"Paris mentioned me in her letters?"

"A few times." She described him as a lawman with a strong sense of duty. He had a wry sense of humor and a way with the ladies. Charming, Paris had written, and he was indeed. Emily felt sick. She'd been such a fool. Yet, she reminded herself, she'd done the very same thing as I. M. Wilde. *Let him who is without sin cast the first stone.*

"But Paris didn't write to say I was coming," Seth said.

"She said Pinkerton was coming."

"He was, but he got sidetracked."

"This is complicated." Her head spun. Mostly with the thought that she'd slept in the same house as the handsome, charming lawman. She'd practically *seduced* him. "I don't think I can take more."

"Sure you can, honey. Just think of one of your adventures. Twists and turns. The plot thickens."

Her thoughts shifted to her own deception. She blushed. "You went thought my chest?"

"I did."

"Were you shocked?"

"At first, though I'd be lying if I said I didn't enjoy it. Especially your latest version of Constance and Antonio's adventure."

Her heart burst with pride, tears stung her eyes. "I was inspired."

"I'm flattered."

He smiled, but his eyes shone with concern. He kept skimming his gaze over her injuries. She wondered if he blamed himself.

"I'm also curious as to why someone capable of writing novels like Verne or Dumas, would adopt an alias to write sensationalized short stories?"

She blinked. Had he really just compared her to two of her favorite authors? "I did it for the money," she blurted. "To finance a grand adventure. For my mother. She was so unhappy and she never really . . . I think she thought of me as more a burden than a blessing."

He reached over and clasped her hand, stroked his thumb over her knuckles. Quiet support. She was glad for it. It helped her tell all.

"I thought that if we shared a grand adventure, maybe we'd bond. I thought maybe a trip to New York or Paris. But I needed money, lots of money. I saw an advertisement in the paper, a dime novel publisher looking for stories. I devoured a dozen issues, read every story, and thought, *I can do this.* But I knew Father wouldn't approve, so I wrote to Mr. Beeslow and asked if he'd act as my liaison. We came up with the name I. M. Wilde. We knew everyone would assume it was a man and we figured that was good considering the writing was pretty . . . frank. I wrote what came naturally, wrote what I knew."

"The Garrett brothers."

Her cheeks flamed. "I didn't mean any harm. I admired them, their work. The publisher loved my stories, kept asking for more. The money poured in and I kept thinking how close I was to making my Grand Design a reality. But then Mother left."

He frowned. "What do you mean?"

"One morning we woke up and she was gone. She left a note for Father and one for me. She didn't want to do this any more, she said. This wasn't the life of her choosing. She wished us well and asked that we not look for her."

She burst into tears. "She went on her adventure . . . without me."

"Ah, honey." He wrapped his arms around her and rocked her.

"She made it as far as San Francisco." This town, Emily thought. With all of the excitement it hadn't occurred to her until now. "She must've had her nose in a book or her head in the clouds, because she stepped in front of a cable car. Father blamed her books. He burned her entire collection. I hated him for that. Told him I'd never forgive him. That's the night he drank himself to death."

Seth made soothing sounds as he stroked her hair. Seth, not Pinkerton, although he seemed very much the same man. He made her heart flutter.

"You've got to let that go, Em. Let them both go."

She sniffed back tears. "I know."

He tipped up her face, stroked her hair out of her face and brushed his lips across her bruised cheek. "I hate that bastard hurt you, Em. I'm sorry I wasn't there to protect you."

"I heard a gunshot."

"Rome."

"Did he kill the man?"

"Yeah."

"There was another letter." She pushed out of his arms, dug in her reticule and passed him the letter with the broken seal. "It got mixed with Sheriff McDonald's mail. He only saw it today. Look at the date and time of the meeting. I thought Mr. Beeslow was in danger. I had to come."

"I know, hon."

"But it wasn't him. The man Rome shot wasn't my *Savior*. It couldn't be. He didn't even know who Mr. Beeslow was."

"The man Rome shot was a hired thug."

"I don't understand."

"Baby, did Mr. Bellamont say where he was staying?"

"No. But he wrote down the name of the hotel." She passed him that information, too. "He seemed concerned about my wellbeing. He wanted me to know that his proposal of marriage still stood, but that, no matter what, I could rely on him for anything. Money. Protection." She faltered, her mind grasping the clues that had been there all along. The expression on Seth's face said he'd already formed the same conclusion. "Oh, my God. Why? Why would he do this to me?"

Seth tucked the address in his jacket pocket. "That's what I'm going to find out."

He rose and she snagged his hand. "Wait. I need to ask him myself. To do what I came here to do. I need to confront my *Savior*." She needed to wrap up the mess of her old life so she could attack her future with a clear conscience and heart.

His gaze flicked over her injuries, a muscle twitched in his cheek. He was furious with Bellamont, worried for her. He was going to refuse her, lock her in the room. Maybe she could argue a gopher into a tree, but a warrior of God was another matter.

He squeezed her hand, infusing her with strength and hope. "On one condition."

CHAPTER 27

Emily clenched her fists and breathed deep. *I can do this.*

Even though he had no hard evidence, Seth had reasoned through the blackmail scheme, convincing her that Bellamont was indeed her Savior. She'd been fascinated by the way he pinpointed clues and presented different scenarios and motives. She went through a like process when she plotted a story.

Only this was real life.

A defining moment for the new Emily McBride.

She straightened her spine and rapped on the ornate door. Room 357 of the Palace Hotel, a seven-story opulent wonder. Her *Savior* traveled in style.

The door swung open and anger replaced trepidation.

Three o'clock in the morning. The resplendent

room was bathed in muted amber light. He was dressed and fully awake. He'd been expecting her. So, why did he look so surprised? "My God, Emily. Your face. Who—?"

"Please don't insult me by playing dumb, Mr. Bellamont. You know who. The man you set me up to meet." The words flew out, terse, to the point. She felt no compassion for this man, this *fiend* who had tried to crush her spirit through manipulation.

His horrified expression cinched his guilt. To his credit and her surprise, he didn't deny the accusation. "I never meant . . . He wasn't supposed to hurt you. Please tell me he didn't—"

"What if he did?" She pushed her way in, careful to leave the door partially open. She itched to slap Claude Bellamont's face, but she knew the appropriate words could deliver the same sting. "Would you still want me? That was your goal, right? To scare me so badly that I'd seek your protection? So I'd relent and marry you? Lord knows, surviving on my own would be a struggle. You stole my savings. You ensured a bleak future by threatening retribution should I pursue the career that enabled my financial independence. You tricked me into believing I could trust you, rely on you. You condemned my chosen life and appointed yourself my *Savior*! How could you be so conniving? So cruel?"

He stumbled back and crumpled into a chair, his face the same purplish-red as his favored merlot. "I didn't mean to take it so far. If only you had agreed to be my wife."

"So it's *my* fault I'm destitute? I deserved to be attacked by a hired thug?" Her blood boiled.

"You deserved a better life, a life that I could give you. A fine home, beautiful gowns. You deserved to be cherished. Your parents never appreciated your unique spirit, but I did. I *do*." He licked dry lips, met her gaze. "Do you remember the first night I brought your father home after he'd had too much to drink?"

She nodded, feeling more ill by the moment.

"You asked me to wait in the sitting room while you tucked him into bed. You'd left your journal on your desk."

"Oh, God."

"I couldn't help myself. So many times I'd seen you hunched over, pouring your thoughts onto paper. I remembered well the stories concocted by Emily the child, but what of Emily the woman?" He pressed trembling fingers to his silver temples and massaged. "You can imagine my surprise when I read those erotic passages. Such naughty thoughts for an innocent. I was intrigued, fascinated by your complexity. From that moment on you became an obsession. I wanted that fire in my life, in my bed."

Revolted, Emily wrapped her arms around her middle, fighting nausea and the urge to escape this man's company. She hadn't meant for those passages to be read. He'd been seduced by an emotionally void experiment!

"I thought we'd established a relationship," he continued. "Working together to keep Walt's drinking problem a secret. When he died, I did everything in my power to keep that from coming to light. You seemed so grateful and, at the same time, so sad and alone. I waited a respectable amount of time before proposing. I thought you would eagerly accept. You would want for nothing."

"I would *want* for love. I don't love you, Mr. Bellamont, and you don't love me."

"You are wrong." He stood and reached for her. When she recoiled, he clasped his hands together. "I loved you enough to bribe Sheriff McDonald and Doctor Kellogg into keeping quiet about the circumstances behind your father's death. I loved you enough to save you from future ridicule. How do you think the citizens of Heaven would react if they knew you were in fact the dime novelist who writes those adventure tales? Violence, obscenity, titillation. Really, Emily. And what about the Garrett brothers? Don't you think they'd feel betrayed?"

She'd soon find out.

Her heart pounded as she pressed onward. She needed to know all, as badly as she needed to tell all. No more lies. No more repressing or hiding or pretending. Seth wasn't ashamed of her writing, no matter how whimsical or graphic. Why should she censure her true self?

"Who are you to judge me? You invaded my privacy. You stole my manuscript pages which means you stole a package meant for Mr. Beeslow."

"I made it a point to know your business. I reveled in learning your secret. It made me feel closer to you and provided me with a means to secure our future. I thought you would break after one letter. I thought you'd come to me for help, but you rallied. Cole complicated matters with his proposal of marriage. Hope rekindled when you refused him. But then that deviant, Pinkerton, moved into your home."

A dark rage bubbled within Emily. "You followed us to Weaver's Meadow. You *shot* him!"

"I'd hoped to scare him away. I couldn't have him tainting you with his abnormal tendencies."

Red hot fury erupted, compromising rational thought. She bolted forward and shoved Claude Bellamont against the wall. "You could have killed him!"

Stunned, he shook his head. "I'm not a murderer."

"Maybe not. But you're an intolerant bully. A manipulator. A man who stoops to criminal tactics to get his way!"

"I did it because I love you."

"Stop saying that!" She balled her fists, but instead of pummeling him, she backed away. Angry tears blurred her vision. "People don't terrorize those they love!"

"I know you're upset," he said, inching forward, "but we can work this out. Give me a chance to make amends." His eyes teared, his hands shook. "Please let me hold you. Let me show you."

"Touch her and you're a dead man."

Seth.

He'd been standing outside the door, listening, waiting. His one condition: to be within striking distance when she confronted Bellamont. He agreed to let her try for a full confession, but had promised to intervene should things get too ugly. She was surprised he'd restrained himself this long.

Drained and shaken, Emily turned away from her tormentor and into Seth's arms.

"You." Bellamont's voice cracked. "This is your doing, Pinkerton."

"Actually, it's yours. And the name's Wright. Seth Wright."

"He's a lawman, Claude, and you're screwed." London stepped in beside them. Emily cringed at his hostile expression, thankful it wasn't directed at her.

"Seth's equally proficient with his fists and his Colt. Given his tender feelings toward Emily, I suggest you come peaceably with me."

The man was flummoxed. "I don't understand."

"I'll explain on the way to the police station."

"But—"

"Because of you, Rome's in a jam with the law," Emily blurted. She turned and faced the winemaker, though she held tight to Seth's hand. "You need to make things right, Mr. Bellamont."

He washed his hands over his weary face and aged another ten years before her eyes. "You're right, Emily. I apologize. I'm . . . It all went so wrong. I only wanted . . . Can you ever forgive me?"

His beseeching gaze tore at her heart. Perhaps he wasn't a fiend so much as a lonely, misguided soul. He *had* been a good friend to her father, right to the ugly end. She reminded herself that she had no right to condemn him. Not when she herself had done wrong at the expense of others. This was the moment to choose the landscape of her future and she would not move forth with a black hole in her soul. Her father had preached, "*Only you hold the power to let the light into your life.*" She was so tired of the dark.

"He, who cannot forgive a trespass of malice to his enemy, has never yet tasted the most sublime enjoyment of love," she said.

Bellamont eyes lightened. "The Bible?"

"Johann Kaspar Lavater. Pastor and poet."

London tossed Bellamont his coat and ushered him from her sight. "I'll meet you back at the Gilded," he called over his shoulder.

Then there was silence.

The last of the starch in her spine dissolved, and Emily sagged against Seth. "It's over."

"Almost." He brushed his lips across her forehead. "Just remember, baby, sticks and stones."

His words baffled her until she angled away and saw Rome and Boston crowding the doorway. They'd promised to wait in the lobby. Patience had never been one of their better qualities. "How much did you hear?" she asked, a stupid question given their stony expressions.

"Pretty much everything," Boston said.

Rome worked his jaw. "You think you know a person."

The shock in his voice proved the last straw. Emily burst into tears. "I'm sorry. I'm so sorry that I made you feel violated. I'm sorry that I got you suspended." She gulped down a sob. "I didn't know Sarah Smith was married. To a politician, no less. I just thought it was . . . brave and romantic . . . the way you saved her and she thanked you and . . . I should have told you I was Wilde the other night. Sooner even. I just . . . I only wrote about you because I admired you. Because I—"

Boston held up a hand. "Emily, stop. Please. It's late. You're overwrought and we're—"

"—impressed as hell."

Emily blinked at Rome, hiccupped over another sob. "What?"

He stabbed his hands through his hair, shook his head in wonder. "After all Bellamont did to you, and you forgave the son of a bitch."

He moved into the room, glanced at Seth who squeezed her shoulders and then left her standing on her own. Her knees quaked as the object of her childhood infatuation came toe to toe with her. "You think you know someone," he repeated in a soft voice. "But I never knew how strong you were, how courageous. I never realized the extent of your talent, Emily McBride."

She sniffed back tears, confused. "But . . . but I'm Wilde. I. M. Wilde. The dime novelist."

His lip twitched. "We got that."

"You said if you got your hands on me you'd . . . you'd . . ."

He pulled her into his arms, a brotherly hug, a comforting hug. "I'm not going to beat the shit out of you. Chrissakes, what do you take me for? Besides, I'm betting Seth would shoot any man who looked cross-eyed at you."

"You're not mad?"

He blew out a breath. "We're not thrilled. You shouldn't have revealed certain specifics. But I'd be a hypocrite if I said I didn't enjoy the fame brought on by your stories, Emily. There are . . . benefits to being a pulp hero. As for Sarah, she was my mistake, not yours."

She shifted her teary gaze. "Boston?"

He offered a forgiving smile. "I'll get over it."

Relief whooshed through her body as she blubbered on her best friend's brother's shoulder. To think she used to dream about being in his arms; now all she wanted was a lifetime with Seth. "I'm sorry if I was a moony-eyed pain all those years, Rome."

"I'm sorry I didn't pay you any mind."

She eased back, took off her spectacles, and sleeved away her tears. "I just want you to know I don't love you, not like a woman loves a man."

"My loss."

Exhausted and relieved, Emily locked gazes with the warrior poet and spoke her heart. "I'm in love with Seth."

Boston grunted.

Rome cleared his throat. "We got that."

By the time they returned to the Gilded Garrett it was a few hours shy of dawn. Wrung out, Emily looked like the walking dead. Ignoring her protests, Seth carried her upstairs and settled her in the guest room. He was almighty tempted to help her undress, but, by God, he wasn't sure he'd be able to keep his hands to himself. He wanted to hold her, kiss her, lay claim to her heart, body, and soul. She'd scared the hell out of him multiple times today. Her courage would be the death of him.

She'd handled Bellamont with grit and grace.

Rome had been stunned by her compassion. Not Seth. Emily McBride was an extraordinary woman. He knew now, without a doubt, that he could be, and would be, faithful to her until his dying day. He'd been humbled and thrilled when she declared her love in front of the Garretts. He ached to tell her his heart, but wasn't free to do so until he made things right with Athens. As spent as he was, he needed to handle this now. This was a big city. Surely he could track down a twenty-four hour telegraph operator.

Midway down the hall, he ran into London. The man motioned him into the study, closed the door. Rome and Boston had already retired. London sat behind his massive desk, massaged his temples. "They're holding Claude for twenty-four hours, but unless Emily presses charges—"

"She won't." Seth braced his hands on hips and swallowed a curse. "You heard her. She forgave him."

"You could probably talk her into—"

"I'm not going to manipulate her."

"Bellamont runs a successful winery. He's not going to tuck tail and run to a new town. Unless Emily moves—"

"Those plans might already in motion."

London shot him a look. "Rome told me about Athens's proposal. My brother means well, but in this case he's misguided. Does Emily know his intentions?"

Seth shook his head. "He penned a proposal, but I haven't given it to her. I wanted to clear up that blackmail business first."

"Do you have it on you?"

"Yeah."

"May I see it?"

Seth jerked the folded letter out of his jacket pocket, passed it over the desk.

Without reading it, London tore up the proposal and deposited the pieces in a drawer. "Emily thinks Paris sent you," he said. "Why don't we leave it at that."

Seth glommed onto his thinking. Nothing would be gained by making Emily privy to Athens's notion of a marriage of convenience. Knowing her sweet heart, she would feel some guilt about leaving Zach and Zoe without a mother. Not that she would marry Athens.

She'd never marry without love, which she'd proven more than once. But now she'd found that love. With Seth. His pulse raced at the thought of making it legal. "I need to get word to your brother."

"Already done." London lifted a dark brow. "I trust I won't have need of a shotgun."

"You're a bossy son of a bitch, Garrett."

"That a problem for you?"

Seth grinned. "Not at the moment."

As tired as she was, Emily couldn't sleep. She lay in the dark, heart hammering, mind churning. Twice she'd declared her love for Seth, the second time in front of Rome and Boston. He'd yet to return the sentiment. He cared for her, of that she had no doubt, but perhaps not enough to pursue a romantic entanglement. He accomplished what Paris had asked of him. He'd vanquished her troubles. Tomorrow he'd probably head back to Arizona Territory.

She burrowed under the covers and squeezed back tears. She'd cried more tonight than all her nights put together. She'd feel better tomorrow, she told herself. Maybe.

The door creaked open and Emily squinted at the backlit silhouette. "Seth?"

"I wanted to make sure you're all right. Go back to sleep, honey. We'll talk in the morning."

"I'd feel better if you stayed with me." If this was their last night together she wanted a lifelong memory.

"I'll bring in a chair and sit with you until you fall asleep."

"I'd feel better if you lay next to me."

"Em—"

"Please."

The pause was so long, she feared rejection. Her heart ached as badly as her head. But, at last, he moved into the room and took off his boots. She watched him peel off his jacket, waistcoat, and shirt. She resisted the urge to put on her glasses for a clearer view. She'd seen him without his shirt before. The glorious image was branded on her brain. She held her breath, wondering if he was going to shuck his pants. She'd definitely need her glasses for that. It was hard enough to see in the darkened room.

He disappointed her by climbing into bed with his pants on. He didn't crawl under the covers with her either.

"You left the door open," she whispered.

"I know."

Her disappointment vanished when he pulled her back flush against his front. Even with the blanket between their bodies, she could feel the heat of his skin. He encircled her waist with his arm, pressed his groin against her rear, and curved his thighs against hers. Spooning, she thought they called it.

She wiggled against him, sighed.

He groaned, and she realized that something had come between them. She smiled in the dark, thinking this was a boner-inducing embrace. Definitely something to remember.

After a long wonderful minute she rolled over and faced him. "You were right about Mr. Bellamont. Thank you for letting me confront him. Thank you for being there with me."

He smoothed her hair from her face, his fingers skimming her skin and fanning desirous flames. "You're an amazing woman, Em. I've never known anyone like you, and that's a fact."

Her heart beat so hard that it bounced around her chest and into her throat. She longed to know his heart, his intentions, but she couldn't bring herself to ask. She'd exhausted her new courageous streak an hour ago. "The bond," she said. "I guess it wasn't artistic."

"Guess not."

"Because, well, you're not a writer."

"Nope."

"You're a lawman."

"Disappointed?"

"Scared."

"Why?"

"Because you're Seth Wright and I'm Emily McBride."

"Yeah." He cradled the back of her head and softly kissed her lips. "And I won't have it any other way. I love you, Em."

A tear slipped down her cheek. "You do?"

"Very much."

"Really?"

"At first I worried I wasn't the right man for you."

"And now?"

"I'm convinced I'm the only man for you."

"I agree," she croaked.

He thumbed away her tears. "For a writer, you're pretty stingy with words just now, hon."

She heard the smile in his voice and smiled back. "Yes."

"Yes, what?"

"Yes, I'll marry you."

He chuckled and framed the side of her face. "Damn, Em. Don't you want me to get down on one knee and propose proper like? Don't you want me to woo you with a poetic declaration of eternal love?"

"Consider me wooed." She snuggled closer. "Are you going to wear pants to bed after we're married?"

He tucked her head into the groove of his strong

shoulder, spoke close to her ear. "I'm going to sleep in the raw and so are you."

"I'm having some pretty erotic thoughts just now. I saw these pictures—"

"Have mercy, hon."

She smiled against his neck. A blissful haze enveloped her. She couldn't ever remember feeling this happy. Fatigued as she was, her mind whirled with several different future scenarios, all of them involving her warrior poet. "Seth?"

"Hmm?"

"What are you thinking about?"

"The one hundred different ways I'm going to make love to you."

She couldn't wait. "Only one hundred?" she teased.

"I might have to consult your book after that."

In spite of her exhaustion, her body tingled with sexual awareness. "I'm thinking we should get married tomorrow."

"After tonight, the Garretts won't have it any other way."

By inviting him into her bed, she'd sealed their fate. "You don't think I—"

"I'm exactly where I want to be."

She released a relieved sigh, kicked off the covers and threw her leg over his in a bid to get closer.

"Em?"

"Hmm?"

"As soon as your lip is healed, I'm going to give you an orgasm-inducing kiss."

Her stomach fluttered as she boldly nipped his earlobe. "Consider me healed."

CHAPTER 28

Territory of Arizona

Athens was convinced he'd never enjoy another sound night's sleep for as long as he lived. He'd wired Heaven the previous day, early afternoon, asking Seth for a progress report. *If the VIP is reluctant*, he'd written, *cancel the mission.*

By nightfall the wire remained unanswered. Athens lay awake for hours obsessing about Emily and Kaila and his unknown future. Leaving it to fate chafed because fate was not his friend. For the first time in three years, he whispered a prayer.

Just before dawn, he drifted off to sleep. Suddenly, he was a performer in the circus. A brightly garbed, smiling idiot juggling two ornery children, eight hotheaded Peacemakers, and one sassy Englishwoman. The gig was challenging, but a *bona fide* thrill.

He scanned the applauding audience, a sea of

blurry faces, save for one. Jocelyn. Smiling and cheering him on. *"I'm so proud."*

Heart pounding, he jerked awake and saw Parker. "Jesus!" Athens bolted upright in bed. "How long have you been standing there?"

"Only a couple of minutes, sir." He pushed open the curtains, welcoming rays of dawn into the dim bedroom. "I knocked, but you were sleeping like a rock."

He threw off the covers, swung his feet to the floor. "What are you doing here so early?"

"Telegram."

His head snapped up. "From Wright?"

"Your brother."

"Which one?"

Parker handed him three folded papers. "All of them."

Athens's heart raced as he opened each one and read.

```
SETH  AND  EMILY  ARE  SWEET
ON  EACH  OTHER.   THOUGHT  YOU
SHOULD  KNOW.  -BOSTON
```

```
JOCELYN  WOULDN'T  WANT  YOU
TO  MARRY  FOR  ANYTHING  OTHER
THAN  TRUE  LOVE.   THINK  ABOUT
IT.  -ROME
```

DON'T MAKE ANYMORE LIFE DE-
CISIONS UNTIL I GET THERE.
THE DESERT SUN'S COMPROMISING
YOUR JUDGMENT.   BY THE WAY,
SETH'S IN LOVE WITH EMILY.   I
GAVE HIM MY BLESSING.   YOU
CAN THANK ME LATER. –LONDON

Athens catapulted out of bed. "What are you standing there for?" he barked at Parker. "Help me pick out something to wear."

"The occasion, sir?"

"I'm going courting."

EPILOGUE

"What about this one?" Emily pointed to a picture in the ancient scholarly treatise on sexual enjoyment. "*The Stag.*"

Using his forearm, Seth dabbed sweat from his brow then slid on his spectacles and examined the exotic position. "He's standing and bearing all her weight."

"So? You're strong enough."

"We're on a moving train, Em. I don't have that kind of balance. Pick another one."

"It looks so interesting."

"That's what you said about *The Knot*."

She giggled. "So now we know you're not as flexible as I am. But look. You don't have to get all bendy with this—"

"Pick another one." Smiling, he brushed aside her

tousled hair, kissed her damp neck, and fell back on the sleeper bed. His wife's adventurous streak knew no bounds. They'd only been married two weeks and she'd already exhausted a good portion of his love-making arsenal. He was one lucky son of a bitch. Although if they kept up this pace, he'd be dead by the time they reached Phoenix.

He grinned thinking there were worse ways to go.

The train rocked and chugged across the tracks, carrying them toward what Emily considered to be her first real adventure. A lengthy stay in the rugged southwest.

They'd decided to keep her house in Heaven as an occasional retreat. Bellamont wasn't going to live forever and Seth liked the idea of their future children running and playing in all that green. Meanwhile, Mrs. Frisbie, who was eager for a taste of country living, had volunteered to move in with Mrs. Dunlap. Emily had been ecstatic, saying she couldn't hope for two better caretakers.

Seth was willing to live on the moon if Emily's heart so desired, but after a long discussion, she'd voted to reside in Phoenix. It was only a few hours ride from Paris, and she liked the idea of living closer to Zach and Zoe. Also, the town boasted a library. Not all towns did and she wanted the option of volunteering part time, even though she'd decided to pursue her historical novel writing full force. Seth had been pleased with her choice as he knew elections were coming up for County Sheriff and he aimed on running.

He'd lost sight of his calling for awhile, but now his mission was clear. It wasn't one of a Peacemaker, but a local lawman. Though disappointed, *Fox* had accepted his wired resignation with grace, replying also with a blessing for Seth's and Emily's union: FATE INTEREVENED AND I'M GLAD. According to London, Athens's new-found optimism had something to do with an Englishwoman. Kaila Dillingham. The woman Seth had ogled while Paris lamented about the troubles of a preacher's daughter. The irony was priceless.

Seth fingered Emily's long blond curls, admired her bare back and shoulders, and the tantalizing curve of her breast as she flipped through the pages of the *Kama Sutra*. He bit back a smile, noticing the intense expression on her face.

She fell back so that she was lying next to him, shifted the book so he could see an illustration. "Do you think you'd pull a muscle if we tried that?"

He didn't even glance at the picture. He was too enamored with his wife's beautiful profile. He plucked the book from her hands, removed her spectacles, and then his own. "As much as I enjoy experimenting with exotic positions, hon, I have a fierce and sudden hankering for a coupling of a more romantic nature."

"Oh?" She offered a smile as he rolled on top of her. "What's this one called?"

"True love." Seth eased inside of her snug warmth, plunged deep and made love to the librarian who'd romanced the west with her hot-blooded tales and roped his heart with her incomparable goodness. Hellion and angel. His wife, Emily McBride-Wright.

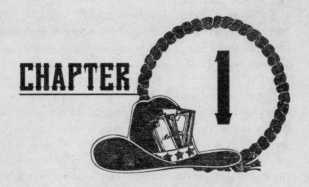

CHAPTER 1

Territory of Arizona, 1877

He'd kill Mason Burke if he weren't already dead. Damn his will and that damned stipulation. Joshua Grant threw back a shot of rotgut, marveling at the dead man's tenacity. Six feet under, and his uncle had still managed to get in the last word.

"Can I get ya' anything else, Sheriff Grant?"

"Yeah, a wife." Josh glanced up from the bullet-nicked bar to the scrunched-up face of its owner. "Never mind. Hit me with another shot. On second thought, make it a double." His future as a wedded theater owner flashed before his eyes. "Hell. Just slide me the bottle and be done with it."

"Sure 'nuff, Sheriff."

1

"Stop calling me that." He snatched up the quart bottle of whiskey Jimmy Hell slid his way. "I told you. I turned in my badge yesterday."

The proprietor of Hell's Drinkin' Hole indicated the rowdy clientele with a flick of his tattered bar rag. "So that's what this party's for?" Smirking, the hairy-knuckled wiseass braced his beefy forearms on the splintered ledge of his bar and leaned forward. "Funny, but I can't recall your reason for leaving town exactly."

Josh leaned forward as well. "That's because I never said exactly." He straightened with a smile and let the taunt settle. Maybe it was the liquor or maybe he was just plain out of his head, but he almost felt giddy when Jimmy narrowed his eyes. He'd been spoiling for a fight for days. Since Mason wasn't available, he'd settle on the nearest pair of fists. Even if those fists were the size of Christmas hams.

Only Jimmy Hell's attention had cut to the swinging doors. "What the . . . ?" His bushy brows cut into a stern V. "Here comes trouble. Good thing you're here, Sheriff. I can't afford another brawl this week. I'm down to six good tables and I'm lucky if I got ten chairs with all their legs."

"Thanks for the warning." Josh ripped the cork out of the bottle with his teeth. Spitting it clean over the barkeep's shoulder, he muttered, "I'll be mindful of where I sit. And stop calling me Sheriff. I'm not the law anymore." That said, he tipped the bottle to his lips and turned to see what form of *trouble* had stumbled into the saloon. Just for curiosity's sake. He'd figured on spying Rosco Timbers or Newt Gibbons, two of Yuma's more cantankerous yahoos, seeing that the mean-spirited Riley brothers were already in attendance. So he near about choked on his half-swallowed drink when he spotted the fresh-faced half-pint standing in the doorway, a bulging carpetbag in hand.

From a distance it was right hard to tell if the kid wearing baggy denim trousers, a faded blue, knee-length shirt, and a dirt-brown fedora was a boy or a girl. A heartbeat later the half-pint stepped forward and tripped over Moe Wiggin's king-sized boot. The hat went flying and ebony, waist-length hair spilled out.

One mystery solved.

Moe scooped up the fedora and plopped it back on the young woman's head. She smiled at the old coot as she elbowed her way through the redeye-guzzling, cheroot-smoking crowd.

Josh knew everyone in and around Yuma. He didn't recognize her. Cute as a baby coon, and his gut warned twice as bothersome.

The kid navigated her unwieldy bag through the maze of occupied tables and chairs, offering apologies as she bumped arms and legs along the way. Intrigued, Josh trained his gaze on the determined runt as she cut a deliberate path through the boodle of pokes and doves, suggesting she knew exactly where she was headed.

"If you got any four-legged chairs in the vicinity of the piano, Jimmy, I suggest you clear 'em out." Josh grabbed his quart bottle and trailed the girl. Maybe he'd get his fight after all. Unfortunately, his progress was hindered by a slew of well-wishers. Assorted doves kissed him for old-times sake. Friends and acquaintances slapped his back or pumped his arm in enthusiastic handshakes. They all wished him good luck. The law-abiding men of Yuma had insisted on throwing him this going-away party. Which was fine, dandy, and thoughtful, except he wasn't all that pleased to be going.

That had been Mason's idea.

"Damn him," he muttered again for good measure. Miserable, and not near drunk enough, he tossed back a healthy swig of whiskey before vying for a spot behind Moe Wiggins, who stood on his one good leg outside a two-man-deep crowd. "What's going on?"

Moe squinted at the kid who was in an animated discussion with the saloon's pianist. "Ain't sure. All I know is that Fingers was in the middle of *Buffalo Gals* and that gal elbowed her way in and put a stop to it."

"Why?"

Moe squinted harder, as though it might somehow improve his hearing. "Can't hear what she's sayin'."

Neither could Josh. His party had grown from loud to deafening. Jimmy Hell was right about one thing. Trouble was brewing. He could see that even in his bleary-eyed state.

"Whatever she's up to," Moe said, "it ain't good."

"It ain't my concern." But, for the life of him, he couldn't tear his gaze from the petite girl. A cute little bunny trapped by a pack of mangy wolves, the sharpest teeth belonging to Burgess and Billy Riley.

Moe drained his beer, sleeved a dribble of brew from his pointy chin. "You've never been one to let a boilin' pot overflow."

"I'm no longer the law in these parts." He figured

4

if he repeated it enough times, he'd get used to the idea. Still and all, he couldn't bring himself to ignore the baby-faced tomboy. The need to protect was a right hard habit to break.

Unable to resist, he moved closer to the action.

"You don't understand, sir." She dropped her bag near the rickety piano and shook a cramp out of her hand. "This is an emergency. I'm in desperate need of your instrument. If you would only accommodate me—"

"Accommodate ya'?" Fingers raised an amused eyebrow above the rim of his wired spectacles. "Ain't never heard it called that before, honey."

His drunken entourage snickered.

"You needn't worry," she hurried on. "I'm very good."

Fingers's other eyebrow shot up. "You don't say?"

She smiled and nodded. "I promise you'll enjoy it."

Josh bit back a groan. How naïve could one girl be not to realize how a passel of men were twisting her innocent words?

"Listen," Fingers said, mopping his brow as though the temperature had shot from eighty to a hundred. "I'm in the middle of a slew of requests. Give me a few minutes and then—"

"A few minutes? It's been days!"

"That long?" Fingers traded a smirk with the leering audience. "Well, now. I reckon I could take a short break." He pinned her with a smarmy look. "Just how good are ya', honey?"

"My brothers think I'm excellent."

The pianist hooted. "Your brothers?"

Owl-eyed and eager for details, the snickering

mob leaned forward. Josh swayed right along with them.

The girl blinked at Fingers. A few seconds later a blush crept up her neck, making a beeline for her cheeks. "I'm sorry. I shouldn't have . . . it's just that I'm . . . " She waved off her words and glanced toward an empty table. "I'll wait over there until you've finished your requests."

Relieved, Josh reached back to massage a crick from his neck. At least the kid had sense enough to vamoose before things turned ugly.

Burgess Riley clamped his burly hand over her wrist and whirled her back around. "What's your hurry, sweet thing? If Fingers there ain't willin' to *accommodate* ya', I sure as hell am."

"Me too!" chimed his brother.

Her face lit up like a noonday sky. "You have a piano too?"

The crowd guffawed.

Josh rolled his eyes. The twinge in his neck pinched.

"No piano. But don't worry. We'll make our own music." Burgess forced her hand over the crotch of his filthy trousers. "Let's put them talented fingers to good use. What do ya' say, wildcat?"

Josh chucked his whiskey bottle and pushed forward. Here comes the fight.

The kid acted faster, kneeing Burgess square in the balls.

For the love of . . . Josh grimaced as the man's wounded howl sliced through him and every other man in the gurdy.

Wide-eyed, the raven-haired ball-buster turned to

run and slammed into Billy's scrawny chest.

Flashing a gap-toothed grin, he snatched her up. "Gotcha!"

She hauled back that same deadly leg and kicked him in the shin. Billy dropped her and yowled. Hopping up and down on one foot, he spewed obscenities raunchy enough to make a hash slinger blush.

Looking only slightly embarrassed, the girl backed into a wobbly-legged Burgess.

Grabbing her by the forearms, the yahoo hauled her backside hard against his injured region and snarled. "You messed with the wrong man, sweet thing."

Josh moved faster this time. When the girl wrenched left he threw a right, ramming his knuckles into Burgess's mouth. The man flew backward, the kid with him.

Quick as lightning, Josh snatched her up and into his arms. The fedora tumbled to the floor, allowing him a full view of her heart-shaped face. The patrons' slurred heckles faded to a drone as he studied the petite minx up close and intimate like. Her smooth complexion, almighty pale in contrast to her ink-black hair, suggested she spent more time indoors than out. A surprise, given her tomboy appearance. Even more surprising was the jolt of lust he felt when he gazed into her walnut-brown eyes, eyes that sparkled with an intoxicating mix of innocence and bald appreciation. Complicating matters, a queer lump lodged in his throat when she quirked a shy smile. "What the hell?"

His gruff words snapped her out of a moony-eyed daze. Blushing now, she struggled like a roped stallion to gain her freedom. "Let me go, you big ape!"

The crowd's whoops and hollers intensified as another skirmish heated up between the Riley boys and a couple of do-gooders. Josh was too busy protecting his gingambobs from Miss Musicmaker's deadly knee and—Christ almighty—*elbows* to pay much mind.

"Watch out!"

At Moe's warning, he dipped the feisty minx just as an empty bottle whizzed past her pretty head. At the same time a chair sailed through the air, shattering the front pane. An out-and-out brawl erupted. Thanks to Mason, he had a lifetime of bar brawls ahead of him. From what he'd heard, the patrons of the Desert Moon opera house were a rowdy bunch.

At least his new life wouldn't be dull.

He glanced down at the pissed off half-pint. "Let's get you out of here, sweetheart."

"I'm not your sweetheart."

"Whose sweetheart are you?"

"No one's." Scowling, she reached behind her and tried to pry his hands from her waist. "I . . . I mean someone's. Some big fellow. An ox of a man who's going to beat you to a pulp if you don't let me go."

"You're a terrible liar." He hiked her higher in his arms and caught a whiff of her glossy hair. Lilacs. The sweet, flowery scent blindsided him, stealing him back to his childhood. A time he preferred to forget. Squashing the bittersweet memories before they reached full bloom, he focused on the swinging doors.

Three men crashed into a nearby table, fists flying. Cursing, he hastened his steps, the girl's best interests at heart. Damn if the menace didn't struggle harder as he hauled her out of harm's way.

"I'm warning you, mister!"

"Warn away."

She elbowed him in the gut.

A second later she kicked him in the shin.

"You're making it difficult for me to behave in a valiant fashion here, kid."

She slapped at his hands. "Don't make me hurt you."

He laughed for the first time in over a week.

Two feet from the doors, she twisted in his arms, reared back and socked him.

"Son of a—" He bit off the curse and worked his offended jaw. "What'd you do that for?"

"I'm sorry. But I *did* warn you."

"So you did. Now I'm warning *you*. Stop fussing. We're leaving."

"But—"

"I warned you." Grinning, he hauled her up and over his shoulder like a sack of grain and whisked her from the saloon. The rowdy mob cheered.

ISBN#1932815287
ISBN#9781932815283
Jewel Imprint: Sapphire
US $6.99 / CDN $9.99
Available Now

For more information

about other great titles from

Medallion Press, visit

www.medallionpress.com